THE GAME OF POWER AND PASSION

WHEN POLITICS MET AMBITION IN THE CORRIDORS OF IIT

NISHANT SHEKHAR

Srishti
PUBLISHERS & DISTRIBUTORS

Srishti Publishers & Distributors
A unit of AJR Publishing LLP
212A, Peacock Lane
Shahpur Jat, New Delhi – 110 049

editorial@srishtipublishers.com

First published in India by
Srishti Publishers & Distributors in 2023

10 9 8 7 6 5 4 3 2 1

Printed and bound in India

To Bhagwan Shiv,
constant source of energy for everyone.

To my Dadiji, Naniji and Mummy,
who all played a significant role
in what I am today.

To all my friends through different stages of life,
for their sustained inspiration.

To all the perpetual storytellers
who inspire the new aspirants.

Praise for the work

"Captures the thrilling side of an IITian's life in this never before heard inside story. It brings to fore how passion and politics come together to make an eventful cocktail in an engineer's life. An exciting and enjoyable read."

– Ajay K Pandey
Bestselling author

"Captivating storytelling that makes you nostalgic... refreshing take on the spirited and dramatic side of IIT life."

– Shantanu Deshpande
Founder CEO,
Bombay Shaving Company

Acknowledgement

I am lifelong indebted to the great institution of IIT Delhi which moulded me into what I am today. There are so many facets of IIT-D life that no one can even come close to doing full justice to narrating the time spent and life learnings acquired in the campus through any form of writing.

I am grateful to my family, which motivated me in all my endeavours at different stages of life. I am thankful to my wife who tolerates my incessant absence while trying to balance multiple tasks in life. I am obliged to my brother, cousin and friends who spent long hours listening and iterating on my story.

I am grateful to Srishti Publishers, especially Arup Bose and my editor, Stuti without whom this book would have never reached this stage.

Finally, I am fortunate that my Papa and Mummy ensured that my formative years were spent with my Dadaji, Dadiji, Nanaji and Nanaji. It's their aashirvaad that holds my hand as I type on the laptop.

Prologue

"You are Abhimanyu Rishabh, right?" He had walked across the lounge to join me at my table. I could barely hear his voice in the loud music.

"Yes," I replied with a surprised look, wondering how I got famous in the firm so quickly. It had barely been a month since I joined this premier consulting firm, after graduating from IIM Lucknow. I had just walked into the party thrown by our employer to welcome the entire new batch who had joined the company.

"You are from IIT Delhi, Karakoram hostel, right?' he continued.

"Yes, but how do you know me?" I had graduated five years ago in 2006.

"Sir, anyone who has stayed at Karakoram in the last four years would know the legend. 'Sarv-shreshtam, Sarv-sundaram Karakoram Karakoram.' Great to meet you!" he completed.

He had joined IIT after I passed out, and he still knew me! I smiled, feeling a sense of satisfaction, similar to what I had felt way back in 2006 at the end of my last 'even semester' at the institute. I was flooded with memories of the events. How – like in the Mahabharata *– every event and character had played a distinct role.*

Year 1: Semester I

July – Dec 2002

Index of characters: Semester I

Abhimanyu's batch (First Year)

Abhimanyu Rishabh	Main protagonist of the Story
Prashant *Gautam*	Abhimanyu's room-mate and best friend; a rare talent of Hindi poetry and debating
Siddharth aka *Sid*	A small town boy; perfect friend of Abhimanyu
Saurabh *Bansal*	Abhimanyu's room-mate and friend; critical mass in Abhimanyu's friend circle
Harshvardhan *Edison*	A good friend of Abhimanyu & Gautam; shared interests in Hindi literature
Vivek	An essential part of Abhimanyu's friend circle
Rudra Rakesh	Dramatics (comedy) and athletics talent
Vishal Arora	Best friend of Rudra; known for his drinking abilities
Pushkar	Expert in fine arts; ardent participant of House production team
Prabhat	Department mate and very good friend of Pushkar
Shubham	Swimming champion; small town boy from Bihar

Aditya *Sanghvi*	Very enthusiastic individual; shared an unsaid bond with Abhimanyu
Makhija	Quizzing talent; acquaintance of everyone in the batch
Rahul	Sports talent; fastest cricket bowler in the institute
Utkarsh	Sports talent; expertise in TT, Baddy, Carom
Thomas	Rare English debating talent; Respected individual in the batch
Bala	Exceptional talent in Music; master of multiple musical instruments
Barnwal	Only person in the batch with prior theatre experience
Mridul	Fine Arts expert; rarely resided in the house consistently
Rachit	Abhimanyu's department mate; a helping hand in studies

One year senior to Abhimanyu's batch (2nd Year)

Shashi Ranjan Singh	Dramatics Club Representative, a major cultural club; immense theatre talent
Vikash *aka Guru*	Enthusiastic soul with a serious approach to hostel work; close friend of Shashi
Rocky	Sports talent: Baddy, Squash, Hockey; Film Club Representative, a minor club

Vatsal	Sports (Cricket) and dramatics (comedy) talent; famous for his sense of humour
Kaushik	Hindi Samiti Club Representative; Most charming and popular senior; close friend of Shashi
Kalra	Best Athlete in the House; represented Kara in most of the sports
Aniket	Music Club Representative
Viks	A good friend of Guru; visible face in the batch

Two years senior to Abhimanyu's batch (Third Year)

Tarun Khandelwal aka *TK*	House Cultural Secretary; one of the best theatre talents in the institute
Aman Awasthi aka *Double A*	House Maintenance Secretary; very close friend of TK
Amitabh Gupta	TK's department mate; close friend of Edison from school
Arora	House Mess Secretary; close friend of Double A and TK
Vir aka *Viru*	House Sports Secretary; close friend of Amitabh
Jolly	A friend of both TK and Amitabh; Theatre talent in the House

Three years senior to Abhimanyu's batch (Fourth Year)

Anirudh Sharma	Karakoram House Secy; facilitated the initial round of healthy interaction

I
'Healthy' Orientation

~ 1 ~

As my jijaji's car entered the campus at IIT Delhi, my joy knew no bound. Hailing from a small rudimentary town, each and every corner of the place appeared meticulously planned and maintained. Within minutes, I could see the main building, standing tall, as if conveying that the place belonged to a few destined ones only. My humble background and upbringing had never taught me to be proud of my achievements, but at that moment, for the first time, I could not debar myself from that feeling. With an eight-floor tall main building and six three-to-four storied blocks flanking it perpendicularly, the institute's framework was unique in several ways. The structure at the top of the annex, that resembled the graduation hat, was like the icing on the cake.

As we reached the allotted hostel, Karakoram, a considerable crowd was already buzzing all over. I could instantly recognise one of the top-ranked guys, whose photograph repeatedly appeared in the advertisement of a reputed coaching institute. Soon, I got to know that he was the 'opener' of the institute – All India Rank 5 – the highest ranked student in the campus.

My jijaji dropped me at the hostel gate and wished me luck before leaving. A couple of makeshift counters at the reception were helping new entrants joining the hostel. I approached the table of the caretaker for the required formalities.

At the counter, a tall, bulky boy with a newly-grown moustache was checking with the caretaker. "Sir, can you please tell me who are my room-mates in B-14?"

He nodded and replied, "Your room partners are Abhimanyu Rishabh and..." Standing next in the queue behind him, I could hear my name, though I couldn't get the other name clearly.

"I guess that's me – Abhimanyu Rishabh." I spoke up.

The boy turned back with a smile. "Hi! I am Saurabh Bansal. Nice way to meet your roommate!"

"Hi! We now need to figure out our third roommate!" I smiled back at him.

We spoke about our hometown, JEE rank and department. Bansal was a local boy from Delhi and had joined Industrial Production. Both of us headed to our room.

As we reached B-14, I realised a two-seater room had been changed to house three of us. A bunk bed was put alongside a single bed, which seemed nicely made up already. We figured, the third person was already there, so Bansal quickly occupied the lower bed of the bunker, and I settled on to the top without any hassle. We then left for lunch in the huge hostel mess on the ground floor.

Post lunch, we headed for the formal registration process. There was a time slot clearly defined for different departments, so the process was quick. After a few customary speeches by the Director and Dean, we came back to Karakoram for a session scheduled with the House Warden in the common room.

I got to know from warden sir's speech that more than 450 people were staying in this hostel. Majority were B. Tech or Dual degree students, along with few M. Tech and Ph.D students as well. All first years were allotted rooms on the ground and first floor.

He also introduced us to the House Secretary, Anirudh Sharma. He must have been one of the tallest guys I had seen in my life. He told us about the six residential wings in the hostel and the other hostel facilities, including the computer room, TV rooms, internet facilities in the room and the mess timings. We also came to know about the other institute facilities such as medical dispensary and multiple canteens operational in the campus.

When I got back to my room, I found a clean-shaven boy standing at the door. He was shorter and slightly on the heavier side. As soon as he saw me, he greeted me with a hand-shake.

"Hi! Prashant...Prashant Gautam."

"Hey! Abhimanyu...Abhimanyu Rishabh," I replied.

"Which department?" Gautam continued with a smile.

"Electrical."

"Aah! You must be in the top 200 JEE rank?"

"Yeah! 155. What about you?" I asked Gautam.

"Textile. And let's talk not about my rank!" He waved the discussion away. "Where are you from?"

"Dhanbad. It's a small town in Jharkhand. Have you heard about it?" I checked.

"Oh, I am from Patna and am fully aware of Dhanbad. I also know how you people never miss a chance to mention that Jharkhand is different from Bihar!" Gautam said with a lopsided smile. I was happy about his sense of humour and relieved to have a roommate from closer to home. And he came across as a confident guy, which helped to calm my nerves.

"So, are you a full toss or *tippa*?" Gautam asked.

"Sorry, didn't get you?" I felt lost.

"Oh, sorry! I have already started using the campus lingo. I am sure you will get a hang of it soon. It is catchy and cool. So, 'full toss' means you have directly joined IIT after XII, while *tippa* means you took a break to prepare for JEE."

"Interesting! I am full toss, by the way. Maybe I was lucky."

"Come on! Don't call your hard work just luck!" Gautam seemed more confident about me than I was.

"Okay, and what about you?"

"I'm *tippa*. This was my second JEE attempt. I couldn't crack mains last time. So, I joined a state engineering college last year. And now I am here," Gautam told me.

"That's why you don't seem to be impacted by a new place!"

Gautam laughed out loud. "Maybe you are right."

We both clicked well together, but back then, I had no idea that this acquaintance would turn into a friendship that would guide me in taking significant and tough decisions in the long run.

☆ ☆

By evening, the hostel was left with just the freshers - *fachas*. We were meeting fellow freshers in the wing, when a couple of seniors came and ordered us to assemble in the TV room after dinner. That started the guessing game about what could be the agenda of the meeting.

"Maybe, we will be asked to dance", "Maybe a night jog for all", "...just another formal meeting." The guesses kept pouring.

At dinner, most of the freshers were easily recognizable. Their faces showed excitement, concern and a feeling of unfamiliarity. It was quite evident from their body language as well.

Finally, at about 10:30 p.m., an announcement was made through the announcement system. "All the *fachas* are requested to come to the TV room in ten minutes."

By now, the feeling of fear of the unknown had started taking shape in our heads.

~ 2 ~

When we reached the TV room, we were asked to sit on the carpet. And then Anirudh, the house secretary, started talking.

"Is everyone's roommate present here?" Anirudh asked. We did not know this question would become banal in the following days.

After a few answers, queries and counting, it was clear that all *fachas* present in the hostel were there.

"Is there anyone here whose parents are still in Delhi?"

That was a bombshell. Where was this headed, we all wondered.

When no one raised their hand, Anirudh said a loud, "Okay!"

Within moments, a group almost as big as ours entered the room with a tremendous roar. The gang of seniors included students from the second and third years. The group occupied the chairs behind us, while a few kept standing. The enthusiasm in their eyes was no less than spectators getting to watch a Bollywood item song, live!

"This is your first day at the hostel. It will be better if you people introduce yourself to your batchmates as well as to your seniors." Anirudh called one of us and commanded to start the procedure. "Your introduction should include your name, rank, department, room number, hometown and anything beyond studies that you are good at – in that order, nothing more or less."

A thin guy sitting in the front stood up to start the proceedings. He was walking towards the mic when he was halted by a cry from the rear. "No mic. Not allowed!"

Stepping back, he started, "My name is Si—"

His name got lost in the hue and cry from the seniors sitting at the other end of the room.

"Hey! Can't you talk loudly? We couldn't hear you. Didn't your parents feed you properly all these years?"

He attempted a couple of times more and we could finally hear, "My name is Siddharth. My All India Rank is 541. Am in the Chemical Department. I am from Bi—" We again lost him in the noise created by the seniors.

Others followed Siddharth. The seniors kept commenting endlessly from different corners of the room at everyone trying to introduce himself.

"Will you ask your parents and then only talk? Idiot!"

"Look at the way he is standing. Have you come for a jog in the park?"

"Hey you big boy, why are you squeaking like a mouse?"

"Uncle, do you have any kids?"

Amidst the noise made by the seniors, everyone had to shout at the top of their voice, and most of them had to repeat twice or thrice.

By the time the introductions got over, it was already 1:00 a.m.

And then Anirudh took charge to make a few announcements before we could leave.

"The most important rule for the next few weeks is the dress code that you guys need to follow. Every facha is ordered to wear formals – full shirt, formal pants and formal shoes – at all times, except in the sports field." If the Delhi's hot weather was not enough for us, we got introduced to a new 'fitting' dress code.

We all nodded and he concluded, "Get your doubts related to the composite sheet containing details of lectures, tutorials and laboratory schedules clarified from the seniors. Otherwise, most of you would miss half of your classes tomorrow. Now go back to your rooms, sleep tight and assemble on the lawn for jogging at 5:00 am."

~ 3 ~

Bansal woke us up in the morning. It was 4:30 a.m., but the entire wing was up. I was still half-asleep, listening to the commotion outside. A boy walked in from the opposite room, all dressed up for the day. Seeing him acted as the trigger for me to get up and get ready.

Soon, the entire batch was in the lawn, standing height-wise in six queues. Proceedings were managed by a group of eight odd seniors from the second and third years. We were asked to start counting. 1, 2, 3..., every person calling his number as loudly as possible. Counting was to become an exercise that would be religiously followed at the start of every batch gathering – at the mess, lawn, common room, hockey ground, everywhere.

"Guys, all of you need to introduce yourselves. But this time, the introduction should be followed by cheering 'Kara ka enthu high hai'." Vir aka Viru, the sports secretary said loudly.

"The intro and cheering should wake up people in the parallel wing too," said the person standing next to Viru.

"Thanks, Guru," Viru acknowledged him. He was Vikash, who was nicknamed Guru for all the fundas he had about hostel life.

What followed was a crazy round of introductions. It was funny to listen to some voices at such a high pitch. One of the boys' squeaky voice made us burst into laughter. We were told instantly, "No one is allowed to laugh here. Is there a joke going on? Instead of being ashamed that you guys can't even cheer properly, how can you people dare to laugh? You, yes you! You are Bala, right? You will show everyone in your batch what you get back if you are caught laughing." Rocky from the second year said.

Rocky took Bala a little away. We noticed some animated discussion between Rocky and Bala. Soon, Bala came back and stood in front of the gathering.

Bala started, "Since I was laughing, I now need to wipe away my smile. Please remember the lines and actions that I am going to do. Anyone who is caught laughing will have to repeat the 'smile wipe' in the future." Bala laughed again.

And then what followed was a hilarious set of dialogues and actions. "I am wiping my smile. I am making a *batti* out of it and putting it up my ass – ahhh!" At that point, the sound of laughter came from different corners of the lawn.

Bala continued, "Now, I am taking it out of my **#* - ahh! I threw it on the ground and crushed it using my feet." He took a pause. "Kashmir is so hot in summers, mother **#**##." I burst out laughing. Guru noticed that as well.

"Good job, Bala! Repeat it, this time in Telugu." Bala did it in Telugu, his mother tongue. And it turned out to be funnier than before.

Guru pointed at some of us and said, "Now between you, you, and you, is there anyone who knows Punjabi or Bhojpuri?" I was one of them. I knew Bhojpuri and Garg knew Punjabi. We did it in our respective languages. And a few more performances in other languages followed.

Including all the drill, we had a long morning – running around the campus and exercise sessions. It was followed by a long cheering session, *"Zor se bolo, Jai Kara ki"*. Barring a couple of sporty people in the batch, everyone was dead tired after the meeting. And then it was too short a time to get ready, take breakfast, walk all the way to the institute and search our classrooms spread across in such a large establishment!

From the detailed course curriculum and schedule provided to us, I could learn that we had a mix of basic science, basic engineering as well as departmental theory and laboratory courses in the first year.

Mornings were fixed for laboratories and tutorials, followed by a quick visit back to the hostel to grab lunch. The afternoon was packed with lectures, one after the other. Along with the huge classrooms, I observed that the departmental courses had students only from my department, while basic science and engineering courses had students from other departments as well.

It was the maths course lecture that clearly set the future expectations for most of us.

A Professor entered the classroom sharp at 4 p.m. and introduced himself. He then announced, "To set the rules straight, everyone who wants to attend the lecture should be in the class within three minutes of the scheduled start time. Three minutes should be enough to reach the classroom from any part of the Institute area." He locked the door while completing his last statement and took attendance. Clearly, a lot of students hadn't made it yet.

"Now I understand why seventy-five percent mandatory attendance is difficult to maintain!" someone whispered from the back bench. It was explicitly mentioned in our curriculum rulebook that if one is short of seventy-five percent attendance in a course, irrespective of the scores in exam, they will be awarded 'Failed' grade in the subject.

The professor continued, "Before we start, let me tell you that all the students who qualify for IIT believe they are better at maths than anything in life. I would request you guys to apply yourself right from day one because whatever you would have learned before may not help you. Last year, I had to get special permission to lower the passing marks to make sure that a significant percentage of students pass this course. I am not sure if we could allow that with every batch."

He went on to start the regular lecture. He had successfully set the fear of MA111 in everyone's mind.

It was post the lecture that we found out that he was not just a maths god! He could be faster than any of our institute bowlers on the cricket field. Also, he represented Delhi in TT in National Games a few years back.

After returning from the classes in the evening, all I needed was sleep. As soon I entered the corridor, I saw Gautam talking to someone.

"Hey Abhimanyu! Had snacks in the mess?" Gautam checked with me.

" I don't feel like eating. Eight-minute brisk walk from the Institute to the hostel in this heat was enough to kill my appetite. I just need water and sleep!"

"By the way, meet Siddharth!" Gautam introduced us.

"I saw Siddharth in the morning when I was half-sleep and without my specs. And without specs, I can't even recognize myself in the mirror!" I laughed.

"Hi!" Siddharth waved at me. He had a very lean and thin body. He was wearing new but ill-fitting clothes.

"I am Abhimanyu. I think you started the proceedings for the batch yesterday night in the TV room."

"Yes, I was that unfortunate fellow. I was so shocked." He was from Bilaspur, Chhattisgarh and had joined the mechanical stream.

"I am going to call you Sid." Gautam had already rechristened him.

"As if Gautam is very cool!" I was not going to miss this opportunity. We all laughed out loud.

The three of us left for our respective rooms to get some sleep. Bansal was lucky to have a free afternoon and was already sleeping. But we had forgotten that we were not supposed to plan days on our own.

Just then, an announcement was being made for the batch to assemble in the lawn. And soon, folks from the second year came looking for us. I woke the other two roommates and hurriedly stepped out. This batch meeting was primarily for finding out the student's interest in different field sports activities and taking them to the respective grounds. As expected, most of the people wanted to play cricket, but soon, only the real players were to become part of the hostel team!

I went for volleyball. Before dispersing for the sports field, everyone was asked to assemble at the mess after dinner at 9:00 p.m., in formals.

At the volleyball ground, I saw a facha playing like a pro.

Viru yelled, "Hey Vivek, where did you learn this?"

"Sir, at Sainik School. Spent most of my school days with the institution," Vivek said.

When we were returning two hours later, someone patted my back. "Hey Abhimanyu! You are quite loud. Looking at your body, nobody expected that." That was Vivek, referring to the introduction sessions.

"Yeah, could manage," I replied with a smile. "You impressed everyone with your game."

"Yeah, I love volleyball. I think we can have a good hostel team."

Vivek was from Udaipur and had qualified under the reserved category. He belonged to the Mechanical Department. We walked back to the hostel.

~ 4 ~

Gautam, Bansal, Sid, Vivek and I had our dinner together. We headed downstairs when the announcement for the meeting was made. Dressed in formals, the batch was counting again. And then we introduced ourselves at the top of our voices, twice.

Guru asked some of us to identify five others from the batch. Not many could do that accurately. Someone standing at the mess entrance was noticing all this. Then he made his entry.

"You guys don't have a voice to cheer as a team. Even after a day, you can't remember even ten people from the batch? Shame! Do you think we are playing some kind of game with you? Your seniors, who are spending so much time with you since yesterday, have no other important work in their lives?" He was Aman Awasthi, the maintenance secretary of the house. Everyone called him 'Double A' and when he spoke, there was absolute silence.

After a pause, Double A continued, "Make a careful mental note *fachho*! Everything you are asked to do has a purpose. If you don't make the most of this, you are cheating yourself."

Double A was in his full form as he announced, "Guys, we will soon have inter-hostel facha events between the seven boys and two girls hostels in the campus. They will be spread across cultural and sports activities. So, you need to know the overall structure that is followed in IIT Delhi for such activities.

"There are 5 boards in the institute – three to take care of cultural activities, sports, and writing skills - BRCA (Board for Recreational and Cultural Activities), BSA (Board for Student Activities) and BSP (Board for Student Publications). Then we have a board to take care of the financial or any other welfare needs of the students – BSW (Board for Student Welfare). Finally, overall management of hostels is taken care by BHM (Board for Hostel Management). All these are headed by their general secretaries, all final year students. Each of these boards has a trophy up for grab, basis the performance of students."

Double A paused for effect and continued, "BRCA in itself comprises of 9 clubs – Dramatics and Dance (D&D), Music, Fine Arts (FAC), Indoor Sports (ISC), Hindi Samiti, English debating and literary (EDLC), Quizzing, Photography (PAHS) and Film Series (FSC). The last 2 are non-competitive ones. Events are organised throughout the year across the first 7 clubs, and hostels keep adding points to their tally, depending upon their performances.

"Similarly, BSA comprise of 10 different sports. BRCA and BSA are the most coveted trophies to win for the hostel. To start the year, all these cultural and sports clubs will have inter-hostel facha events. The more we add to our tally during this period, the better will be our chances for the overall trophy. Also, to complete the *gyaan* on these two boards, BRCA organizes Rendezvous, the cultural fest of the institute, and BSA organizes Sportech, the sports fest of the institute."

Arora, the mess secretary, took over. "The other 3 boards have different ways of evaluating the hostel's performances, which you can understand by getting in touch with any of us separately."

Double A continued, "Overall, there is a Best House trophy, which is a result of house ranking across all the 5 boards. So, it is now time for you guys to show some enthu and prove your skills across activities, culminating with the largest event of them all – facha skit."

Double A was not done yet. "Beyond these 5 boards, we also have something called AIC (Academic Interaction Council) which is a student body to discuss course curriculum, courses to be offered during different semesters, etc. AIC organises Tryst, the technical fest of the institute. This year, the general secretary of AIC is from Kara, so we will have the responsibility to organize Tryst in February next semester. Now I will let house representative of these BRCA clubs and BSA sports to introduce themselves so that you guys get to know whom to reach out to. *Kara ka enthu high hai.*"

The next couple of hours were spent in understanding every cultural club and sports activity. It was only by 1 a.m. that we got back to our respective rooms.

Back in our room, Gautam and I drew a simple diagram to get a hang of all the information we had just received.

Board Structure

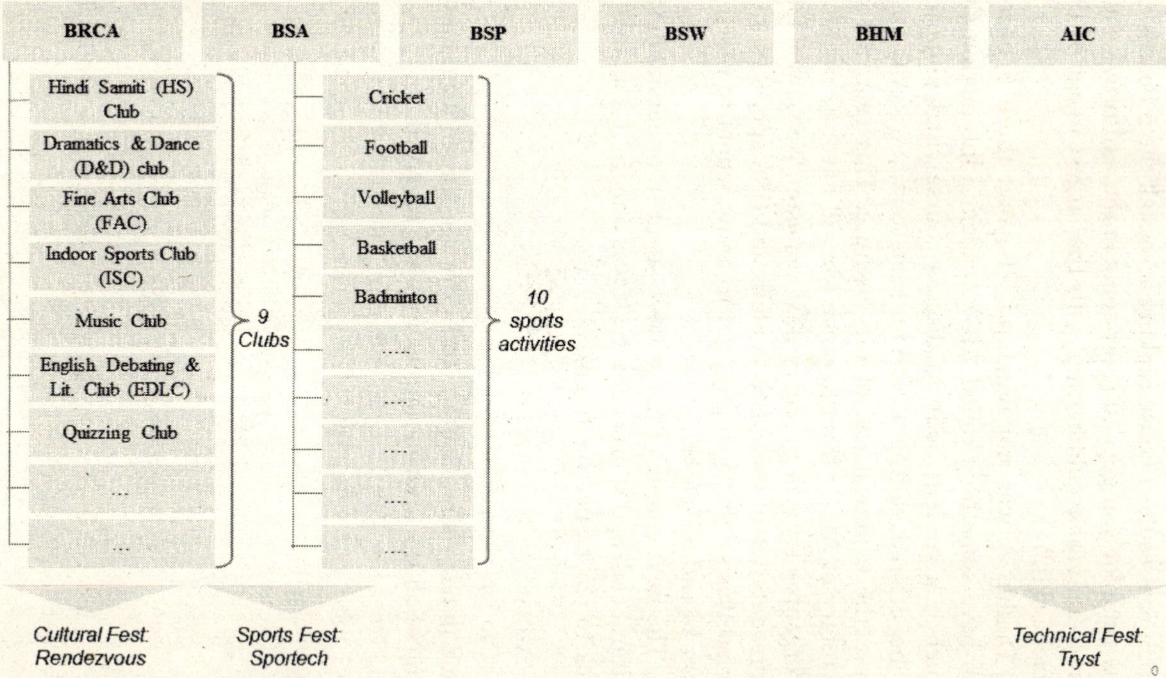

~ 5 ~

Jogging in the morning, batch meetings twice a day, 'healthy interactions' during the day, selection for cultural and sports events in the evening and cheering during the batch meetings became part of our daily schedule.

At one instance, as we were entering the mess for the batch meet, a senior stopped us. He kept his hand on my shoulder and said, "Come with me!"

I got worried, but didn't have a choice. He took me to the cycle stand behind the lawns.

"Sit down!" He pointed at a broken chair. "Do you remember me?"

Thankfully, I did. "Yes sir. You are Shashi Ranjan Singh, dramatics club representative."

Shashi was one of the most authoritative seniors in the second year. He had this unique wicked laugh and a deep voice, which when raised, was enough to make people run.

"Good. Do you smoke?"

"No sir." I was being honest.

"I don't believe you," he said. "Why don't you try this?"

"No sir."

"Trust me, you'll feel better." He lighted and offered it to me.

I took it from him hesitantly. As soon I took the first puff, I coughed out loudly.

"Oh my god! Seems you have never tried it before."

When I could breathe, I replied, "I told you sir."

"Yes, you told me, but you were not assertive enough. Be confident, otherwise it's going to be a difficult life. Learn to say no! Come, let's go!"

An individual 'healthy interaction' tuned out to be interesting learning conversation for me.

Search for talent among *fachas* helped folks from the batch build their reputation and name. It became evident across all the sports and cultural activities that we participated in. Cricket was one sport which most people in the batch wanted to give a try. A lengthy trial session was set up in the evening for the thirteen hopefuls – I was also one of them. It was being conducted by Vatsal and Kalra, both from the second year, well-known as the backbone of the hostel team.

Vatsal was the tallest in his batch, a bit on the heavy side. We had always seen him in the track pants in the hostel as well as in the institute.

Kalra looked the fittest of all and took a round of the cricket ground before addressing us. "Batters will be tested first. You guys will be facing Vatsal."

First ball was enough to set up the day. The first batsman got hit on the rib cage and fell on the ground holding his chest. Kalra took him off the pitch.

"Who is next?" Vatsal asked, as if nothing happened.

Four out of eight backed out and joined the rest of the batch, sitting at the boundary. I was one of the four left. Rahul emerged the best in the bunch, as he was able to withstand Vatsal's bowling well.

Then the bowler's trials were conducted. This time Rahul volunteered to go first.

Vatsal and Kalra padded up. The first ball from Rahul zipped past Vatsal's face. It was a well-directed bouncer. It was followed by a massive roar from the boundary. Vatsal was now getting the dose of his own medicine.

"Great job, Rahul!" Kalra also joined the cheering.

Vatsal made a comeback in the next few deliveries. He was followed by Kalra who also handled Rahul's deliveries well. Overall, Rahul left a definite impression during the trials.

During one of the batch-meets Aniket, the music club rep, announced, "We are lucky to have the best possible musical talent among the freshers in the Institute."

Viks, his batch-mate, quizzed him in his own self-assuring and charming style. "If that's the case, please let us all know about this rare talent."

Aniket continued "We had the music trials yesterday, and I didn't have to make any effort to select people who would be representing the house. We have the best drummer in the institute or possibly Delhi, Bala. I don't know if there is any musical instrument Bala doesn't play. To partner Bala in singing, we have Thomas. I am confident Kara is going to rock this year!"

"*Kara ka enthu high hai!*" We all shouted in unison.

Bala was the most soft-spoken person in out batch. He was from Andhra but had lived his life through the country. He could speak better Hindi than many north Indians in the batch.

Thomas was tall, dark, handsome and a person with unmatched presence.

We had the TT and baddy trials next night. Rocky took charge of the same.

While in TT, Utkarsh emerged best in the house defeating Rocky; in baddy, Rocky remained unmatched. Rocky and Utkarsh duo was now the best in the house.

Rocky was also part of the Institute hockey team.

Just like a common enemy unites even the oldest of foes, the entire batch came together to share their woes about the seniors!

We bitched and whined amongst us, but knew that the whole exercise had helped us a great deal.

During these early days, Gautam found a Hindi-literature bonding with Harshvardhan Edison, who had his room on the ground floor. Edison belonged to Banaras and was a firm speaker, with excellent knowledge of Hindi literature.

We often wondered how his second name came to be Edison. He told us he was the oldest of three siblings and all the children were named after historical personalities that his father was fond of! His other brothers were named after Da Vinci and Washington. Edison's response left us surprised and the story was told and retold multiple times on the campus.

Gautam, Vivek, Edison, Sid and I started spending a lot of time together post classes, with the centre of gravity lying with Gautam and me. Bansal spent a lot of time alone after the classes, primarily focusing on studies, but would join us whenever we asked him to. His presence brought sanity to our randomness.

II
Preliminary days of 'Enthu'

~ 6 ~

It was 9 p.m. when we all assembled in the mess. Someone with average height, light build and slight moustache entered the mess, a big smile on his face. Nobody noticed him at first, and then, just as suddenly, everything in the mess came to a standstill. Most second years let go of their catch for the evening and asked us to settle down in the centre.

He came through the little space, where we were sitting and took his position at the front of the crowd. He had a hint of a smile on his lips and seriousness on his face. All those seniors who had been behaving like bosses until now, waited for him to take the proceedings from there. This was weird!

"Fachas, how is it going for everybody?" he started with a big smile. "Am sure you are enjoying the healthy interaction with your seniors," he said with a shade of mischief in his eyes while stressing the word *healthy*. "I got the answer," he said looking at us with a wink. "Facchho, it's time for some serious gyaan, something that could shape how you are going to approach the rest of your time here in Karakoram." At that point, for the first time, I noticed the gravity and effectiveness in his voice.

"Have you all been thinking why you are made to cheer so much in the campus, on the ground, at the seminar hall, in the activity centre, everywhere? What am I achieving by being so loud and hurting my throat? As a student here, in the best institute in the country, am I not supposed to be studying with the brightest people and emerge as one of the best engineers? From where and why has all this fell upon me? I came here to study! Probably your biggest question is, what sense should I make out of *'Kara ka enthu high hai'*, if at all it makes any sense?" Most of us had approval in our eyes, but we dared not say it out loud.

"Ok, boys!" He broke the pin drop silence. "Can any of you answer one question – what would be the collective set of characteristics by which you'd be known here at IITD? Do remember, you will end up competing with proven *bonds*." I picked up another college lingo jewel, *bond*, which we got accustomed to soon.

Everyone had a different answer in mind, I am sure. I had my own version, and I feel lucky that I was corrected that evening.

"Maybe I can answer all your doubts," he said very softly. And then his voice boomed through the silence. "Hello everyone, I am Tarun Khandelwal, Cultural Secretary of Karakoram. Everyone in the campus calls me TK." This guy was definitely the decision-maker kinds.

"Welcome to Karakoram, your new *home*!" He scanned us all and said firmly, "Don't ever forget this – Karakoram is not your hostel! Karakoram is your home."

"Nobody will ask you which department you're from, what is your rank or where are you from! Everyone will be interested in your hostel, maybe even before asking your names. This hostel will be your new identity from today, your new home - Karakoram. And trust me, from whatever I have learned from my seniors, even after moving out of the campus, the only thing that you will be able to connect yourself with at IITD would be your hostel, your present home. You may be having one or two brothers at home, but this hostel gives you hundreds of brethren. And I mean it!"

Every single word he had uttered was echoing in our ears. Although no one had realized this then, the intensity we witnessed was going to make a lot of difference later.

"And the most important thing of all, Kara ka enthu high hai. Kara ka enthu..."

"...High hai," we said in unison. Everyone said this without any trigger, as if it came coherently from inside.

"I hope you all have realized the expectations and responsibility that you must carry. They will, for sure, define your life at the Karakoram. Any questions?"

There were none, so TK concluded, "So boys, time now to head back to your rooms. And be there for the morning jog at 5 o' clock."

"Do you expect people to take TK's fundas seriously? At times all this looks funny," Gautam remarked the moment we entered our room.

"I am not very sure, but his ability to inspire and bring out the *enthu* and *passion* in everyone is clear. Did you see the people sitting in the Mess? And as far as I am concerned, I have already started feeling at home here, so things made sense. Maybe that's the case with others as well," I replied.

"Yeah, Double A was impressive, but TK was at a different level. It seemed his words came straight from his heart," Bansal was also inspired by him.

"Exactly! TK's definition of hostel life and his ability to link emotion to practical aspects of living in a hostel resonated with me. I am sure we will get to see more of him in the future," I concluded the discussion.

We had absolutely no hint back then how that man was going to influence our future actions, purpose, and lives.

~ 7 ~

Hindi Samiti Club had dumb charades as the fachcha event. It was a difficult selection for Kaushik, who was the Hindi Samiti Club Rep. We had many contenders for the three-member team. So Kaushik carried out the practice session for three consecutive nights.

Gautam stood out in his ability to guess the correct movie and we all knew he'd be there. For the other two places, it was a fight between six people. Kaushik was so confused for the other two places, that he drew chits. Edison and Bala made the cut.

Quizzing was the most transparent objective selection. In the multiple quizzing rounds, Makhija emerged as the champ. There was nothing in this world on which Makhija didn't have an opinion and he made sure he shared those with as many as possible.

Gautam had a great track record in quizzing, but he couldn't make it through the cut. He felt the topics focussed on were so different from what he was used to. Like he knew Hindu mythology, but had no clue about Greek mythology. He about Bollywood and Indian music, but little about Hollywood and global music. It inspired him to broaden his horizon and try again.

For indoor games carom and cards, Utkarsh emerged as the clear winner.

I won the chess competition, and was expected to represent Kara in the facha events for the same.

Thomas shone bright in the English Debating and Literary Club (EDLC). Experts in the senior batches believed "EDLC trophy for the year is definitely going to come to Kara this year."

Kalra conducted the Athletics and Football trials as well. Rudra Rakesh emerged as the best athlete from our batch. Surprisingly, he had come across as a non-serious chubby fellow during facha interactions. He surprised everyone with his energy and agility in the trials.

Shubham emerged as the raw talent in swimming. He came from interiors of Bihar and had spent his childhood swimming in the village pond. Now, he was going to polish his skills in the swimming pool.

By now, we knew who was gifted in multiple arts and those who were unmatchable in their field. All of them were going through the busy schedule of preparation, practice and performance for their respective cultural and sports activities.

I had presumed that everyone at IIT would be more academic than inclined towards all these extracurricular activities. I was surprised by the capabilities of the students in general.

~ 8 ~

Another team, the enthu squad, also emerged from the batch during the events. It included those who were present in all competitions, cheering their breath out and maintaining the team spirit before, during and after the performance of the house. Aditya Sanghvi and I enjoyed being the loudest of them all.

Sanghvi was Sid's roomie, whose average build hid a powerful voice. A football enthusiast, he was a local boy from Delhi, but rarely went back home on weekends. Instead, he would spend his time attending all the events planned over the weekend. Very few could match Sanghvi and my energy at the top of our voices. We were the *enthu* kings for the house.

It was Utkarsh's badminton league match against a fresher from Nilgiri. His opponent had won the first set when we decided not to cheer Utkarsh, but anti-cheer his opponent, Aman. Anti-cheering was about picking the cheapest of expletives targeting the person or his performance.

Sanghvi started, "Did you check with your mother before entering the court against your *baap*?"

"He first has to check who his father is!" I joined.

Everyone started in sync after we raised a slogan to anti-cheer him. Soon, Aman started losing his concentration – reason being the creative choice of words for his mother and sister. 'Nil bulls' – as people from Nilgiri called themselves, also tried the same, but Utkarsh was trained enough by our seniors during the practice session and was able to easily ignore them.

It went to such an extent that Aman turned back and threatened me, "Will see you outside the arena tonight."

It resulted in the entire Kara gang getting further united vocally and breathlessly tearing him apart for the rest of the match. The final result was 2-1 for Utkarsh, with the last set getting over in the shortest time.

A similar situation prevailed after we won the musical event. The Student Activity Centre (SAC) has many student facilities, including the swimming pool, badminton court, squash court and an open air theatre. The huge first floor was the venue for the music event. Bala from our hostel was representing us in both competitions – solo singing and solo instrument player, for which he had chosen drums. Bala was at his best in the event.

We bagged the first position. And as soon as the results were announced, the entire campus started echoing with *"Kara ka enthu high hai"* and *"Zor se bolo Jai kara ki."*

The Kumaon fachas were trying hard to compete in the cheering, but we were double in *enthu*. The tension was slowly building, and it reached its crescendo when both the groups arrived near the roundabout in the hostel area. Had it not been our seniors from both the hostels, things would have turned ugly. Thankfully people were brought under control, but cheering continued in its full swing until we reached Kara.

It was still early days of our strong rivalry with Kumaon.

During a basketball match, things went out of control. We were leading against Aravali aka Ara by a considerable margin, and almost the entire batch was cheering for Kara. When five minutes of the game were left, Ara was losing hold in the match. Plus, the double dose of anti-cheering was making them lose their cool. Sanghvi and I didn't realize that during the sequence of events, we had reached too close to the place where Ara boys were sitting. And before anyone could realise, they surrounded us.

"Both of you need to be taught a lesson." By the time the rest of our batch could run and reach us, Ara boys had already punched us and tore our T-shirts. For the next few minutes, no one was aware of who was hitting whom.

The seniors pulled us apart, there were a couple of bleeding noses, torn clothes and many others nursing internal injuries.

As soon as we gathered senses, the Kara cheering started with our victory.

The performing teams of Kara were supported with cheering and anti-cheering in full enthusiasm. It was one thing that was constant during the facha period. Everyone in the batch was cheering for the other without any inhibition.

People in the batch were selected to represent the hostel in different events basis their performance during the practice sessions. There were multiple such instances when one lost out closely to someone else. Rahul lost out to Gautam for a Hindi Samiti event. Similarly, I lost out to Utkarsh for the TT event, Garg lost out to me for the chess event, Gautam and Bansal lost out to Makhija for the quizzing team – the list grew on a daily basis.

But we all cheered together without any negative feeling for losing out. The best in the bunch should serve the hostel. In the field or on the stage, it was one Kara, the United Kara. Given the Kara unity showcased by our batch, no one at that point of time could even think that some of these instances would be remembered for long by certain individuals.

~ 9 ~

The first month of the semester was coming to an end. I was relishing the enthusiasm, team spirit and bonding, among other things. We were doing well overall – better in the cultural activities than sports. EDLC and quizzing turned out to be our strengths, well supported by music and indoor sports. In outdoor games, we did well in basketball, volleyball and TT.

There were two things common to all the inter-hostel events – the presence of a significant number of fachas and TK. We always saw TK being part of all the action, both cultural as well as sports – cheering, helping, leading, making decisions, coordinating – making his presence felt. Even when there were two events taking place simultaneously, he would attend both. TK had this uncanny ability to come up with out-of-the-box ideas every time. And one could notice the confidence that club representatives and other participants could showcase in TK's presence. He was becoming a role model for us.

~ 10 ~

It was Friday evening. We were returning from the volleyball final match, which we had lost in the dying minutes of the game. Everyone was asked to assemble in the large storage hall right above the mess. It was surprising because we always gathered in the mess. People were tired, but on a Friday, we had all the time in the world.

Gautam, Sid, Vivek, Edison, Bansal and I went together. The entire batch was present there. Among the second-year people, Shashi, Kaushik, Guru, Vatsal, Viks and Aniket had also joined.

As I entered the room, I heard them discussing, "We need four good people. We have two, and we need to identify two more. Rest can be managed."

"Let TK take that call, but where is he?" As soon as Shashi finished, TK made his entry.

"Is everyone here or are we waiting for someone?" TK took over. It looked as if something big was to follow.

"Everyone is here except a few locals who have gone home," Shashi replied.

"Okay, then let's do this! Facho, I am proud of all of you. The kind of enthusiasm we have shown as a team in the past few weeks is unmatchable! Our performance has been great. It's not only a reflection of our talent pool, but also shows the team effort behind the performance." Everyone had a beaming smile on their face.

"It's now time for the mega event – the facha skit. This is the last one, since nothing comes close to this. Here, the role of every individual is bigger, as we will have the largest team of performers, and everyone's responsibility to help us deliver as a team will be important. I promise, it will be as much fun as the hard work. Going by our past records, each one of you will cherish the next ten days for a long-long time, besides the new names that many will get and be known by for the next four years!" All of us burst out laughing.

"So, who all have ever acted in a skit or a play?" TK was hoping to find some enthusiasts.

Three hands were raised – Barnwal, Makhija and Sanghvi. Our batch was surprised to see Sanghvi among them. TK and others waited for some more time, hoping that a few more hands will be raised. And then TK talked again, "Great, so we have some starting point. Barnwal, do you believe in what I said about the coordination and team effort required for the skit and plays?"

"Yes, sir. Absolutely! You just cannot move ahead as a team if anyone is missing – there is so much of interdependency. Even if they're playing the role of a tree." Barnwal said from experience.

TK was smiling, "Very good Barnwal. In fact, even if someone in the production or support team in back-end is missing, the next set of actions get jeopardized. What all have you done earlier, Barnwal?

Next, Barnwal explained his prior experiences followed by Makhija. Barnwal was more experienced of the two.

TK turned to Sanghvi, "What all have you been into, Sanghvi?"

Sanghvi reverted, "Sir, I have been on stage twice before. I am glad Barnwal made it easier for me to say this – once as a tree and the second time as part of the crowd behind a politician!" The entire batch broke out in laughter, including the seniors.

Bringing things under control, TK continued, "I am thrilled to see your enthu, Sanghvi. We will require so many like you. You guys need to give this a try, all of you. It doesn't matter if you have done this before or not. We need to push ourselves a bit more to identify the hidden talent here."

TK changed his tone and continued, "Enough of gyaan folks. Now, it is time for some action. Each one of you will be a part of this – some in the on-stage lead roles, some in smaller roles and the others in the off-stage production support. Shashi, Kaushik, Guru and Vatsal will work with you, identifying people for different roles. And we will take it from there."

Shashi briefly shared the storyline of the skit with us. It was a comedy with a mix of mythology and history in the backdrop of an engineering college. There was less of logic and more of fun. We all were left impressed by the theme. There were four lead characters and multiple supporting roles. TK auditioned Barnwal and Makhija for the two lead roles, and they did well in the same.

Shashi and Kaushik then divided the rest into two groups under Shashi and Guru, and Kaushik and Vatsal.

Gautam and I were part of Vatsal and Kaushik's group. Kaushik was looking for the third lead role. He tried auditioning a few people, but their performance was not satisfactory. As Bala was doing decent, Kaushik selected him for another role. He then started looking for the next actor.

"Abhimanyu, why don't you try?" asked TK. He was watching the proceedings from a corner. I was left surprised. "I think you will be able to pull this up. Go for it!" he was pushing me.

I gave a blank look to Gautam. He nodded, which gave me confidence. With a deep breath, I got up and took the script from Kaushik's hand. Few people had already tried their luck by that time, so the dialogues had become familiar. I read the conversations a couple of times and then closed my eyes. Imagining the sequence in my mind, I went for it. The dialogues came out in a natural flow with a few breaks in between. I didn't hold myself back and acted with full enthusiasm

I went on for the next few minutes without break, and then stopped suddenly. An awkward silence encapsulating the room with my loud voice echoing from all the corners had rattled me. After a strange silence of about ten tense seconds, everyone clapped. Shashi and Guru were also applauding from the other end of the room, where they were auditioning the other half. That was my first stage performance in life, if it can be called a performance, and the response was just right to make it worth.

I turned to see TK's reaction. His smile was quite reassuring. I thanked him inwardly.

"So, we have the third lead actor," Kaushik summed it up.

I didn't know then that this act would turn into my passion and purpose, a medium to channelize my enthusiasm and ambition, an integral part of my life in the times to follow.

For the fourth lead character, we had Rudra Rakesh. Rudra was a typical character in himself. He was very talented, but everyone knew about his insincerity. He possessed a strange ability to irritate others – he would never do what he was asked for, never stick to the written script and dialogues, always came late and acted important. But during rehearsals, Shashi and Rudra had a showdown, after which the latter mellowed down a little.

Another person who left a mark with his unique performance was Vishal Arora. Vishal was playing the role of a drunkard, and he was playing it so effortlessly. It was exposed later during the semester, why it all came so naturally to him.

~ 11 ~

Since the skit practice began, all evenings were spent in the storage hall. Over the weekends, we practiced in the afternoon as well. Sometimes we also occupied the TV room. Multiple teams were working in tandem. Gradually, I developed a habit to discuss the developments in the skit with Gautam and Sid at the end of the day.

"Among the four leads, Barnwal is able to understand and deliver scenes faster than others. He is playing the character of Indra, the most important one, roaming around the hall all the time."

"Rudra is still continuously reminded of sticking to one dialogue. As such, the other actors in Rudra's scene always look confused. Otherwise, he is quite funny, with all his unique actions, in his role." I was honest about Rudra.

"Barnwal is so good, yar. He is quick and efficient with his dialogues delivery. For me, two things have come naturally – learning the script to the last word as well as delivering dialogues loudly. Playing the role is really tough. I am working on my modulation and movement on the stage. Every day I get scolded by Shashi for showing my back to the audience while changing location." I was working on my weak areas.

The funniest night was when people who were supposed to play the role of the opposite sex were selected. Since it was the hostel performance, all the female characters had to be performed by us only. So the fairest and the smoothest of the batch were selected and taught to walk, act, behave and even dance that way. Many folks from the second year, including Rocky, Kalra, Aniket, Viks and Vatsal joined us that night, just to have fun. The loudest cheers of the night during the practice sessions were reserved for these female leads.

"O chhamiya!"

"Where were you last night?" "

"I am sure you will find a new boyfriend in the college."

"He doesn't even require waxing!"

"He is just so natural. Go on, baby!"

They were like the energy boosters for the batch during those long nights.

New names started emerging for each one of us with every passing day. We no longer had Barnwal, Vishal and Animesh in the batch. They were replaced by Indra, Bewada and Apsara, respectively.

TK planned the next step for all of us. "Guys, we have done enough practice for individual readiness. Now, it's time to prepare for the overall film. We have fourteen scenes in the skit. We now need to get them in the right sequence."

TK and Shashi were quite familiar with the size of the hall. They wanted us to get used to the same.

"Guys we have marked lines on the floor of the storage hall to create the deck as well as the wings. It closely resembles the seminar hall, where we will be performing. You all need to plan your entry, standing positions, movements and exits as per these marked lines now."

Soon, the integration process started – sequencing and synchronization of scenes were fun because we could see things falling into place.

As the days passed, people became comfortable with their roles, started identifying ways of improvement in others, and most importantly, began looking at the bigger picture, beyond their individual roles. The best part was the enthu and cohesiveness in the batch – none of us missed the practice sessions and were punctual, avoiding any loss of time or delays.

The last 3 days were spent only in the run through, without any breaks. During these days, the importance of the production team became evident. From arranging and managing props to handling stage lights through the controls in the wing and spotlight from the first floor, playing background music using the laptop and coordinating support in the backstage as well as at the entry and exit points. It was amazing how everything came together to give that great experience of watching the skit.

Multiple customized props were created by the production team for the skit. Pushkar from our batch was an integral part of this activity. He was from Jaipur and had qualified under the reserved category. He was a tall and thin guy who always had a smile on his face. His nights were as long as ours, especially as we came closer to the event date.

"Pushkar has been working so hard," I pointed out to Gautam.

"Agree. It is really tiring as it requires a lot of patience. And Pushkar somehow fits in that role really well." Gautam was right "Does Prabhat also support him in his work?"

During these initial days, one could notice Pushkar hanging out with Prabhat, his department mate. They had developed a great bonding.

"Not really. But Prabhat hangs around until late during the practice, even though he is not participating. Pushkar is sometimes supported by Mridul. But unlike Pushkar, Mridul is not present consistently." Mridul was from Delhi. But unlike Sanghvi, he rarely stayed in the hostel.

A night before the event, everyone got their dresses for the role they were playing. Indra was trying to adjust his unique white dress and the special crown, Narad was wearing an orange dhoti, and others got their own laptops made from thermocol. These props brought so much of visual appeal to our skit. And then we had the practice session. People involved both on-stage, and off-stage wanted to give their best.

Anirudh, House Secy, had told us during a batch meet that the skit would let us experience the true spirit of working together. He was so right! We were creating memories for a lifetime.

The night before the event, every house was given an hour in the seminar hall for final dress rehearsal. These slots were spread through the whole night for the 9 hostels. We were eighth in the queue and had our slot at 3:00 a.m. The excitement had kept us awake. I had been in that hall as a spectator, but for the first time, I was on the stage running from one wing to the other, visualizing a crowd of more than one thousand people spread across the ground and first floor of the hall, watching our performance. It was getting as real as it could get!

III
Witnessing the 'Real Enthu'

~ 12 ~

The day had arrived! For the seniors, it might have been a regular thing, but for a fresher like me, it was a different experience. The excitement along with a sense of anxiety made me visit the restroom frequently.

That day, we attended the morning classes as usual. In the evening, we had the last round of run-throughs with the full props. After finishing with the practice, we left for the seminar hall. Ara's performance had started. They had the fourth slot. Shivalik was to perform next. They were already backstage. The changing rooms were bustling with actors busy getting ready for the show. We had the sixth slot in the queue of nine hostels for our performance.

Lot of dressing and make-up work was required for the cast of our skit. So, we had to start the preparation as soon as we reached there. The most complicated part of the overall process was to change the gender of a few people. Going literally, it would have taken a lifetime, but here it was just to attach, or hold the twin assets on the bare chests of some of my fellow fachas.

Depending on their chest sizes, fitting bras were bought a day earlier. The process involved tying up bras and then filling each cup with either lemon, oranges or tennis balls depending on the role requirements. For the role of a woman, an orange was sufficient, but for a dance item number, tennis balls along with a bunch of papers to keep them stable were essential to have the "size does matter" effect. And people were not leaving any opportunity to tease the poor guys, even at this hour.

Our slot was announced soon after. We rushed towards the stage. As we entered from the backstage, everyone took up the allotted task – Pushkar started fitting backdrops, TK began marking positions and setting the scene, Guru and Shashi got on to testing light controls, and so on. We were allotted ten minutes for setting things up and we used it well.

All the actors were left on their own to concentrate before the final performance. I was nervous, but showcased confidence on my face. Within a few minutes, all of us took our positions. We were all set.

Audience lights were slowly switched off. TK, standing in the wing, made the announcement with the skit introduction, "Karakoram House presents before you, a skit that will take you back to the time when you had entered this campus for the first time. Do re-live that unforgettable period while this performance recreates those magical moments. Ladies and gentleman, Kara fachas present before you, *Yaadein.*"

The stage was wholly transformed into a mythical grand court of Indra. The opening of the stage curtain was accompanied with cheering by the Karaites sitting amongst the audience. All of us got pumped up. As soon as the lights turned on, Barnwal as Indra started the proceedings from Swarg lok.

The light setting helped the performers on the stage in a strange way. With lights flashing in our eyes, we couldn't figure out the size and spread of the crowd. That was comforting for a fresher!

We were soon comfortable in our roles, the initial nervousness having given way to normal execution. We could hear loud laughs from the audience for our punch lines, which helped us gain confidence.

The first four scene-changes went smooth. As we were approaching the end of the fifth scene, Barnwal was supposed to stand, and then while having an animated discussion, both of us were supposed to walk out of the right wing. But Barnwal didn't get up at the moment he was supposed to stand up from his chair. I thought maybe he had forgotten. So, while completing my dialogue, I went closer to him and tried signalling him quietly for our exit. He didn't budge. Our original plan was to switch off the lights as soon as we walked out, to set the stage for the next scene which had Rudra and Makhija. But, with Barnwal not ready to move, TK had to get the lights switched off before our exit. I then saw Barnwal getting up hurriedly, holding on to his *dhoti* and running to the wing. As I walked to him, I realized that the elastic of his *dhoti* had given away – thanks to the size of his tummy. And Pushkar was finding an alternative to make it work. No one in the audience noticed this unplanned intervention.

Our next entry was in less than three mins. As we could not find an alternative, I got my leather belt strapped on top of Barnwal's dhoti. I was hoping it would hold his dhoti for the next nine scenes.

My leather belt didn't disappoint for the rest of the skit. Every aspect of the fresher life that we enacted was duly acknowledged by the crowd. With every applause, our level of confidence kept soaring. Other than the Barnwal gaffe, everything went as planned and practiced. Surprisingly, even Bala did not forget his dialogues.

The skit helped me learn for the first time that there was nothing more satisfying for the performer than the applause from the crowd during the performance.

The skit was a hit. As soon as we walked around the hall to join Kara *junta,* Double A walked up to us and said, "Rocking performance guys. Kara ka enthu high hai."

And soon, one of my department-mates from Kumaon walked up to me and said, "You really surprised me Abhimanyu! Never expected you could be so lively on the stage. Great job, man!"

The performance after us was solid, but the one later was at best average. Kumaon had the last slot – theirs was always an awaited performance. We had heard a lot about them. The history of Kara-Kumaon rivalry in cultural activities, especially dramatics and music, had already been narrated to us several times by our seniors. We had witnessed the same last week during the musical event for the freshers. With the seeds of the rivalry already sown in our hearts, we watched their performance with full attention.

Kumaon left a lasting impact with their performance. It made me realize the importance of the script for an act to be more than successful. Their actors also did justice to the script with their comic timing. Overall, I felt they had performed better than us. Somewhere deep within, it left me with an encouragement to play a larger and more significant role in this rivalry.

As the points from the judges were being summed up, every hostel had enough time to go back to their cheering ways. The entire seminar hall was falling small for the high decibel voices. The air was filled with one-liners from all the hostels. Each had a few of them, and the respective hostels kept changing them at regular intervals.

And then, the announcement for the declaration of the results came. The Judging committee comprised of a final year student from NSD, an IIT Delhi dramatics club alumni and IIT Dean for Student Affairs. Dean Sir had the mic.

"Each and every performance that we saw today had something in it. It was tough for us to judge and award only one, but as for every competition, there are winners and losers. Although, we have come up with the top three, the others were in no way inferior." We held our breaths, anticipating what would follow. Sensing our impatience, the judge cut his talk short and lifted the paper in his hand.

"We will start with the third place." After a moment of pause, he said, "The third place goes to Vindhyachal." The left half of the middle rows were in thick of the action. I could notice my department-mates cheering at the top of their voices.

"The second place goes to Shivalik," This time the upper floor of the seminar hall echoed with a huge roar. A synchronized thumping with the feet immediately followed, giving a feel as if the balcony of the seminar hall would soon come down.

Few of us Kara freshers looked at each other. I could now guess the winner. I could see TK standing in the front, closer to the stage. He was entirely composed, listening to the announcements. I was looking at him for his final reaction.

"And the winner for today is... Kumaon." The pause was deliberate. The right-most front part of the seminar hall erupted. Kumaon's celebration knew no bound.

On hearing the final results, TK simply blinked and took a long breath. There was no other emotion visible on his face.

The announcement of results dropped our spirits. I could predict Kumaon as the winner and knew that Vindy (Vindhyachal) had given us tough completion. But I didn't expect Shiva to be ahead of us, though I couldn't see their performance. Most of us felt as if all the hard work that we had put in had ended up nowhere.

But someone was not thinking on the same lines. The one who had put in the maximum efforts, who owned the entire responsibility, and who had taken care of the enthu that he had instilled in others - TK, the enthu king.

Immediately after the announcement, in between the cheering of hostels that had won, TK's loud, unique voice came up with a thrust, "Kara ka enthu high hai."

This cheer was enough to break us free from the state of disappointment. Seeing the other victorious hostels cheering, the infused enthu and the urge to show that we were always the best, needed only a trigger and TK provided the required spark.

"Kara ka enthu..." TK cheered again.

"...High hai!" This time he was not alone. Gautam and I joined him in the chorus. And then, Sanghvi and everyone else joined us in the next round of cheering.

In that loss, the kind of spirit TK maintained was indeed inspiring. He didn't let us feel down and out in the situation. His behaviour also imparted a sense of courage in me. It taught me to be prepared for any setback, irrespective of the honest efforts one could put in.

~ 13 ~

With conclusion of facha skit, the 'healthy interaction' period was over. A freshers' night was organized to formally welcome the first-year students. Although every fresher's ice-cream coupon was taken away by a senior at the hostel, there were no more sirs, formal wears, orders, batch meetings or healthy interaction. It was for the first time that we saw some of the most brilliant minds of the country stand in long queues, just to get free ice creams. It reminded me of an aged person once telling me that till date, he always found IITians not give up easily on things available for free!

The first year students had fully integrated with the hostel by now. That night was reserved for the bumps session. It was our chance to take out our frustration with the seniors. We had the opportunity to beat up seniors of our choice. It was as if the tables had turned.

Rudra started the process, "Let's start with Shashi."

He immediately pulled Shashi in the centre. Vishal, Prabhat and Gautam joined to raise Shashi in the air. Rest of us had our share of slapping his bum with whatever we could get in our hands – slipper, boots or brooms.

"TK, it's your turn now. You can't be left now." I pulled up TK.

Prabhat was after Guru's life, "I have reserved my maximum time for you, Guru."

Sanghvi and Rahul pulled up Rocky and Vatsal.

And then we had a long queue of Kaushik, Kalra and many others. All of them got the beating for all the pain they had given us in the past 4-5 weeks.

The seniors also felt proud in getting pulled in by the juniors. In a way, it was a sign of their popularity. At the end of the bumps session, we were asked to call every senior by their first name, to set the transition rolling.

TK and Shashi had told me earlier, "Those who rag you the most would eventually turn out to be your closest friends in the house." It was turning into reality. Shashi, Guru, Vatsal, Rocky, Kaushik and others - all had become our close friends.

Edison got us introduced to a senior from the third year. Amitabh Gupta was from his hometown Banaras. Edison used to share with us the *fundas* he received from Amitabh on all matters. Amitabh was the Common Room Secretary who was visible intermittently during the facha period.

Amitabh was an avid contributor of Hindi articles for the BSP magazines. He was also part of the house football team. One could notice him getting people together every evening for the football practice. The two enthusiasts from our batch to join those practices were Rudra and Sanghvi. He possessed gyaan on almost all the matters of interest for a fresher – studies, priorities in daily lite, fitness, leadership, courses to choose, and so on.

Basis few interactions with Amitabh, we realized his core funda of hostel life was "studying is the most important thing here in the institute. Enthu for other activities is important, but you need to prioritize studies, because there are higher chances that you may not end up gaining as much from passion for the hostel as you may end up losing on studies." Owing to his gyaan, he had gained respect from select people in the batch, especially Edison.

Gautam and I also became close to Amitabh, but for a different reason. It was our common interest in Hindi literature that brought us close. I could notice a great bond developing between Gautam and Amitabh over time.

Amitabh was from the same department as TK. Therefore, many a time we could see both of them together. Though in the hostel, Amitabh used to hang-out with another set of people as well. Jolly was the only person from Amitabh's group who had left any impression on the batch as he used to join us during the batch meets and interacted independently with freshers.

~ 14 ~

Until now, the fun part of our new lives in the campus had kept us busy, but the reality of the first 'Minor' was going to hit us shortly.

"It's hardly a week from now." Sid was already getting hyper. "We were so busy in hostel and extracurricular that we didn't see it coming. Seniors should have told us before."

Bansal seemed well-prepared. "How come you didn't see it coming? We were handed over the timetable for the semester on the first day itself. And it's clearly mentioned that every semester at the institute has 3 scheduled exams – 2 minors in between and 1 major at the end of the semester."

"I only noticed the planned mid-semester break. Now I realize that both the minors are scheduled before the break," Sid cribbed. "Let's gear up now."

"For me, the biggest challenge is to get over the sleepiness during class." I had a different problem to overcome.

On the weekend before the minor, the tempo was set for the exams. It was like a curfew in the hostel. Not many were visible loafing around – they could be seen reading either in their rooms or in the studying areas of the institute, i.e. exhibition aka exh hall in the main building, or reading room in the library.

For every department, the *junta* was in the process to identify one or two people in the hostel as the go-to man for all the notes and doubts. In rare cases, people had to identify someone from the other hostel. The most popular were those who were sincere and didn't mind sharing their notes. The ones who came up with all the excuses to not share and help others were nicknamed RG. This name came from the concept of relative grading (RG) that was used to evaluate students in the institute.

Bansal explained the concept of relative grading to Sid. "Under this concept, there is no absolute range of marks to get a certain grade in a course. Instead, a range is defined for every grade purely basis the performance of the overall student group, and so one will end up getting a grade relative to how others in the group have performed."

"So you mean, I may score 80 in a course but may end up getting 'B' grade because there may be many who would have scored more than me, while for the same score, I may end up getting 'A' if there are few who would have scored in that range?" Sid clarified.

"Bang on, Sid!" Bansal replied with a smile.

Rachit was my go-to man in Kara for my department. Unlike a few others in my department from other hostels, who were RG, Rachit was very helpful. Be it notes, be it explaining the subject matter, be it assignments – Rachit never refused to help.

Minor I was a bit of a reality check for me. I got to know that some papers would require real-time investment going forward.

I was discussing with Sid and he consoled me. "Doesn't matter. It's just the beginning. The next couple of days are like freedom from jail for all of us. Let's go out for a movie. We have been in Delhi for one-and-a-half months now and have not been to any cinema hall."

"As if you went for a movie every week in Bilaspur. Do you even have a theatre there?" Gautam always made fun of Sid's hometown.

"We have a few. Although it is better to go for morning shows there," Sid confessed honestly. We all burst out laughing.

"Sid, now you have a computer room for that. So, no morning shows. But let's go out for dinner in *Mezbaan* and then late night show tonight at Sangam?" Vivek had a plan.

"Yes, but no English movie please. It is so difficult to understand their accent." It was Sid again.

"Agree. It's time to go for a Bollywood masala movie. And let's give Sid this semester's time to prepare so that we may watch a Hollywood movie at the end of this semester," I was aligned with Sid's preference.

Bansal and Edison joined us in the plan.

Barring Bansal, who was from Delhi, it was the first time all of us were stepping outside the campus. And we didn't call it off until dawn.

☆ ☆

Soon, the results of Minor I started coming, and with it, the early academic toppers in the batch also began emerging. For the ones who had already made academics their goal for life – Bansal, Rachit, Thomas and Mridul – it was being reflected in their results. Sanghvi and Rahul were turning out to be the other strong performers in academics.

For my department and me, the most depressing results were in MA111. "Considering everything, I could proudly say that I was well above average with a score of 4.5. The average score for the department with all students under IIT JEE rank of 200 was 1.7!"

"It sounds a bit insane." Bansal didn't like it.

"Wait till you hear this. After distributing the papers, Professor announced that in the major exam, we will not have any time limit. We would be allowed to sit for hours. In fact, we could go back to the hostel and come back to continue writing the paper, if required." I told them.

"Oh my god!" was a common expression on the faces of all three of them.

As far as overall results for the rest of us were concerned, Gautam, Sid and Edison estimated that they belonged to the top half of their department. Interestingly, Sid had topped the other maths course meant for all other departments in the institute. He was pulled down because of his performance in the rest of the subjects. Vivek was struggling in most of the courses. I estimated myself to be the part of the top twenty-five percentile in three out of five courses. I could feel the need to pull up in others.

~ 15 ~

Every club had a calendar of events spread throughout the year between the first and the second semester. After the facha events and Minor-I, inter-hostel events across clubs commenced. I experienced many high-quality events of different BRCA clubs. I attended competitions like music duo and dumb arcades because of personal interest, while others like Hollywood quiz, English debate and oil painting to serve my inquisitiveness.

I realised there was so much to learn from each of these events. Either you learn from the content or from the participants.

I sat discussing with Sid in his room, along with Sanghvi. "If there is time at hand, there is so much to choose from." I was honest.

"Time is critical. That's one resource we are always short of!" Sid was bang on.

We also realised how along with individual talent, teamwork was required to excel in cultural activities.

"So when do we get to see the Kara versus Kumaon battle next?" Sid asked.

"It has to be a dramatics or a music event," Sanghvi stated the obvious.

"I know that. I am asking when we get to see the next big event."

"If I remember correctly, Shashi had mentioned that apart from the facha skit, the dramatics club has four large-scale competitive inter-hostel events – Hindi stage play, street play, English stage play as well as Music *Manoranjan* which it shares with the music club.

"And then, there is this Institute Stage Play production that acquires participation from the best performers and enthusiasts from the campus. Among all of them, the Hindi stage play followed by the street play are the other two events scheduled for this semester." I remembered it by heart.

"So basically we will get to see the rivalry in action next in the Hindi stage play." Sid was looking forward to the same.

Given the long lead time required for practice in the drama events, it was a matter of days to pick up the pace.

~ 16 ~

As expected, the date for the Hindi stage play was announced soon. And who else to lead such an important event other than TK!

TK called for a script reading session for all the known enthusiasts and surprise talent, if any. He had chosen a script and most probably decided upon the cast as well. Usual suspects from the first year – Barnwal, Makhija, Rudra, Vishal and I – and the second year – Shashi, Vatsal, Kaushik and Guru – joined TK, our director, in the TV room.

TK distributed a copy of the first chapter of the script to all of us while instructing the way forward. "Everyone will try different roles of the play as part of script reading exercise. I will keep changing the reader for a role as and when required. We will stick to the first chapter of the script for now. To start with, please go through the whole chapter."

After about fifteen minutes, TK asked Shashi, "Can you share your understanding from the reading?"

"To me, the play looks like a philosophical drama with a central character who has four people in his life. And it seems each of them will have different influences on this character. Of these four people, I guess that the character of his family doctor and older brother seem to be more prominent than that of his neighbour and childhood friend," Shashi briefly summarized what we all read.

"Anyone else wants to add anything?" TK wanted more.

"Just a minor addition from my side. I am not sure if the doctor and his elder brother are more prominent because this is just the first chapter. Although, it seems like the doctor is going to have a negative influence on the central character compared to his elder brother," I added my view.

"Interesting. Anything else?" We waited for a few seconds.

"Okay, if no one has anything else to add, then I will talk. It is indeed a philosophical drama. Let's not get into the discussion of which character is prominent and which is not. As Abhimanyu rightly pointed out, the first chapter is not enough to figure that out. In fact, there are three more characters in this play. As we do the reading now, please don't judge the character by how much airtime he is getting; rather try to make that airtime as effective as possible. After an hour of reading and trying different combinations, I will decide who is going to play which role in our performance," TK clarified the objective and was able to set the expectation.

For the next one-and-a-half hours, all of us kept reading the script as different characters of the play. We were expected to be as loud and forceful as possible. Our roles kept changing. I got the chance to try all the characters, except the central character. Shashi, Kaushik and Barnwal got the chance to try the central role. Obviously, TK knew what he was doing.

"I don't know about you guys, but I loved this session. It's fun to observe from outside." TK was wholly engaged during the reading.

"It was a learning experience for me. I could gain so much from others. Am sure others would have felt the same way," Vatsal expressed.

"True for me." It felt as if I spoke out of turn.

"Let me now tell you guys my first choices for the roles." TK had decided. "So, Shashi is going to play the central character. I was pre-decided on this, and none of you were able to challenge my starting point basis the reading exercise." Everyone knew Shashi was the best amongst us and so none of the other two who tried during the reading would have minded. "Then we will have Kaushik for the younger brother, Barnwal for the doctor, Abhimanyu for the childhood friend and Vishal for the neighbour. Vatsal is going to play another important relatively shorter role in the play, which you guys have not read yet. Now, there are a couple of more characters in the play that Rudra and Makhija should play. Guru, you will handle the production this time," TK stated clearly.

I could see the disappointment on Rudra and Makhija's face. Guru didn't show any emotion.

"Also, this requires everyone's commitment. Let me know if there is any constraint, especially for you - Shashi, Kaushik and Barnwal." TK gave away the importance of characters.

"Great that you raised this point TK. I am sure this is going to be a one of its kind of experience. My only concern is that I have to go home for the first half of the next week. I really want to be part of this group, but don't want all of you to suffer because of me," Kaushik raised his concern.

"A committed stakeholder available for seventy percent of the time is more valuable than a non-committed one. You will be part of this play, Kaushik, but let's do a swap. Abhimanyu you will play the role of the younger brother and Kaushik will play the role of the childhood friend. Collect a copy of the full script from my room tonight. Let's rock this one," TK announced his decision. The change in the role allocation was instant, and TK didn't leave any scope for discussion.

We collected the script from TK's room. He had one copy for each one of us with our names clearly written on top. He emphasized on "Please keep your individual copy with you all the time. Use the same copy to takes notes, underline important parts or make any edits. It will serve as a master for you." TK's methodical approach was quite clear to all of us.

As soon as I reached my room, I told Gautam and Sid what had happened. "I feel like I have received a promotion out of turn in my first job. I am very nervous about the role, though."

"Don't worry. Settle down and start preparing. Now that you have been promoted, try to make the best out of it. You can't get a better learning opportunity." Gautam calmed me down. I knew he trusted my talent more than myself. It raised my confidence, but it took me longer than usual to go to sleep that night.

~ 17 ~

We started practice the next day. It took me a day to realize what I have gotten into – there was a huge difference between a skit and a play.

A skit was more about reciting the dialogue with full energy without any inhibitions on the stage while maintaining your stage presence even when you were not talking. I was able to learn it quickly during the facha skit. The stage play that I was now part of was different level. It required an actor to develop deep understanding of the character, underlined thought process of the director, role build-up, dialogue delivery and modulation, on stage timing – the list was endless. There was so much of mental preparation required. It had no comparison to a skit.

Among all the participants from the second year, the experience of Shashi and Kaushik was clearly visible. Vatsal also seemed comfortable in his short role.

For most of us from the first year, it was a challenging experience. Even for Barnwal, it was no longer comfortable. Vishal, Rudra and Makhija had relatively lesser stage time, so they were comparatively relaxed.

I was not able to meet even half the expectation that TK had with my role. TK knew it was my first time and so he was investing a lot of time with my body language, voice modulation, actions, dialogues, as if he knew the character in and out.

And in between all this, the talk about the rivalry between Kara and Kumaon enhanced the pressure. "Is this the best that you can do? Kumaon audience will rip you apart during the performance," TK screamed as I completed the monologue scene. "Abhimanyu, you are representing Kara! I can't believe you still don't understand this. Either you are not trying enough, or I am not able to communicate what is expected." The only satisfaction was that TK still did not raise any question on my abilities.

We were at the end of the first week. The TV room was converted into a makeshift stage with a set up comprising of all the essentials of a drawing and bedroom meant for different scenes of our play. The setting was as per the size and dimensions of the seminar hall. I was trying to put in as much effort as possible. That night, when we were packing up, TK was not happy with the progress. "Abhimanyu, we need to spend more time. You've made a lot of progress, but we still have a long way to go. Apart from the daily night practice when everyone is here, we need to spend more time individually. Let us meet in the evening post snacks, before dinner. And then Vishal, we two should spend some time together after I am done with Abhimanyu."

"TK, what about your tutorials in the evening?" Shashi raised a query.

"I have enough attendance. I will manage," TK replied swiftly. "Okay let us pack up, will meet tomorrow evening."

And then for the next one week, TK made me go through one hell of a routine.

"It seems you are practicing dialogues even in sleep," Gautam and Bansal pointed out to me.

Everyone was all praise, but nevertheless, it was taking a toll on my body as well as the mind. It was taxing to make so many choices and prioritize between classes, extra-curricular, hostel spirit and own personal time.

"Can someone really bother so much about the hostel? Does this thought of hostel being the second home really make any sense? Does anybody care about what you do for the hostel? How can one invest so much time for the hostel? What does one gain by going through all this?" These were the thoughts boggling my mind while sitting idle at Wind T, the breeziest, windiest spot in the campus during a free lecture.

"Hey, Abhimanyu! Already started bunking classes? You have not even completed three months in the institute," I heard TK tease me.

I turned back to find TK with Amitabh. Amitabh had a class, I suppose, so, he went asking TK to meet in one of the afternoon classes.

"No! Haven't bunked a single till now. But I think I will start soon," I replied with a smile.

"Why? Got a partner to do that?" He asked with raised eyebrows.

"Partner?" I didn't understand.

"I mean, girlfriend. Already made one?" He said with a smile.

"No no! Not possible for me," I quipped.

"It is possible for everyone, though it is difficult to get a decent one. It's just two girls for every nine boys here in the institute, and most of the decent ones get fixed within a month." He knew the statistics.

"Coming back to the hostel for lunch?" TK asked. I had classes only after lunch, so I joined him.

"So, why will you soon start bunking classes?" TK asked again.

"It is getting difficult to manage late night practices along with the morning lectures. Either of these two needs to be avoided," I replied in short.

"Welcome to the world of time management, boss! Everyone here has the same complaint. A 9-pointer complains about the lack of time to accommodate every subject in his schedule, which leads him to miss out a 10. An extra-curricular stud complains about simultaneous participation in so many events at the same time. A 5-pointer complains about missing out time to study in between his daily doses of games, browsing, movies and other activities," he tried to calm down my confusion.

"Then, what to do?" I asked with a blank face.

"Try to manage both. That is what you are supposed to do for the rest of your life – managing multiple activities and tasks at the same time. And most importantly, you should neither miss the part of life which you may be enjoying in the present, which help you live a fulfilling life; nor the one which is important in the long run." He tried to answer my query.

"So, you mean I should continue with plays and skits only if I enjoy them? Then what about hostel spirit that you had been speaking about in the initial days?" I had queries.

"That pep talk was a part of my duty. Someone must do it to pass on the traditions to the new people joining the family. And for your batch, I was the one. You will learn more about it as you grow senior.

"Let me tell you an important thing. Interest in such kind of activities is essential. But if you don't have the hostel and team spirit, you will not enjoy these activities in the same way. It is an opportunity to work in groups, develop our thoughts together, give an output under a single umbrella and a chance to represent an institution, hostel in our case. In fact, this spirit will help you enjoy and celebrate smaller occasions which you may not have done or even thought of otherwise. In fact, you must treat the hostel spirit and interest in such activities as two sides of the same coin. It just makes whatever we are doing more enjoyable."

"I think that's a much better way to think about this," I concluded as we had reached Karakoram. It started to make so much sense now for a fresher.

~ 18 ~

The conversation with TK helped me clear my mind from the surrounding noise. It reflected in the practice sessions.

"It feels someone has got his focus back." TK knew it.

"Not only focus. The future also seems to be clear." I was confident now.

During the last two days before the event, I learned a new important element of the stage plays. For these two days, I found TK highly invested in the light settings. TK and Shashi knew the spread and location of floodlights and spotlights fitted in the seminar hall. They spent a lot of time planning the exact location of the cast on stage during different scenes to create the best possible lighting impact. Guru was asked to control the lights from the wing. He got Sanghvi for assistance in the Wing and Pushkar for on-stage support. Aniket and Viks were brought in to control the focus lights from the first floor. It was only during the practice slot in the seminar hall that I felt the real impact of TK's homework. I could understand the feeling of contrast between lightness and darkness, the effect of floodlights and spotlights and the intensity driven by the sheer direction of light.

On the day of the event, we didn't have any practice. TK wanted us to save all our energy for the final performance. Sitting in a circle, the whole team went through the script recital twice.

At the seminar hall, we found the audience in huge numbers. But unlike the facha skit, the crowd was sane, with limited cheering between the performances. We waited backstage for out slot. As soon as our performance was announced, Guru with the help of Sanghvi and Pushkar got the stage set. Shashi set the tone for the next one hour with a powerful opening scene. It got the attention of the crowd. There was drama, there was emotion, there was humour, and above all, there was a connection between the actors as we performed. There was pin drop silence through the performance. Change in stage settings between breaks, lights and scene changes went smoothly. The plan was perfectly executed and was well applauded.

This time we had the eighth slot for the event and was followed by Shivalik. They had a monologue which was an exciting concept for me to experience for the first time. It was hard to believe that a single person was able to keep the attention of the crowd for more than forty-five minutes. I got to know later that he was from the fourth year and was the cultural secretary of Shivalik last year. He had brought all his experience on to the stage today. We couldn't see Kumaon's performance. But whatever we heard from others, it was a gem.

The jury was a combination of people from NSD and IIT Delhi alums. Soon we had the results announced by them after the customary appreciation for all the performances. "We don't have the third position this time as we have two hostels sharing the second position. These two hostels are Kumaon...." my heart was beating hard ".... and Karakoram." The moment Kara's name was announced, I looked at TK. TK was looking at Shashi. He then turned to me and gave me a smile. I smiled back. All of us from Kara then cheered together "Kara ka enthu high hai" which overlapped with "Jai Kumaon".

"And the winner for today is... Vindhyachal." The announcement was followed by claps, whistling and cheering by the Vindy junta.

After a minute, the Jury resumed, "Now for the best actor, it was really tough for us to choose one single performance." This was surprising for me because I didn't know that there was the best actor award as well up for grabs.

"Before announcing the best actor, we would like to call two other performances which deserve a special mention. One is Ajit from the Shivalik House. Monologues are always a tough act, but he did a splendid job. The second one is Abhimanyu from Karakoram. It's challenging to maintain an identity in a play with so many important characters. And he deserves mention for creating a spark while being continuously surrounded with others."

As soon as the jury announced my name, I was awestruck. I just couldn't believe. Kara junta looked at me and showed me a thumbs up. I could only smile back.

The jury continued, "Now coming to the best actor award. It goes to Aditya from the Vindhyachal House. He is the prime reason for them being the champion today."

My feeling of being surprised immediately converted into being competitive - it was funny.

"Also, among so many impressive performances, it was difficult for us to choose the best director." Again a surprise for me, but I immediately started praying for TK.

"But we finally decided to give it to Sanjeev from Kumaon. He deserves it for leaving an impact with such a simple story. He has an eye for detail. Keep it up, Sanjeev!" I looked at TK. He was still smiling. He went to Sanjeev and congratulated him.

Soon, the crowd dispersed. And then came the most boring part of the whole exercise – taking everything that we had brought as part of the stage setting back to the hostel. No one had any enthu for this useless activity, but Guru ensured to get it done.

~ 19 ~

Soon, we had the Minor-II exams of the semester. Like the last time, it was marked with intense days of study followed by night outs, one after another. By this time, everyone had got a clear idea of who was the go-to-man for each course. Rachit remained my notes man!

One explicit learning from Minor-I days that junta applied during Minor-2 was giving notes to the Xerox shop a night in advance. This was the time when Xerox shops in the institute did the bulk of their business, and so they worked round the clock.

As soon as the Minor II was over, people left for their homes for the mid-semester break.

When we were back after the Dusshera holidays, the biggest experience of the year awaited us. *Rendezvous*, the annual cultural festival of IIT Delhi, organized by BRCA was scheduled over the coming Friday to Sunday. Every fresher looked forward to Rendezvous, given they were going to witness such a large-scale fest for the first time in their lives. We had an exciting agenda spread over three days – professional musical nights, rock show, Haasya Kavi Sammelan, inter-college group dance, fashion show, and stage plays among others.

The crowd expected in Rendezvous was always the prime attraction. One could get to see and meet a lot of girls, especially from DU. It was a unique experience for a small town boy to witness events like RDX, where only couples were allowed to dance on the DJ music stationed near the swimming pool. Despite large girls' crowd to keep one interested, we were only able to hang out as a gang of boys overwhelmed with things around.

"Sid, any luck with making friends with girls today?" Edison had already tried his luck last night.

"Not really. I am going to try RDX today, though," Sid had plans.

"RDX? You know that you require a girl partner for that?" Vivek was surprised.

"Come with me. I will show you," Sid said confidently.

All six of us went together to SAC in the evening. Euphoria band was going to perform that night. As was the case last night, a considerable crowd was stationed outside the SAC. As soon as we reached there, I asked Sid, "So what's the plan, Sid?"

"Nothing. Just be confident," Sid said while walking away from us. He went to a group of three girls standing at the SAC entrance. We were left behind.

"Are you guys waiting for someone?" Sid reached out to them.

"Sorry?" one of them replied.

"No, I was just checking if any of you plan to go to RDX?"

"Actually yes, but we don't have partners," the other girl replied to Sid.

"I can help," Sid offered.

"Either the three of us go together, or none of us will join," the girls seemed interested, but wanted to stick together.

"Okay, here is the plan. Security Volunteers are checking for couples at the entry, But not at the exit. Why don't I take you girls one by one? One of you may have to wait for some time though. But still, it's better than not getting in at all," Sid came up with the best of plans.

"That's brilliant!"

We still don't know why they agreed only after a small discussion within themselves. Sid came back and joined us just after an hour while we were watching the band performance.

"Great Sid! Had fun?" Gautam checked with him when he was back.

"Not bad. I deliberately waited inside before getting the next one so that I get to spend some time with the girls. When all three of them were together inside, I soon realized that I wasn't required. So here I am with you guys!" Sid confessed.

"Hats off to you Sid, I can never pull that off," I said.

"Honestly, I wasn't sure either. I had thought that I may have to try a few times before being successful. Maybe it was my day, so it clicked in the first time itself!" Sid sounded very happy.

We had the night of our lives that day – watching a live band performance for the first time ever was exhilarating.

Next day, we planned to attend the inter-college group dance event in the convocation hall (Convo) in the night. Unlike the open-air theatre in SAC, Convo had limited seats. So events in Convo required passes for entry, which we failed to collect. We were still optimistic but were proven wrong in the evening. Finally, we decided to spend the evening watching Rock Show in the open air theatre. Edison didn't join us as he continued trying his luck at Convo.

When we got back to hostel, Edison was already there. He was furious with his experience. "I must tell you the power that these Jwala (Jwalamukhi hostel) guys are enjoying. The security volunteers are all from Jwala. They don't allow people from other hostels, but it's a free passage for the junta from Jwala. And then most of them are carrying an official card, anyway."

"All fachas from Jwala were also allowed?" I checked with him.

"Yeah. All of them, and we were asked for passes. Damn!"

"I didn't mind missing the inter-college group dance. I loved the rock show. I have created my new playlist as well." Sid was in a different zone altogether.

"It's not about what we missed, Sid. It's about the privilege that comes along naturally. I could see it must be special. Let's see, if we can enjoy any such privilege in the next three years," Gautam was thoughtful.

Overall, we could appreciate the talent from other campuses who participated - dancers, speakers, artists and several others. We could also acknowledge the effort that went into organizing such a large scale event.

☆☆

One fine Friday night, the photography club had organized for a telescope to experience the appearance of a celestial body, that happened once in several hundred years. A decent crowd gathered on the terrace of the main building.

It was mesmerising to watch the body make an appearance and vanish again into a long hibernation. It was close to 1 a.m. and most of the people had already gone back. As the club secretary was one of my department seniors, he agreed to let us use the telescope for a little longer. Thus, it was only Gautam, Vivek, Edison, Sid and I on the top of the main building along with the telescope.

We started with having closer looks of Qutab Minar and other tall buildings in the vicinity. While focusing the telescope on the top floor of Qutab Minar, Sid came up with his brilliant idea.

"Why are we going so far off when heaven itself can be traversed close by?"

"Heaven, what heaven?" Edison quizzed.

"See, though we losers could never consider girls' hostel as a place where beauties reside, still we can try our luck," Sid said with a wink. He took the telescope control from Edison and said,

'I will show you something which you have never seen in your life, that's my bet."

The aim was set at Himadri, one of the two girls' hostels in the campus. The target was thoroughly searched from top to bottom. Sid finally set it at the second floor as most of the windows were open on that floor.

"Hey guys, someone just entered her room. I guess she is from the third year. I have seen her in the institute! She's just come from somewhere, I guess." Sid almost shouted. He had located a girl of his department who was two years senior to him.

"She must have gone to meet one of her boyfriends." Gautam broke his silence. He sounded excited.

"Wait, someone has come at her door... She is animatedly chatting with the visitor. She gave her something, I think a book."

We were all listening intently. "The other girl is gone now... She's locked the door from inside. She is drinking water..."

Sid had been speaking to us as an experienced commentator. Soon Vivek forcibly removed Sid and sat on the spectator's seat. It was a kind of tragedy for the rest of us because only one could see through the telescope at a time.

"She's looking into the mirror... There she goes!" Vivek shouted at the top of his voice. "She has opened the top two buttons of her shirt and is still looking mysteriously into the mirror."

At this, Vivek was forced to leave because of his inability to make us visualize the drama going on. Gautam immediately took his seat.

"Hey guys, she has almost unbuttoned her shirt. But she is facing the other side. So no luck so far." Gautam's version of the drama was very expressive.

"She is walking back and forth in front of the mirror. I think she is analyzing her walking style along with her other assets. But still, nothing substantial is visible in the side view," Gautam was excited.

"She dropped her top!" Gautam was getting too excited.

"Edison, this is your only chance to experience something big. I doubt you will be able to do anything otherwise," Sid pushed Edison to go for it and he took control from Gautam.

The way things were shaping up, I was planning to go last to experience the best possible visuals. So I didn't show any urgency to get into the spectator's seat.

Edison almost jumped off his seat. "What am I seeing? I can't believe this. Why is she bending now? I think she is trying to unbutton her skirt." The latest observation was enough to blow off the lid.

Though Edison sounded very ordinary, everyone jumped on him. I was the only one left who hadn't had a view till now, so I was confident that next chance would be mine. But this unbuttoning of skirt forced everyone to go out of control. And because we all were trying to get the best view, the telescope itself got disturbed from the set position.

"Why did you change the position, Edison?" Vivek shouted.

"I didn't, Abhimanyu pushed me," Edison shouted back.

"It was my turn!" I sounded disappointed.

"Fine! Let's just shift it back to the same position" Sid started to set it to an earlier position.

After it was set again, Gautam informed, "Hey the lights of her room are off."

"Hey, lights are on again," he shouted in a few seconds.

"Shit man!" Sid sounded disappointed. He immediately got up.

I took up the seat at last. Megha was sitting in front of her desktop in her night suit. "I could get nothing out of this."

At that moment, a guard arrived at the rooftop.

"What are you people doing here when the event was over long back?" He asked us to leave the place and go back to our respective hostels.

I kept back the telescope where it was supposed to be. And then we left the terrace to return to the hostel. We cursed Edison as he was the one who got to the see the best view. And I, not being able to see anything but the night dress, was the centre of all the fun.

~ 20 ~

A week after the Rendezvous, the final set of inter-hostel events for the semester picked up pace. That's when the dramatics club announced the date for the street play – another large-scale event. We had two weeks to prepare.

TK took up the responsibility of the script. "Let me first write the script. Will update you guys next week when am done with it."

I checked with Shashi separately on this. "Why do we need to spend so much time on the script?"

Shashi explained, "Abhimanyu, a street play is very different from the stage play. Here, we need to write a new script from scratch as well as practice the execution. Writing the script is core of the overall effort. Without a good script, we can't pull off a decent performance. On ground execution is of different style but relatively simpler compared to the stage plays."

TK called Shashi, Gautam and me a couple of days after the event date was announced. "Looks like TK has a special role for you in his script." I teased Gautam.

TK looked disturbed when we met him, "Guys, I had started writing the script. But there is some personal emergency at home which I need to attend to. The script is not even close to completion. Shashi, you know, if we don't get the script right, we have already lost the battle. So, you will have to take it up from here. Sorry for this unplanned development." TK explained the situation.

"Totally understand, TK. We will try our best." Shashi assured him.

"And TK, let us know if you need any help with the personal situation as well," Gautam was concerned.

"Thanks a ton. Will let you know in case I need any help. All the best," TK left in the afternoon after handing over all the pages that he had written.

Within a couple of days, I realized that it was too much left for Shashi to take care of. My ability, being a novice, to contribute was limited anyway.

Shashi got Gautam on-board. "Gautam, I will need your help in writing the short couplets as the punchlines for our performance. Your command over language is way better than anyone."

With the delay, Shashi had to start the practice with an incomplete script. In parallel, he worked along with Gautam to complete the same. It was not an easy job. Scenes were changing and new dialogues were added or refreshed as we progressed.

Finally, given the time Shashi and Gautam had in hand, they pulled off a decent entry for the house. All of us, including Gautam, Rudra, Vishal, Makhija and Barnwal were part of Kara's execution. We also roped in Edison, Bala, Sanghvi and Rahul from the first year to form the team.

It was also the first time that Gautam and I did something together. Overall, thanks to Gautam's creative writing I felt we had created an entry where we had few high points. Again, it turned out to be an excellent learning experience for me. But our entry was not good enough to end up in the top three. Kumaon, Vindy and Jwala grabbed the top three positions.

The street play was the last big cultural event of the semester. Sports events for the semester were also concluded after that. We bagged some and lost some, but made great bonds in the process.

It was soon time for majors for the semester. It was a week-long affair. The night before the MA111 was the most stressful night for me. Though I was above average in the class basis combined score of minors I and II, getting a decent grade remained a challenge.

Sid walked into my room stating, "I hate tomorrow's exam course. It's just theory after theory."

"You don't have an option. Likewise, I don't have an option to avoid my exam tomorrow," I had my own problems to sort out.

"Do you have MA111 tomorrow?"

"Yes!"

"Show me what you are studying." Sid was interested. He grabbed a chair next to me and started looking at my notes.

We started discussing the problem that I was trying to solve from one of the lists of sample questions. The discussion soon made me realize that Sid's mathematical aptitude was brilliant! We spent close to one-and-a-half hours discussing questions. Sid helped me solve a couple of them which I was trying to figure out until now, before getting back to his own course that he was not liking.

I realized the worth of spending time with Sid on the subject the next day. Whether it was my luck or learning from the time well spent, I could crack more questions than my own expectations.

In the evening when I met Sid, I thanked him. "Thanks, Sid. I could perform better than I was expecting – thanks to the time spent with you! How was your exam?"

"My exam went as I was expecting. I always found it difficult to write long explanatory answers, and this was no different. But to tell you the truth, I just wanted to get over with it!" Sid had his own way of dealing with stuff. It defined his character - effort put in utterly proportional to the level of interest.

Majors gave all of us an accurate picture of where we stood in academics as the overall semester results were available. For me, there were subjects where I could pull off despite not paying attention in the classes. While in others, not attending classes regularly and procrastination at my end was coming to bite me.

In the maths course, I ended up with a good grade. Overall, I ended up in the top twenty-five percentile of the department which left me wanting more from myself.

Gautam, Edison and Sid ended up in the first half of their respective departments. Bansal was in the top three of his department, while Vivek's struggle continued. I didn't dare to ask details from Vivek directly, but Sid told me that he couldn't clear all his courses of the first semester.

I made a point to myself from what I had learned from TK. "One needs to multi-task, and I can't run away from it."

Year 1: Semester II

Jan – May 2003

Updated Index of characters: Semester II

Abhimanyu's batch (First Year)

Abhimanyu Rishabh	Main protagonist of the Story
Prashant *Gautam*	Abhimanyu's room-mate and best friend; rare talent of Hindi poetry and debating
Siddharth aka *Sid*	A small town boy; perfect friend of Abhimanyu
Saurabh *Bansal*	Abhimanyu's room-mate and friend; diligent and logical individual in the group
Harshvardhan *Edison*	A good friend of Abhimanyu & Gautam; shared interests in Hindi literature
Vivek	An essential part of Abhimanyu's friend circle
Rudra Rakesh	Dramatics (comedy) and Athletics talent; Insincere and insensitive in approach
Vishal Arora	Best friend of Rudra; known for his drinking abilities
Pushkar	Expert in fine arts; ardent participant of house production team
Prabhat	Department mate and very good friend of Pushkar

Shubham	Swimming champion; small town boy from Bihar
Aditya *Sanghvi*	A very enthusiastic individual - shared an unsaid bond with Abhimanyu for the hostel work
Makhija	Quizzing talent; acquaintance of everyone in the batch; self-proclaimed multi-topic expert
Rahul	Sports talent; fastest cricket bowler in the institute
Utkarsh	Sports talent; expertise in TT, Baddy, Carom
Thomas	Rare English debating talent in the institute; respected individual in the batch
Bala	Exceptional talent in music; master of multiple musical instruments
Barnwal	Only person in the batch with prior theatre experience
Mridul	Fine Arts expert; rarely resided in the house consistently
Rachit	Abhimanyu's department mate; always a helping hand in studies

One year senior to Abhimanyu's batch (2nd Year)

Shashi Ranjan Singh	Dramatics Club Representative, a major cultural club; immense theatre talent
Vikash *aka Guru*	Enthusiastic soul with a serious approach to hostel work; excellent friend of Shashi

Rocky	Sports talent: Baddy, Squash, Hockey; Film Club, a minor club, Representative
Vatsal	Sports (Cricket) and Dramatics (comedy) talent; famous for his sense of humour
Kaushik	Hindi Samiti Club Representative; Most charming and popular senior; close friend of Shashi
Kalra	Best Athlete in the house; represented Kara in most of the sports
Aniket	Music Club Representative
Viks	A good friend of Guru; visible face in the batch

Two years senior to Abhimanyu's batch (Third Year)

Tarun Khandelwal aka *TK*	House Cultural Secretary; one of the best theatre talents in the institute; Individual with an unmatched passion for the house
Aman Awasthi aka *Double A*	House Maintenance Secretary; best friend of TK; Tag team with TK for all the Housework
Amitabh Gupta	TK's department mate; close friend of Edison from School
Arora	House Mess Secretary; Close friend of Double A and TK
Vir aka *Viru*	House Sports Secretary; close friend of Amitabh

Jolly	A friend of both TK and Amitabh; theatre talent in the House
Spidy	Rare English debating and quizzing talent in the Institute
Lakhan	A very good friend of Amitabh

Three years senior to Abhimanyu's batch (Fourth Year)

Anirudh Sharma	Karakoram House Secretary; facilitated the initial round of healthy interaction
Narayan	Partner of Anirudh in the House politics during their times Referred as Godfather of the House

IV
Early signs of the future - I

~ 21 ~

The second semester started in the first week of January. It was the peak of Delhi's winter, which made it awfully tough to make it to the early morning classes. Many found it easier to attend them after staying up the whole night, rather than waking up and getting out of the blanket in the morning. Although heaters were not allowed, rules didn't stop people from smuggling them into their rooms.

We were upgraded from three people to two people per room. Gautam and I remained roommates; Bansal shifted with Edison; Sid and Vivek were now new roommates too. Similarly, new pairs of roommates emerged in the batch – Sanghvi & Makhija, Pushkar & Prabhat and others.

January soon turned out to be a month of proxies. There were three types of people in the batch – those who couldn't attend the classes; those who attended but couldn't mark proxies; and those who were regular and could signal proxies. The third type was popular, and I was proudly one of them.

Now we knew that there were 9-pointers like Bansal and Rachit; talented people in creative fields, like Bala, Thomas, and Gautam; sporty people like Utkarsh; and few who had managed a balance between studies and extracurricular activities, like Rahul. And then there was a set who were identified by their enthusiasm and hostel spirit like Sanghvi and me.

Unlike 'Odd Semesters', inter-hostel events were planned only for the first 2.5 months in the 'Even Semesters'. Rest of the semester was meant for institute elections, year-end awards, and the passing of the baton to the next batch. As such, events started early in the second week. Few events including group dance and Indian musical night were planned in the starting weeks. TK continued to plan, lead, coordinate and put his best foot forward for the events.

Gautam and I were returning from the Hindi Samiti's parliamentary debate event where Kara didn't end up in the top three. TK was also with us.

"It didn't go as expected?" I asked Gautam.

"No yaar. This was a new format for me." Gautam didn't hide the disappointment.

"Don't worry, you will get to learn," I tried to cheer him up.

"Abhimanyu, I met the Institute Dramatics Secretary the other day. He told me you hadn't come for the Institute play auditions, so he reached out to you and you still refused?" TK changed the topic.

Institute play was a stage play production by the BRCA Dramatics Club. It brought together the best talent in the institute from across the hostels.

"Yeah, I refused," I said softly.

"Why?" Gautam looked at me with surprise. He didn't know about this.

"Because I didn't have the motivation," I responded impulsively.

"What do you mean?"

"I need to prioritize between so many things happening around me – both in studies and extra-curricular activities. Within extra-curricular, I would any day prefer spending my time and energy for an activity where I represent Kara than spending time on Institute production. House performances are associated with natural, intrinsic enthusiasm for me. I failed to identify any such rationale for myself in the Institute Production."

"But Institute production will help you learn and grow within the Institute's theatre group. Also, in a way, it's a recognition of your talent." Gautam had a fair point.

"You are correct Gautam. But the motivation of being popular at the institute level is nothing compared to winning events for Kara."

"I am not going to say if it's right or wrong, but I respect your choice Abhimanyu. You continue to grow as an individual." TK's words meant a lot for me.

"Completely agree with you, TK. Today's Abhimanyu is so different from the one I met the first time. From a person who was not very confident about himself to the one who can make such a choice, he has come a long way," Gautam made it even more significant.

"Okay, okay! But don't think that we have forgotten your performance in the parliamentary debate." I was trying to overcome the unexpected massive moment.

TK and I then continued pulling Gautam's leg until we reached the hostel.

~ 22 ~

February was the time for *Tryst*, IIT Delhi's technical fest. As this year AIC G. Sec. was from Kara, we were the hostel responsible for holding the fest. At the start of the semester, people from the first year were picked as volunteers for the different teams. We worked day in day out for the fest. For all of us, it was the first instance to work for the hostel beyond representing it in the cultural or sports events. It helped us experience the power that the organizing hostel enjoys while organizing such an event.

Tryst was marked with events across different technical topics and departments of the institute. And given it was a tech-fest, the fun quotient was bound to be much lower.

"Inter-college Robotics competition was the most popular event of the fest." Sid was correct in his evaluation.

"Hats off to the participants. There were so many robot

entries which were out of the world. The assigned tasks were also interesting. I watched the whole event." Bansal had loved it.

"I liked the musical night, with the local Delhi band. They performed all the hit numbers." Gautam had his own choice.

For Tryst, all the activity heads were from the second year - Guru, Rocky, Viks, Vatsal and others. We noticed that Guru stood out among all in handling responsibilities and getting the work done.

"Let's see if they can leverage it going forward," Gautam was thinking about the future.

"What do you mean?"

"Abhimanyu, this is the semester for power and politics. I know it is still early days, but one needs to start connecting the dots for sure."

It was for the first time that I was introduced to the concept of politics and power in the hostel.

Gautam elaborated, "I don't know how politics is played out here in IIT Delhi and Karakoram in particular, but irrespective of that, if someone has to start getting visible for the same, it has to start now. And I don't think there was any better opportunity than Tryst to pull that off. It has put a few ahead of others."

Now I was both curious and excited. Until now I had looked up to Gautam as a talented friend who I could trust. This conversation reflected his maturity and experience. Not only did he have interesting takes on every development, but he could also foresee future actions and reactions. He could read beyond the obvious. There was so much more to come from Gautam for me.

"Sid, between the theory and the lab courses, which one do you find more stressful?" I checked with Sid while preparing my report for the PH130 lab the next day.

"Obviously lab courses. Even the institute rank 1 holder will agree on this." Sid responded immediately.

"Exactly! In this semester every Tuesday night, I am so stressed because of this lab course. I don't mind preparing the report, but it's so stressful to undergo viva every week. And given the nature of experiments, anything and everything can be asked. It's like being evaluated continuously. At least in theory courses, we are evaluated only in Minors and Major, without facing any embarrassment during viva." I was thinking about the potential questions tomorrow.

"I always struggle in these lab courses. But then I feel it's good for people like me who otherwise will never talk to professors. It forces me to build confidence to interact with them." Sid again had a unique view about these lab courses.

I liked how Sid forced me to think differently. We soon had the minor-I of the even semester.

Learning from the last semester, this time I had put in an honest effort to be regular to classes since the beginning. The last-minute preparations and associated night outs didn't change during the minor, but awareness about the subject matter helped me considerably.

Post the Minor-I slowdown, juggernaut was back to business.

Two big events were planned at the end of the series of events that had started seven months earlier. One of them was the English play for the dramatics club and the other one was called Music Manoranjan (MM), a joint event for the dramatics and music club.

MM was an interesting concept – the right mix of theatrical creativity and musical talent. TK explained the idea to me. "In the event, hostels are supposed to perform a skit with a twist. The dialogues of the cast are supposed to be parodies or actual songs, and they need to be performed live in the background. So, there will be a team of musicians and singers playing the music and singing the parodies live in the background, while actors will perform their roles on the stage."

As it was clear from TK's explanation, a performance of this kind required the height of creativity, coordination and management.

The English play and MM were scheduled too close to each other. Though technically they belonged to different clubs, but had almost the same participants. Apparently, MM could only be prepared by TK. He had the prior experience, could write the script as well as bring in the right set of people. So, he gave the English play's responsibility to Jolly, his batchmate.

Jolly was a charming person with excellent control over English. He was quite visible during the facha period. Shashi had once told me, "Jolly was a strong contender for the position of Cultural Secretary last year, but then, their batch unanimously elected TK owing to his track record."

Soon, we saw Jolly preparing for a mono act play - an exciting concept. He used to practice alone in the common room, with sometimes TK or Amitabh accompanying him. Jolly and Amitabh were close friends.

But Gautam brought to my notice, "Amitabh is quite visible during the event, though it is supposed to be a solo performance by Jolly."

"Come on Gautam! I think you are over thinking!"

"Maybe you are correct! Anyway, from what I saw in the practice session, I think Jolly is pulling off a decent performance."

While Jolly's performance was really appreciated given his concept, we didn't end up in the top three spots in the English play event.

~ 23 ~

MM was TK's last hurrah as the Cultural Secretary. The format of the event required preparing the script with songs and parodies before any practice could start.

"My knowledge of Hindi songs could be put to great use while preparing the script. So, I offered my help to TK on the script." I told Gautam.

"Yeah it will help you learn this format as well," Gautam bucked me up.

TK completed his script with some help from me and Shashi. Maybe TK was over-cautious from the debacle of the street play, so he kept Shashi and me involved in it, right from the start.

TK then built two core teams – music team and drama team.

Music team comprised of synthesizer, tabla, drum, guitar and flute players along with the best singers in the house. It had Aniket, Bala and others who were pulled from different batches. He also got Debo from the third year, who was possibly the best guitarist in the campus, on board.

TK then assembled a big drama team comprising of people beyond the usual stage performers – Shashi, Vatsal, Rocky, Guru, Kaushik, Rudra, Vishal, Barnwal, Makhija and I among many other first years. Rocky was an exciting addition because I had not seen him in any drama event until now.

"Guys, before getting into action mode, to set the tone I want to share the few deliberate surprises I have made regarding the role allocations." TK announced. "As the norm, first-year guys are always picked to play the roles of girls. This time, along with Animesh, I am picking Rocky as well to play the role of a girl." Animesh had played the role of a girl even in the facha skit.

There was a massive roar in the Common Room when TK announced this. Though one could notice a loud "NO" on Rocky's face.

"I know Rocky may not agree. So, to convince him, I am myself going to play the role of a dancing girl."

This time there was even a bigger roar "This is going to be epic." People expected a blockbuster.

And then, TK listed out the others in the acting team. Other than the obvious choices, he named eight to ten supporting cast members primarily from the first year.

The practice sessions revealed the other side of TK. For the role he had promised to play, TK was investing his time to learn, and copy moves from a leading item song, setting up the example for the others to work just as hard."

TK acted like a Captain managing an army of thirty people between the music and drama teams.

During one of these practice nights, I asked Rocky, "So how did you land up here? Seems like TK was eyeing you for long!"

"I also don't know. But when you see what TK is doing himself, how will you say no to him?"

"Agree."

"Given the stakes, he is pulling everything that's possible."

"Stakes?"

"See, we have only one event left beyond MM for the year now. Realistically, we don't have any chance to win BRCA. But still, we can end up second in BRCA. For that, we need to end up in top 2 of MM. Obviously, the position of Vindy and Shivalik in MM will also matter. But I am counting on Kumaon that they will surely be in top two."

"I didn't know that we don't have any chance to win BRCA anymore." I was disappointed.

"Second is also worth the fight buddy. In the BHM night at the end of the year, both the winner and runners-up for BRCA are awarded trophies. So, we should aim for the second now."

"Got it! What about BSA?"

"We don't have any chance in BSA. Thanks to Hockey and Volley Bronze, overall, we will end up fifth or maybe fourth. In other sports, besides Baddy and TT, we didn't end up at any respectable position. Anyway, beyond the top two, it doesn't matter."

The stakes were indeed high this time.

~ 24 ~

For the next one week, the music and skit teams practiced separately. TK was coordinating for each of them.

For music team, it required a lot of effort. First, they had to prepare the original song music that was picked as part of the script and then adjust the new lyrics that were written as parodies in place of the original words. TK had to make some edits during music preparation to suit the team's requirements. Observing it from the outside was such a learning experience.

Then for a week, both the teams were brought together. This week was critical, and it took time for stage performers to sync their movement with the live playback singing. It was a pure fun experience, especially for the people who were part of such an act for the first time. The performance of the music team brought out the best in everyone. Every time Debo played his guitar, people were forced to get on their feet and dance. Every time Aniket sang, people listened to him spellbound. Among all the celebrations and chaos, TK kept his focus. He kept reminding people of the common purpose and did not let them waste their time and energy.

Such a large team with people from all the batches practicing with a common cause and enthusiasm was unmatched for me. Even people like Rudra and Vishal were forced to act sincerely this time.

The entertainment quotient was also unrivalled, especially during the last few days when things started falling in place slowly.

TK also brought in Double A in the last week to manage the production requirements. Coordinating time for everyone, arranging food for late night practices, making props, buying costumes – an endless list of activities were being managed by Double A efficiently. We were told to reach out to him for anything that we required for our roles. He was also given the responsibility to control lights in the Wing. He got in Arora, Mess Secy and Viks to control the focus lights on the first floor of the seminar hall.

The day of the event felt as if the whole of Kara was present in the seminar hall. It was the maximum crowd for an event that I had seen throughout the year. People had occupied every inch of space.

We had the fifth slot this time. We took maximum time to set the musical instruments in the Wing. TK made sure that everyone in the music team, singers as well as the instrument players, were able to see the stage entirely. Double A got the scene ready and was in control of the lights along with Arora.

Finally, Karakoram house performed as per expectations. All our high points, both concerning the musical highlights as well punching parodies marked with on-stage delivery, were applauded. There were a few minor glitches, but nothing noticeable, which was an achievement. Many people predicted that we would be in the top three this time.

Kumaon performed immediately after us. And this time, they were out of the world. While they didn't have many high points, they connected with the audience through their story. They were inevitably going to be in the top three.

Vindy also performed reasonably well. Surprisingly, Shivalik was a let-down. It seemed they didn't have anyone in the hostel who could have taken care of their entry for the event.

Soon, the results were announced by the jury in between all the cheering. "For us, the winner was quite clear, but it took some time to decide between the second and third." I could see tension building on Double A's face, though TK was still calm.

The jury continued, "So the third position goes to Karakoram House." It was followed by a huge cheer from the Kara junta, "Kara ka enthu high hai." TK also joined the cheering but was apparently not the best of self. Double A was visibly upset. Not everyone knew how close we were to claim the second spot in BRCA. And it wasn't discussed either after the event.

Vindy was second, and Kumaon came first. I made a mental note that going forward, we would need to create the right team for every club to compete with Kumaon.

~ 25 ~

Eventually, all the events for the year were over. We bagged the third position in dramatics, EDLC and quizzing. But in other clubs, we did not end up in the top three slots. Thanks to MM, we were placed third overall in BRCA, though beyond second, everything else was equal. Kumaon, expectedly, won the BRCA trophy. Vindy was second.

TK was disappointed that we could not end up in the top two for the BRCA trophy. "When I reflect back over the year went by, I can point out so many instances, where we could have done better." TK so desperately wanted to do well.

Personally, I was disappointed after listening to a few people from my own batch.

Prabhat told me, "Even after putting up so much fight throughout the year, we could not even win the runners-up trophy. I don't know if TK had a focussed plan."

Even Edison once mentioned to me and Gautam, "TK tried hard, yes, but the fact is that he does not have results to show."

I couldn't take this comment, "He has the results to show at many places, Edison. You need to refer to the full last year. He cannot do everything on his own. If we don't have natural talent in all the fields, we will always be constrained."

"Why are you taking it personally? I am just saying that we didn't end up in the top two, so TK doesn't have results to back his efforts."

I couldn't understand where Edison was leading to.

I spoke to Gautam separately later, "Gautam, from what I have been hearing people say, I realize that only effort is sometimes not enough. At times, it needs to be backed by results. TK did everything. Still, I can hear murmurs in the air."

"You are right, Abhimanyu. You need to have an eye on the results, but an honest effort is always required. All of us, who have worked closely with TK, know how much he has given to Karakoram in the last one year."

"I think we need to have the right people for the right challenges. That's where I see a mismatch in our effort. Of course, we cannot make up for lack of talent otherwise. And this participatory culture needs to be built and driven from the top. Probably this is the biggest learning for us from the year." I was thinking about the change in action going forward.

"Aren't we too junior in the system to think and drive this as of now?" Sid was pragmatic.

"Yeah, true. But people from our batch would be cultural reps in the next year," Gautam said hopefully.

"Hmm, but it has to be driven from the next cultural or house secretary," Sid stated.

"Agree! We can action this whenever we have chance on our side," Gautam said mysteriously.

"I don't know about the future, but we don't have time right now. If we don't go to the mess now, dinner will be wrapped up." Sid broke the seriousness and we all left for dinner.

It was now time to get ready for the year's next big thing. TK's next move was going to be critical.

~ 26 ~

With all the hostel events over, it was now time to look forward to the potential candidates for the new leadership team in the house. And TK was the natural contender, for us.

"We did not see the house secretary in action for most of the year. Also, mess and sports secretaries were relatively less visible during the year. I found maintenance and cultural secretaries together serving as the godfather of the hostel. But TK, the cultural secretary was the man of the year." I summed up my take on all five critical people with positions of responsibility in the hostel.

"Totally agree with you on this. If we go by the last year, TK was a champion of all the three potential ways one could serve the hostel – by leveraging own skills and capabilities, by ensuring that the right team of deserving talent is developed, by maintaining and driving the enthusiasm of the team as the leader. No one could beat him in the enthu that he wore on his heart at all times," Gautam summed up well.

TK emerged as the man whose enthusiasm was infectious – his own participation, visibility, style of motivation, everything seemed unmatchable.

Within a few days post the last inter-hostel event, one could feel the unsaid tension everywhere. Soon everyone was part of the discussion related to who could be the next music club rep, the next dramatics club rep, the next cultural secretary, who are the possible candidates for the house secretary, etc. In a nutshell, the first political or *poltu* season for our batch had arrived!

The first and foremost thing for us was to understand the political structure and process, both at the hostel as well as the institute level. So, Gautam and I reached out to Guru and Kaushik to find out more.

Guru, as always, had all the gyaan. "It is a bit complex, so pay attention. There are two parts of the political hierarchy – internal to the hostels elected by the people of the house, and external to the hostels at the institute level. All external posts have a defined electoral college comprising of elected people from the house."

"Let's start with internal first." I was mentally taking notes.

Guru continued, "BRCA is the largest political institution. Internal to the house, at the bottom of the hierarchy, each of the 9 BRCA clubs has house representatives or reps. BSW has 2 house reps. Similarly, BSP has 2 house reps, one each for Hindi and English. For BSA, each of the 10 sports has a vice-captain, but they are selected consensually without elections. All of these positions belong to the second year."

"So, basically you have 13 political posts in the second year – 9 BRCA, 2 BSW and 2 BSP reps," Gautam summarized.

"Correct! In the third year, there is a house cultural secretary and a house sports secretary, who are part of the BRCA and the BSA, respectively. Alongside there are two more essential political posts – mess and maintenance secretaries.

We nodded in understanding, and Kaushik added, "Then externally, each of the 9 BRCA clubs has a club secretary at the institute level, again from the third year. A defined electoral college comprising of club reps from all the hostels vote to elect them. BSP also has 2 secretaries at the institute level. Each sport has a captain at the hostel and institute level which are again non-political, and the teams decide within themselves."

"Got it. Interesting! So overall, BRCA has the highest number of political posts?" Gautam queried.

"Absolutely. Now coming to the fourth year, every house has a house secretary. Externally, there are general secretaries for BRCA, BSA, BSW, BSP and BHM. Then there is SAC general secretary, which is technically the highest post in the student body. And then there is AIC general secretary, responsible for technical fest along with contributing to academic and course curriculum decisions," Guru told whatever he knew.

"I am sure you would have understood by now which is the most coveted post!" Guru quizzed.

"It has to be BRCA General Secretary. Whoever has experienced Rendezvous, would understand that. All the privileges and power would lie in the hands of the people from his house." Gautam was right. We knew who enjoyed the power during the last Rendezvous.

"Technically, for all internal hostel posts, we can have elections, where all five hundred plus people in the house can vote. But in practice, especially in Kara, reps and secys are elected within the B.Tech batch. And then they file the nomination so that they are elected for hostel either by default or by winning against M. Tech or Ph.D. candidate, if any. House Secy is the only election where entire house votes for the candidates. This tradition has been there for some time," Guru explained the dynamics.

"Also, the elections are held at the end of the academic year so that people can take over from the next year. So, you will have an election now, so that you are up and running as cultural club reps when you are back to the campus in the second year," Kaushik told us.

"Internal is relatively simpler then. I am sure externals would be much more complex." I was getting interested.

"Yes, for externals, houses form coalitions and then they go after different posts at all levels divided among themselves. Sometimes, a house is united and sits as a single entity in the coalition. Kara has such a tradition. Similar is the case with Kumaon. They are, therefore, called 1.0. Few houses get split internally and sit in different coalitions, and then you call them by fraction depending upon how much vote-share they have. For example, 0.3 or 0.7," Kaushik explained the external dynamics.

"This sounds like a matter of really high stakes," I was impressed.

"Yes, it is. And therefore, you will find Anirudh and Narayan taking control of externals for Kara this time. Narayan was the kingmaker internally last time, and hopefully, he will be the kingmaker externally this time." Guru told us.

"So, which posts are you guys gunning for?" Gautam was generally inquisitive.

"Not to be discussed with the first years, yet. You will figure out after the elections," Guru closed the discussion.

Key positions of responsibilities

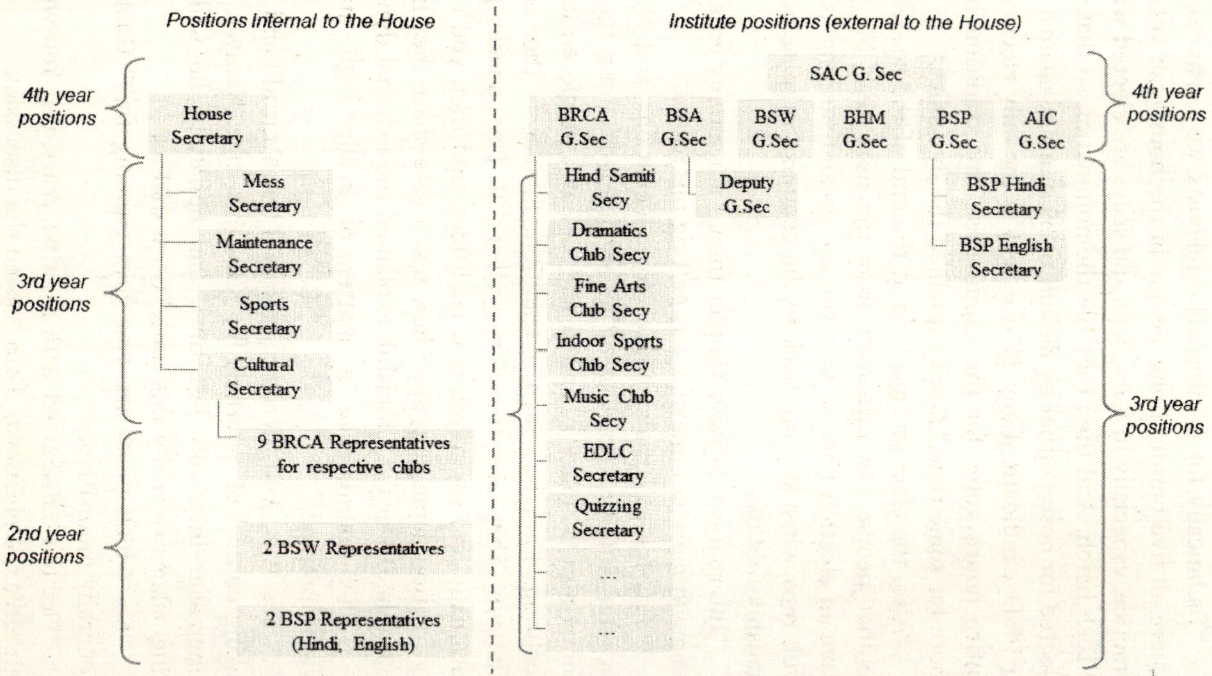

~ 27 ~

When we came back to our room, we drew a diagram to understand the critical external and internal political posts for our understanding, basis what we heard from Guru.

"The more I listened from Guru and Kaushik on this, the more I got fascinated," I said honestly.

"I agree. Though more interesting is the informal rules that we have defined as part of Kara traditions. You feel so much of respect for the people who maintained these rules, batch after batch."

"True. So, in a way, the effort of Guru and others during Tryst which impressed the juniors in our batch will not have any impact soon as secys will be elected within Guru's batch, and juniors will not vote for them."

"The effort during Tryst was more to create a case for himself within the batch."

"But then elections are not won in days. And there is not just one election to win," I said proudly.

"Right! Now you are thinking the way I would like you to," Gautam said with a mischievous twinkle in his eyes.

We were excited to witness what was in store for us in the next few weeks.

~ 28 ~

In between all these randomness of poltu shaping up, Minor-II was knocking at our doors. With the mind space getting split between multiple agenda items, it was the worst time to prepare for exams. And the early interest shown by few individuals in the batch was not helping the cause.

Makhija was the most vocal about politics in our batch. He always acted as if he was aware of all the equations.

"Maybe batch neutrality is what he is striving for so that his position could remain secure." Gautam had his view about Makhija.

Makhija's proven record in quizzing provided a high starting point to him for the position of the quizzing rep. My discussion with Makhija was an eye opener for me about how people can think about their political participation.

"Sanghvi is always present in all the events. No one can match him in enthu for the hostel" I said as I genuinely respected Sanghvi.

"Yeah, that's true. That way Sanghvi's funda in life is quite clear. He knows that it is the best way to get a position of responsibility," Makhija was crisp.

"Interesting. Best way to target a position of responsibility by getting respect from the batch," Gautam understood.

"Possible. He is quite clear in his thinking. Anyway, I need to run for the class." Makhija left in a hurry.

"Respect from batch?" I questioned Gautam.

"See, there are two ways to be the choice of the batch. Either you need to be talented like Thomas so that nobody can beat you in the field, or you need to earn the respect of the batch by showing unbeatable enthusiasm. And Sanghvi has chosen the second option," Gautam clarified.

"There is nothing wrong in that, I would say," I quipped.

After a pause, I added "I don't know if you realized, but these early discussions are eating away one night after the other. And I don't think with Minor-II starting from the day after, this is going to help us."

Both Gautam and I tried avoiding poltu discussions for the next few days while exams were on. We were not entirely successful in our effort.

Once Minor II was over, and we were back to the daily routine of classes and labs, politics took centre stage.

I was completing an assignment when Utkarsh and Makhija walked into my room. It was quite late already.

"Hey, Abhimanyu! Long night? What are you up to?" Utkarsh got talking.

"Yes, need to complete this assignment. I have a submission tomorrow."

"Gautam seems to be chilling," Makhija quipped at Gautam.

"Yeah, only lectures tomorrow," Gautam clarified and called Makhija over to a corner, though I could still hear their conversation.

"I am sure you must be preparing for the Hindi Samiti rep," Makhija started at the right note.

"Preparing?" Gautam was surprised.

"Yes, I should rather say you are almost confirmed," Makhija was not one to mince his words.

"Looks like you are deciding for the batch! Then I guess you must have chosen yourself for the quizzing rep," Gautam took him one-on-one.

"Come on Gautam! I am not deciding. But few reps are quite easy to predict, including EDLC, music, Hindi samiti and quizzing may be. I think it's clear to the seniors as well."

"Seniors? I thought our batch would decide," Gautam differed.

"Yeah, the batch would decide, but seniors will make the final call. And they think these four reps should be clear," Makhija showed off his connect with seniors.

"It's great that they do not want any early groups in the batch," Gautam concluded.

"They will soon call for a batch meet to finally choose people," Makhija continued. "We will have to form a view in the batch before that."

"I was thinking for the indoor sports club," Utkarsh communicated his intentions.

Gautam kept silent.

Makhija continued, "Abhimanyu should go for the dramatics club. After all, he has participated in all drama events for the year. And everyone knows the enthusiasm that he has shown for the house. Abhimanyu and Sanghvi are the two most spirited guys in the batch."

"How will the reps be finally decided?" I could not resist and finally joined the discussion.

"I think the batch will be asked to vote as per their choice. Still, in the end, only Narayan and Anirudh will decide," Makhija explained.

At that point, Sanghvi and Rahul also walked in and joined the discussion.

"I guess, there will be a few surprises, though. Some unexpected people will surely stand for different posts," Makhija felt.

"I am sure, Rudra will go for dramatics. Fine arts can be between Pushkar and Mridul. Photography and film series club will be open for everyone," Gautam put forth.

"And then, we will have BSP Hindi and English reps as well as BSW reps," I concluded.

"Sanghvi will go for one of the BSW reps. Everything else, I think, is quite open," Utkarsh clarified.

"Do you sense anyone else trying for indoor sports?" I checked with Utkarsh.

"Maybe Garg, but am not sure. He participated in a chess tournament, but he is an individual without any group," Utkarsh replied.

"I don't think so. You are missing the Pushkar and Prabhat combo," Gautam clarified for him.

"What do you think about Rudra?" Makhija checked with me.

"Frankly, I didn't give it a thought. This is the first time I am thinking for the dramatics rep. Rudra is a great candidate for the same. If he could be a bit more sincere, I am sure he would be the best bet," I replied.

"That is a big if," Gautam quickly corrected, "and dramatics is the most crucial rep position, given the tradition of Kara and how everything rallies around the same." I was surprised by Gautam's reaction. He was almost pushing my candidature in the discussion. And simultaneously, he was buying me into the decision. I could see it on his face.

We were all fully engrossed in our discussion.

"Rahul, I think we both should go for BSW rep. We can together bring in the trophy as well," Sanghvi clarified his intention for the first time. As expected, he linked it with the house spirit.

Rahul acknowledged Sanghvi's suggestion but did not say anything.

"We are discussing this as if we will decide everything. Am sure 2-3 rooms are having the same discussion at this point of time," Gautam tried being realistic.

"And I am sure that Makhija has already been part of those discussions as well," Sanghvi did not lose this easy chance.

Everyone laughed aloud. Given the time, it was the signal for everyone to get to sleep. And for me, it was going to be a night out – I still had to complete the assignment and prepare for viva.

~ 29 ~

"I think you made the decision on my behalf," I checked with Gautam the next day. Edison, Vivek and Sid were also in the room.

"The same way you took the decision on behalf of Edison," Gautam had a ready answer.

"What is this about?" Edison asked.

"Reps for the next year," I said.

"So, what is the big deal? I think you guys did the right thing. I wonder where was I! Otherwise I would have proposed names of all three of you," Sid mentioned.

"You were busy with your favourite pastime – sleeping while Linkin Park playing at full volume. I don't know how you manage that!" I answered him.

"Come on! Let's not talk about my hobby now. I hope we will have Hindi samiti rep, BSP Hindi rep and dramatics rep together in one room, charting plans for the hostel next year." Sid was already thinking of the future.

"It's not that simple, Sid. I think yesterday night's un-invited discussion forced us to take things more seriously. Good that we also threw our hat in the ring. Let's see how it pans out," Gautam was weighing all chances, I felt.

"I am glad that you guys represented me in my absence. I was thinking about discussing this with you guys." Edison was happy.

"Discuss what?" Gautam checked.

"Which post should I try for? I want to be a part of this," Edison clarified.

"I couldn't guess that you wanted to be part of this. Anyway, Abhimanyu proposed your name for the right post. I don't think you will face any opposition for BSP Hindi rep," Gautam was honest.

"I was hoping that Gautam and I did not end up eyeing the same post. It is good that we will be trying for different posts." Edison looked relieved.

"In case you both had, I do not know what would have happened to your chances Edison!" Sid never left the opportunity to pull Edison's legs. Edison did not like the joke.

"Let us see who all are planning to be the reps in the batch. That will define what is in store for all of us," Gautam summarised.

~ 30 ~

Shubham once caught me and Gautam in our room for a discussion. 'Abhimanyu, I am sure you are going for dramatics. I am thinking of photography."

"Photography? Why Photography? I am not sure if you'd have a chance, as you were rarely visible in any of the hostel cultural activities throughout the year. I think few others in the batch may also go for the same." I did not hold my words. Although Shubham was doing well in swimming events for the hostel, he didn't contribute to any of the cultural activities of the house till date.

"Why others? Would you not support me?" Shubham asked directly.

"Yes, you should stand, Shubham. Many in the batch will support you," Gautam tried calming the situation.

"You guys should also support me. We are friends, after all. One Bihari should always think about another. And am sure you will need support from me too." Shubham left after spending a few minutes, trying to convince us.

Gautam signalled to me not to react and patiently listen to what he was saying.

After Shubham left, Gautam took me to the task. "Try to listen to everyone. It will help you understand their way of thinking. And for god's sake, don't get into the discussion of who is right and who is wrong."

"I get it! But it is so difficult to accept people who were not visible through the year, who are now wanting to stand for such posts shamelessly. Shubham is trying photography because he cannot try anything else. He is a swimming champ and should concentrate there. It is difficult for me to not express my anger when I am convinced that they are not eligible." I tried to explain my point to Gautam.

"Please do not wear any emotions on your sleeves during such discussions" It was clear, strict advice that Gautam dished out to me that day.

I had another similar discussion with Garg. As Gautam was not a part of it, I ignored his advice and did not resist myself in pointing out Garg's opportunistic behaviour in the discussion. Garg left the dialogue, fuming.

For the following two weeks, I was part of many such discussions. And it helped me understand the ambitions of many individuals in the batch.

One day while walking back from the institute, I met Pushkar on the way. We ended up discussing our participation in the ongoing campus politics.

"I am going to stand for dramatics rep. I am sure Rudra and Barnwal will also stand for the post, though," I was frank.

Pushkar responded with a smile. "I don't think Rudra would be the right candidate for the post. Let us see what our batch thinks about this position." He was non-committal to my chances.

"What about you?" I checked with him.

"I am going to stand for Fine Arts Club. I do not think there is anyone who would stand for that profile. In any case, people have seen the efforts that I have put in throughout the year." He was quite confident.

"Yes, Pushkar, you contributed a lot, especially during the facha skit."

"Yeah, that was the peak time."

"Did you also participate in other events through the year?" I tried an honest discussion with him.

"Yeah, in a couple of them," he sounded hesitant.

"Who participated in the rest?"

"Folks from the second and third years only."

"I think Mridul also participated, right?"

"Yes, he was there in some of the events, but he was not in the hostel most of the time. Everyone knows he is rarely visible in the house." I could notice Pushkar defending his chances for the Fine Arts Club rep.

"Yes, I agree with you. Actually, I was surprised to know that he had participated in the events as well. You should try for the Fine Arts Club, for sure." I had witnessed his efforts, and so, wanted him to give it a try.

We did not discuss the topic further once we reached the hostel.

I was having some evening snacks at the mess after classes. Vishal was also in the mess.

"Long day?" Vishal asked me while sipping his coffee.

"Yes. Had a lab today. What about you?"

"Nothing much. Just had the tutorial today. So, have you made up your mind for the dramatics rep?" Vishal got to the point.

"Yes. Nothing to lose for giving it a try."

"Then I think there will be 3 people for this position. Barnwal, Rudra and you."

"Have you talked to Rudra and Barnwal?"

"Yes. I convinced Rudra to go for the dramatics rep. Barnwal has motivated himself."

"Okay. Are you not going for anything?"

"Dramatics is the only place where I have contributed, but it has to be only one between Rudra and me. I am not trying anything just to fool myself. Anyway, it's not a big deal this time. Things will get serious only in the following year." Vishal was frank.

"Yeah. It makes sense." I concluded. Vishal seemed to be thinking long term

In the days that followed, one of my afternoons was free. I was lazily lying in the room. I decided to walk across the wing to see if there was anyone else free that day. Finding no one in the 'Long' wing, I made my way towards the 'Short' wing.

Peeping into Rahul's room, I saw him sitting alone and surfing on the internet. I entered his room. "Seems you are also free today."

"Yes, just had the lectures in the morning. What about you?"

"Nothing in the afternoon. Rare day for me. I was feeling very sleepy after a long night yesterday."

"Why was it a long night?"

"There is only one thing that is keeping us all awake these days. Makhija wanted to talk about the batch dynamics and politics. I had to literally push him out of the room to catch on my sleep."

"What was he saying?" Rahul seemed intrigued.

"The same old stuff. Which rep positions are clear? Which rep positions will witness a fight? He also said that BSW reps are also now clear, as you have made up your mind for the same along with Sanghvi," I briefed Rahul on my conversation with Makhija.

"Yes, but the only thing bothering me is that BSW rep position is not as great as the BRCA rep positions. And I think I have a chance there as well. Though overall it would be better to go for something which will serve the purpose of the house." Rahul was not very convinced with his own decision.

"I don't know how you define something better than the other. At the end of the day, there is a definite role and trophy to seek for every house rep." I was not aligned with Rahul's point of view.

We ended up discussing potential names for all the positions. I also told him about Gautam's, Edison's and my candidature.

~ 31 ~

It was a Saturday morning, the best sleeping time of the week, when less than five percent of the hostel turned out for breakfast. None of us had any clue about how this Saturday was going to be very different from the ones we had lived in the campus so far, a day to set the ball rolling for the agenda of the future. It started with an early morning knock at the door. One could clearly hear the voices of the fourth-year seniors – Narayan and Anirudh were in the wing.

"Fourth-year folks rarely visit our wing. So this must be a special cause," Gautam woke me up.

Everyone was asked to assemble in the TV room immediately. It was time to discuss the reps from the batch. The timing of the batch-meet surprised everyone, and so no one could lobby for himself.

Anirudh and Narayan took control once everyone assembled. Anirudh started the affairs. "Guys, I'm sure all of you were expecting this to happen, maybe not in this manner! Today, we need to elect BRCA Club and other reps from your batch. And as per the Kara tradition, your batch will elect the reps among yourselves. Before we get into the details of the process to follow, I want to share something from my side." The last line caught everyone's attention.

Anirudh continued, "Your batch is the most talented batch among the seven batches of Kara that I have seen during my four years in the house. Some of you may consider my statement to be business as usual, but I seriously mean it! You will rarely get a hostel batch comprising of so many folks talented in so many different fields. I will not take names because that will bias the people in this room, but we have individuals sitting here who

I would rate as the best talent that the institute has witnessed in the last several years." It was a great compliment coming from the house secretary himself. "I hope that the entire batch acknowledges the same during the batch elections, given the elected representatives will personify the house going forward."

A momentary silence followed in the room.

Narayan continued from where Anirudh had stopped. "Thanks Anirudh. Now, let me brief you guys about the process that we will follow for the elections. We will go one by one for each of the rep positions. For every rep position, people who are interested can stand up for others to take notice. All of you can then mark the preferences in the chit that will be passed on to you guys. Post that, you need to drop the chits in this box. We will repeat the same procedure for all the rep positions. There are different boxes to drop your chit."

It was first of a kind experience for most of us. And it was going to be the stepping stone for all those interested in a political role in the hostel in the future.

I don't know whether it was deliberate, but Narayan started with the least controversial rep positions. "Let's start with EDLC. Who all are interested?"

Everyone started in the chorus, "Thomas...Thomas..."

Surprisingly, Mridul also stood up. Many people started pulling his leg. "You stand no chance Mridul,"... "Sit down Mridul, sit down!"

Finally, Mridul gave up. "Okay okay! I don't think I have a chance."

It was such great batch camaraderie to set up the session. No voting was required for the EDLC rep. Even Narayan and Anirudh acknowledged the same. "Great start guys! I hope every rep is elected by voice vote".

Similar simple elections took place for music – Bala and quizzing – Makhija. No opponent stood against them. Both were purely elected by voice voting.

Then followed the Hindi Samiti club rep's election. Apparently, Narayan was expecting similar voice-based selection for Gautam, but this time Rahul also stood reluctantly. Rudra passed a joke on Rahul, but given it was Rudra, no one took it seriously.

Rahul was one of the respected guys in the batch, and so his action was somewhat unexpected. I looked at Gautam with surprise, but he seemed calm. There was a pause, and then Narayan took over. "So let's circulate the chit. You guys can write your preference here." There were few murmurs, but it set the pace and uneasiness for the things to come in the next hour or so.

I murmured into Sid's ears, "Maybe Rahul still remembers losing out to Gautam for the Hindi Samiti event during the facha period. And he thinks this could be his chance for redemption."

Narayan moved to Indoor Sports Club – this time Utkarsh and Garg stood to face each other. Some people asked Garg to step back, but he was adamant. The chit was again circulated.

Then followed the Dramatics Club Rep's position with Rudra, Barnwal and I pitted against each other. Some of the guys tried to deter Barnwal, but he ignored. So, chits were again floated. People were asked to jot their preferences in descending order as there were three candidates.

Fine Arts Club was surprisingly late in the queue, as Pushkar was expected to be the natural candidate, but Mridul again pulled a surprise. The batch also did not protest. Maybe, those like Sanghvi and I could notice Pushkar's contribution, but it went unnoticed by the larger crowd. So, the preference sheet was again circulated.

Then followed Photography for which four people stood up, including Shubham. The entire batch made fun of them. Sanghvi had not stood up until then.

We then had the BSP Hindi and English reps up for grabs. Surprisingly, Edison was elected unanimously as the Hindi rep. Gautam and Edison stuck to their plan. Gautam did not get influenced by Rahul's surprise move and didn't interfere in

Edison's chances. Mridul was on a spree. He stood for BSP English as well. So, it was between Mridul and Srini for the English rep.

Finally, it came to 2 BSW reps. Four people, including Sanghvi, Rahul, Barnwal and Sid aimed for the coveted position. To me, Sid's attempt was quite surprising, as he had never revealed anything to us before. Still, I was happy for him that he was showing confidence.

After all the chits were collected, Narayan summarized everything that had happened so far and concluded, "Now everyone here is free to go their rooms."

It left everyone amused. We thought that the results would be disclosed, but surprisingly, we were asked to leave. When Rudra checked with Narayan about the tentative time for the declaration of the results, he retorted angrily, "Everyone will get to know from the notice board."

No one had the guts to cross-question Narayan. Through the day, people kept discussing, debating and making fun of everything that had happened in the morning.

~ 32 ~

The following day, just after lunch, Narayan came to our room. He asked Gautam to join him. On the way, he also asked Makhija, Bala and Thomas from our wing to follow him. He also checked for Rahul and was informed that his room was on the ground floor.

After some time, Gautam came back and told me, "Narayan asked all of us to fill the nomination forms. I filled for the Hindi Samiti rep."

"And Rahul?" I asked as I could guess for the others.

"Rahul filled for the BSW rep," Gautam sounded uncomfortable this time. "Narayan has also asked you to meet him sometime later during the day."

"Why? Not now?" I was left surprised.

"I don't know. I also saw Rudra, Utkarsh and Mridul waiting in Narayan's wing when I was leaving. So I am guessing Narayan wants to meet you for some other reason," Gautam was trying to sound optimistic.

In the evening, while coming back from dinner, I met Narayan in the lawns. "You were looking for me, Narayan?"

Narayan was with some other folks from the fourth year. "Yeah Abhimanyu. I wanted to meet you. Great that you caught me. Should we go to my room?"

"Yeah, sure."

He did not say anything on the way. As soon as we reached his room, he started, "You must be aware of the results?"

"I can figure out. I know the people you called." I was honest.

"Great! So Abhimanyu, I will try to be as transparent as possible. Multiple people were standing for multiple posts. Obviously, your batch voted for those who were the right choice as per them. Now, we also know what would be best for this hostel as well as your batch going forward. So, we had to finally decide taking everything into account. Now, as expected, those like you who wanted but could not eventually become a rep would be disappointed." He paused to check my expressions before continuing, "We, as your seniors, also have a responsibility towards the house – that it should be one unit without any fractions. Moreover, people should willingly contribute to the hostel spirit. So, disclosing voting results for every post doesn't make sense. It was also done in a way that none of you could act independently basis the results."

I was still not getting what he wanted from me. "Narayan, I understand the role you guys have played, and I am fine with the results. I am not going to do anything going beyond the norms, if that is what you are hinting at."

Narayan came back to me at his authoritative best. "I have already told you. We did it in a way that none of you could anyway go beyond what the hostel wants. Today was the last day of filing nominations."

"Sorry, I did not mean to be rude," I tried to calm him down.

He let out a long breath and came to the point. "That's okay. Good that you told me what's in your mind. My only point is that you are an enthu guy. We all know about it. All of us have noticed your vigour. I just want you to continue with the same spirit and not get disappointed with the outcome this time. Just believe it has been done for the greater good. Trust me, this is coming not only from me, but from every senior that you have worked with."

I quietly listened before attempting for the last time. "Can you tell me if I won in the voting?"

"No, I will not tell you. I have not told anyone in your batch. The only thing that I want you to take away from our chat today is that you just need to keep your spirits high and continue with what you are doing for the house. Do not take this to heart. You have a long way to go in the house."

"Long way?"

He finally smiled. "Abhimanyu, the year I joined Karakoram four years ago was the year when Kara won the last BRCA. I still remember the celebrations. Everyone was at the top of their world – both on the night of the last event as well as the awards night. It was a surreal feeling. Now when I look back, I think maybe it came too early in our hostel life. Three years have gone since then, and we didn't win anything. Within a month, I will be gone, so no more chances to get a shot at BRCA. You have just started, and you have a long way to go, three years to be precise. You need to maintain your spirit if you wish to contribute and win BRCA for the house. So today, it is more important to maintain the enthu than to know the results of the voting," Narayan concluded.

"Understood Narayan!" I thanked him and left. The last point that Narayan made was intriguing for me. On returning to my room, I told Gautam about the chat with Narayan. He listened and slowly responded, "Maybe, they balanced out the available talent and the batch dynamics. I cannot predict the actual voting results."

"Absolutely, I might have won, but as per them, favouring Rudra could help maintain the batch dynamics, and avoid any unwanted reaction. I would anyway contribute toward the hostel. Or I might have lost, and the seniors wanted me to become the dramatics rep but respected the batch decision. Both the possibilities hold a chance." I tried to analyse the situation.

"Yeah, both things are possible. Anyway, one thing is common – the seniors acknowledge your contribution, and they want you to keep doing the same. So let it be," Gautam concluded.

In the wee hours that night, the list of house rep nominations was put up on the notice board. Given only one nomination per position was filed officially, all of them were going to be elected unopposed at the house level.

EDLC	Thomas
Music	Bala
Quizzing	Makhija
ISC	Utkarsh
Hindi Samiti	Gautam
Dramatics	Rudra
FAC	Mridul
FSC	Parikh
PAHS	Grover
BSP Hindi	Edison
BSP English	Srini
BSW	Sanghvi and Rahul

One could clearly notice that every wing and group in the batch was represented in the list.

The list included few unexpected ones as well. The most surprising was Mridul becoming the FAC rep instead of Pushkar, given the efforts Pushkar had put in through the year. Eventually, Pushkar was made the 'Kara Forum Rep', which was not an official position but was expected to help with any production support required for any event or club. Shubham also didn't make the cut.

There were long bump sessions at night, concluding with all the reps throwing a treat for the batch in the canteen.

V
Early signs of the future - II

~ 33 ~

Reps from our batch were decided couple of days before the final elections. In parallel, beyond our internal batch election, house secy election was the talk of the town. Maintenance, mess and cultural secys were elected by the Second years among themselves. So, for them, only the final verdict was awaited, but the House Secy's election was a much larger affair for the whole house.

All of us in the first year anticipated TK to be one of the obvious candidates for the house secy's position. With 'Double A' being his closest friend, one didn't expect Double A in the race.

Then there was Sankalp Verma aka Spidy, who was a rare talent in the institute. He was the EDLC club secretary in the institute and was regular with both EDLC and quizzing clubs. Everyone was expecting him to get nominated for an external post, though. Jolly was another expected aspirant. He was quite popular given his charm and friendship with people in our batch. Viru, the Sports Secy could have been a surprise package as well.

During the poltu discussions, everyone in the batch could only guess the possible candidates and potential groups.

And then arrived the day when the prospects contesting the house secy elections disclosed their candidature. It came as a big surprise for most of us, if not all.

Amitabh and Double A – two good friends were pitted against each other for the post of House Secretary.

For the first year, TK not contesting the elections was the biggest surprise of the season. No one would have even remotely guessed that. In his place, Double A's candidature was less of a surprise given the 'working duo' approach they showcased throughout the year.

Amitabh's candidature was also a surprise, given there were more prominent names in the batch. Maybe Amitabh was able to rally people behind him.

House secy candidates soon became the topic of discussion in the House.

"Gautam, for me Amitabh's candidature was as surprising as TK's non-participation. Amitabh has always come across as someone who has set priorities in life – studies, sports, literature and helping juniors whenever they approach him. And politics never featured in the list," I said.

Gautam intervened, "But Amitabh was a key contributor to BSP articles. He was an integral part of the football team. And how can you forget his visibility during the English play? Let's see which side Jolly finally falls to."

I was still not able to accept Amitabh as a candidate.

"I don't know if you guys know this, but there is a large fan following of Amitabh in the second year," Edison joined our discussion.

"Of course, you know this. Amitabh is your chuddy-buddy from school," Gautam caught him.

"Then your loyalty is also kind of confirmed?" I directly concluded.

Edison did not respond.

I was hoping that Edison would not campaign for Amitabh against Double A internally within our batch. For me, it was like Double A was contesting the elections in place of TK.

~ 34 ~

Team members of both the candidates became clear when they started campaigning across the batches in the house. Both had a team of heavyweights.

Double A's team, as expected, had both the key individuals, TK and Arora, the cultural and mess secys, respectively. They were joined by Lakhan. We could not figure a rationale for Lakhan supporting Double A because he seemed as close to Amitabh as TK. We guessed, "Maybe Lakhan is more of an idealist and so took the side accordingly."

Amitabh had the support from other talented people in the batch. Viru, sports secretary, and Jolly were part of his team. Jolly's support for Amitabh was surprising, given his friendship with TK that we had witnessed during the English play. Viru and Amitabh were football-mates – an obvious link. A set of *maggu* people – Pondy, Tau and others – who had only spent time studying till date and had no evident existence in the hostel throughout the year were part of Amitabh's gang.

Unexpectedly, Amitabh's team looked as equally strong as Double A's team on paper.

"Have you got this big news?" Gautam excitedly announced as soon as he entered the room. He was perspiring heavily. We couldn't guess if it was because of the long walk from the institute or the news that he was going to share.

Sid and Edison were with me in the room.

"What happened?" Edison asked Gautam.

"It's in public now. Kara is going to contest for the BRCA general secretary and Spidy is the designated candidate." Gautam spoke without taking a pause.

Sid jumped from his seat, "Isn't it exciting? If Spidy wins G Sec, Kara will be organizing Rendezvous. We will enjoy all the privileges."

"Yes, it is. But given the situation, it also brings along the other complexities." I was thinking beyond Rendezvous. "I am sure it will impact our internal house secretary elections as well."

"You are right!" Gautam got the hint.

"How?" Sid was curious.

"As of now, both the teams for the house secretary elections look solid. But given Spidy's current position, his role and support become critical. The team that gets Spidy's backing will surely become stronger," I explained it to him.

"Why? If Spidy wins in the external elections, in his capacity as BRCA G Sec, he should act for the whole house without any bias. And for the house secy, I will vote for Double A and TK for the work they have done for the house, irrespective of Spidy's position. Both the elections should be mutually independent events." Sid was transparent, but we knew that's not how politics worked.

"Great that you think like this, Sid! I am not sure if everyone would share the same thought process. People may vote for the team that has Spidy believing that the new House Secy, who will be close to Spidy, would play an important role in constituting the core organizing team for Rendezvous, in case Spidy wins the G Sec elections." Gautam stated my worry more clearly. "I just hope it works in the best interest of the house," Gautam finally said.

Both Gautam and I knew that this event had the potential to be the decider in Kara's political game. We could only hope that it plays a decisive role in line with our expectations.

One day, I happened to be walking back from the institute with TK.

"House secy election is like the talk of the town these days," I started.

"Yeah, it should be. It's time one gets to learn so many things." He was in a chit-chat mood.

"Hmm, then why did you lose the chance to learn? Everyone was expecting you to challenge. You were potentially the strongest candidate."

"Oh, come on! It's not that easy. I had my own reasons for not going for it, though," TK paused.

"That's what I want to know." I was eagerly waiting for his response.

TK waited for some time before talking. "Okay, let me explain it to you. I have two reasons for not contesting the elections. Firstly, I don't have enough energy left in me to take this forward. It's not an easy job and the last year has taught me that very well. I don't want to go for something when am not sure that I will be able to give 100% to it. Mere participation is very different from leadership.

"Secondly, we had put in much effort but did not end up in top 2 in BRCA. You know, I am aware of the areas where we could have done better - Street play being one of them. Still, in the end, I could not win the trophy for the house. It was my responsibility. If I contest, it will be talked about again and again, and I don't want to face that. I am happy to be in the background only." TK's face carried his emotion. He had taken it personally and seemed exhausted to explain it further. After a pause, he added "Also, no harm in prioritizing study for some time"!

Two distinct styles of campaigning were evident in the days leading to the elections.

One was purely based on the sheer amount of work done for the house, contributions, sacrifices, and an opportunity to leverage the experience to make it even better. People who were touched by Double A's team, TK in particular, agreed with this style."

And then the other team's campaigning was based on taking everyone along, irrespective of whether one commanded stature in the batch or not. Apparently, the team knew that every vote was significant – of those who worked for the hostel and those who didn't care.

In the beginning, I could not relate to Amitabh's style, but discussion with people like Kinwar from our batch helped me understand the logic. Kinwar obviously was indifferent to the hostel spirit and work. Given his persona, he was also not among the most famous people in the batch. He could identify more with the group that was supporting Amitabh's team.

~ 35 ~

Unlike the house secretary elections, where it was an all house affair and candidates were known, one could only guess the results of the internal batch elections among the second year students.

"Going by history, Shashi seems to be the favourite for cultural. TK was also the dramatics rep in his time." I was drawing a simple parallel.

"But then, we also have Aniket, the music rep. And, why are we forgetting Vatsal? He has been quite active during the year in the cultural activities." Gautam put forth his thoughts.

"Vatsal has been an avid contributor to sports as well along with Kalra and Rocky. He can go for sports secy as well. I believe he rightly deserves one of these posts." Vivek also joined the guessing game.

"Going purely by skill, Kalra may have the upper hand for sports. But what about Rocky? Am sure he will get one post. If not sports, maybe maintenance." I always thought Rocky was one of the visible guys in the batch.

"I think the other unexpected trump card can be Kaushik. He is the most charming and popular person within their batch." Gautam was right in his guess.

"The only other name that comes to my mind is Viks." Edison was now stretching the list.

"There seem to be quite a few possibilities. It would be interesting to see the final results," Sid was excited.

"We will only get to know the final names of the secretaries as it will be an election within the second year batch. Then it all depends upon the personal charm of Sid to get the background information from the right sources." I was trying to pull Sid's leg.

"Don't worry, we will get all the information. But let's first get to know the final results." Edison was confident.

Two days before the house secy elections, the internal batch elections for the second year secys were held. Only the elected people from the batch were then allowed to file nominations at the hostel level.

First years got to know the final names from the notice board, without any hint of what happened in the batch of the second year students.

Mess	Guru
Maintenance	Viks
Sports	Kalra
Cultural	Aniket
Common Room	Kaushik and Vatsal

Given no M.Tech candidates had filed the nominations, all four of them were elected by default.

Guru as the mess secy and Kalra as the sports secy were the most expected results. Aniket as the cult secy was surprising, but not as surprising as Viks as the maintenance secy.

"To me, the biggest surprise is Rocky and Vatsal not being among the most important four secys. They were the most visible people from the second year along with Guru and Shashi. Then they are friends with almost everyone on their own as well as the junior batches." I mentioned the surprise for myself from the list.

"Given Amitabh's current position, I am sure people will now start thinking of a long-term prospect there," Sid was right in evaluating the new common room secys.

In a couple of days, details of the second year batch elections started emerging. And who better than Edison to tell us the particulars!

"Guru, Kalra and Aniket were consensus candidates. Shashi didn't contest for cultural. Vatsal and Rocky didn't try for sports."

"What! How come Aniket became the consensus candidate for cultural in the batch and no one stood against him. No one would have expected that from Shashi." I just could not believe that.

"I am not sure why Shashi did not fight." Edison had no clue.

"Same here," Gautam said.

We couldn't arrive at any rationale for his action then. It was still early days for us in the political game of the house.

"In my priority order, Viks would have been the last to get the maintenance secy position. How come he got it ahead of the other deserving people?" Gautam had his own doubts.

"As far as maint is concerned, Rocky originally won the internal elections. But Narayan and Anirudh want him to contest one of the BRCA club secy positions in the externals. So, Viks, who had originally lost the batch elections was elected." Edison had a profound insight.

"Probably, Narayan is banking on Rocky's personal relations and charm in the institute. He can bring in a lot of carpet votes," I spoke my mind.

"Carpet votes?" Vivek didn't understand.

"These are the votes from the girls' hostel that you can bring based on your personal connections. Rocky can play his charm there." Gautam explained it to him.

"Sid, we are hoping that you develop a similar charm," I poked Sid.

"Don't worry. I am working on it. It will be a game-changer in our time," Sid was serious.

"So Vatsal and Kaushik didn't even contest for any post. I can understand that Kaushik may not be interested, but why did Vatsal settle for less?" I was curious.

"There is still a year to go, Abhimanyu. We may not get all the answers today, but am sure a clear picture will emerge during the year." Gautam was right.

"You mean, we need to use this time to work on Sid's charm for the carpet votes next year!"

We all burst out laughing.

~ 36 ~

Only two days were left for the final house secy elections.

Double A and Amitabh both came to our wings with their teams and completed a round of campaigning. It was a usual pitch that we had heard before. Then we all were back to our rooms.

"It's going to be tighter than I was expecting." I shared my honest evaluation of the situation with Gautam.

"Absolutely," Gautam was in violent agreement.

After a couple of hours, we heard Amitabh and his team returning and knocking at the doors in our wing. "Guys, can you please come out again?"

It was quite surprising that they wanted to talk again. "I bet there is some serious development which has made Amitabh and team return so quickly," I told Gautam while unlocking the door.

As soon as we came out, it became evident why they had come back. It was probably the most significant moment of this year's election.

Spidy was standing right in front of our room as part of the team that had re-assembled. Spidy had now come out openly in support of Amitabh.

"Sorry guys for the trouble! But we thought it is important for you people to know that I'm backing Amitabh. I always wanted Amitabh to be the next house secy but took some time to make it public. But better late than never," Spidy said clearly.

"I just wanted to let you guys know that even the most talented guys in the batch belong to our team. And I am assuming you guys understand that well now," Amitabh kept it short and crisp.

☆☆

The night before the house secy election, we had the SOP (Statement of Purpose) of the candidates. It was an hour-long affair where the candidates had to talk about their agenda and plan for the house.

Double A emphasized on his past work right from the first year, his awards that were an acknowledgment of his work and his contribution in creating an ecosystem where people could contribute towards the hostel.

Amitabh talked more about the compassion and his involvement in creating an environment where people were much better connected to each other. He touched upon his work for the hostel without being in the limelight and ability to build relationships with the more extensive section of the hostel.

Listening to Double A and Amitabh in the SOP session gave me a kick. I had loved the experience of the last ten days, and this was like an embellishment.

I told Gautam that night, "I am finding this to be a battle between teams with real agendas. It has all the elements of politics, but is as clean and transparent as it can be. I don't think politics can get healthier than this."

~ 37 ~

The D-day had arrived.

As soon as I reached the mess on the ground floor, I felt different. The season had reached its peak. An air of suspicion enveloped each one of us. People were trying to read each other's mind. Everyone out there was either trying to influence the other or getting affected. That depicted the beauty of an election in a small place. The loyalties of sizeable numbers were already decided. Many of them were making last-minute efforts to get more supporters on their sides.

While leaving for classes after lunch, I found TK standing with Double A and a few others in front of the mess. He was greeting people as a last moment effort. This TK appeared very different from the TK that I had seen the previous year - always assertively instructing others, humble but not submissive, and confident. It was a paradox that the same TK who was there for the hostel till yesterday desperately needed the same hostel to support him today!

"Gautam, don't you feel that TK has been acting too cautious since the beginning of this election season? I believe he does not require such efforts to win the elections for Double A. He is the most popular person in the house." I could not resist sharing what was going in my mind.

Gautam offered a counter perspective. "Abhimanyu, you are making simplistic assumptions. Your suppositions would have been correct had TK himself stood for the elections. Here, it's 'Double A' who is fighting the elections and TK is only his good friend."

After greeting TK, I moved ahead and left for the institute.

In the class, the intensity of the discussion was visibly gaining headway. Every group was sharing the scenario in their respective hostels, but their conversations were very different from the one that I had experienced in Kara.

Two people belonging to the same hostel were talking. First one was confirming with the other "Are you sure about voting for him?"

The other fellow replied in confirmation "Yes, I must think about my future. See, I am going to be the music rep next year. He has promised me that he will take care of me in next year's secy elections."

These kinds of conversation made me uncomfortable. I had not witnessed anything like this in Kara. We all had zero political alignment to any group or section of their seniors. Although many of us might have decided about the vote for a candidate or a group, the respect for the other candidate or interaction with the other group remained intact. This did not seem to be the case with other hostels.

As I was walking back to the hostel, I saw Gautam ahead of me. I paced up to catch up with him.

"Decided?" I said with a pat on his back.

"Hey! It was already decided long back for us, right?" he said with a laid-back attitude.

"Yeah, I think for most of the freshers, TK will be the man. He has always been a god-like figure for us through the entire year," I replied in the same tone.

"But you know, in politics, the immediate past matters much more than history," Gautam chipped in with a sneer.

"Maybe, but in this case, immediate past is similar to long-ago times. Isn't it?" I checked.

"If you consider a month, then you are right. If you just consider the last ten days, you may not be right," Gautam reverted bluntly.

"Hmm. You know, my fellow classmates knew a lot about their candidates. I felt as if they were playing an important role in the elections as well. In fact, Bhanu even knew the second-year equation of his hostel. You know Bhanu, right?" I again started.

"Yeah, that Vindy guy with spikes." Gautam knew most of the people on campus.

"Yes, the one with spikes," I was aware of his contacts.

"Abhimanyu, do you ever feel we should consider ourselves fortunate?" Gautam sounded a bit emphatic this time.

"Why?" I was not able to get his hint.

"...because out of all the 7 boys' hostels, we have landed in Kara," Gautam replied. The freshers at Kara are still united. We may have decided our vote, but that's the end of the matter. That's not the case with other hostels. Maybe Kumaon is another exception like us. Everywhere else, people have been fragmented by their seniors in their very first year. Remember, none of us knew the candidate till late? We were only guessing. That's because no one from the senior batch tried to win us from the start, and so, no seeds of fragmentation. I am not saying that we will remain the same in the future, but the first year is too early. I had always felt that freshers should be kept away from this as this could sow seeds of partition very early between us. We all will be striving for the same goal next year, together. And in a way I think this will contribute to a better hostel life as well."

Considering what I had seen in the morning, I immediately got settled with his opinion. "You are bang on, Gautam! One great thing in Kara till date is that every individual is making his own decision between the third-year candidates with very little influence from either the second year or the fourth year."

"Even the godfather of the final year – Narayan, and others are far from the internal elections. No one knows whom they are supporting. They are busy with externals most of the time."

We both ended up reminding ourselves of something that could have been missed in the chaos that prevailed. Another important aspect of the 'healthy politics' in Karakoram was quite evident.

38 ~

Eventually, beyond Double A and Amitabh, another person Ram, enrolled in the Ph.D. program, was contesting for the House secy position. Apparently, no one was taking him seriously. The ballot paper had three names, and every voter had to tick their one preferred choice.

Voting for the elections started sharp at 4:00 p.m. in the common room. It peaked post 6:00 when people were back from classes. It continued until 8:00 p.m. and the last one hour witnessed a long queue for voting. More than five hundred voters were listed in the voting list. This included the day scholars, local Delhi folks, who were attached to the hostel but didn't reside there, and few others, who were assigned to the house for dining while living with family in accommodation provided by the institute.

Post 8:00 p.m., the counting process started. It was overseen by the house warden, mess supervisor and a fourth-year student nominated by the house secy. Every candidate was allowed to have two representatives during the counting process to ensure that the results were validated by all the parties.

After counting of every hundred votes, the mess supervisor announced the updates and pasted the same at the glass door of the common room. It contributed to slow and uneasy build-up of the tension.

Gautam, Sid and I went for dinner in the canteen after casting our vote at around 7:30 p.m. When we came back by 9, we saw a large crowd gathered outside the common room.

Post the counting of 300 out of 421 polled votes, the mess supervisor announced, "Amitabh is leading with 135 votes over Double A with 125. Ram has 35 votes while rest 5 have been declared as invalid votes."

As soon as I heard the update, I reacted, "How come Double A is lagging?"

Gautam immediately signalled me to keep my emotions in

check. "We still have one more round to go. It's going to be a close fight. Let's go for a walk."

As we stepped out, Gautam scolded me, "It is going to be really close. You need not be emotionally vocal in public. There were so many from our batch standing there. Did you see anyone else reacting like the way you did? Not even Sanghvi showed any emotion."

"What do you mean?" I was surprised.

"You need to realize that it's anyone's game now. Double A, Amitabh, TK, all others were standing there. There is no point in being transparent about who you voted for. We don't know who wins, so don't burn bridges. We must aim to work for the house and its new leader. That will be helpful for all the stakeholders," he explained patiently.

"Hmm." It made sense.

"Please ensure one more thing," Gautam said. "You should not tell anyone who you voted for. I may guess who you voted for, but you should not tell it openly even to me. And similarly, don't expect me to disclose the same."

We had completed a round of the ground and were back to the house entrance. A big hurrah inside the house pulled our attention. Results were out.

We hurriedly walked towards the common room entrance. We were astounded to find that neither Amitabh's nor Double A's team was celebrating. It was the junior batch that was making all the noise. Results posted on the door read:

Amitabh	176
Double A	176
Ram	62
Invalid votes	7

Our warden was engrossed in discussion with Anirudh on how to handle this.

Mess Supervisor shared his view in private conversations. "We made a mistake. We should have asked the voters for a second preference as well so that votes of the last candidate could get redistributed if required."

Finally, the warden came out to announce that re-election will take place the next morning. This time between Double A and Amitabh only.

The election fever had got extended by another night.

Post the results were announced, there was a word-of-mouth wave in the night.

'Amitabh was a far better candidate, and so, an equal number of people voted for him.'

'Amitabh was leading until the last moment despite Double A being visible through the year.'

Amitabh's team, including Spidy, played a vital role in contributing to this wave. No one knew how the non B.Tech votes, who voted for the third candidate the first time, would swing this time.

Thankfully, the next day was Saturday. Voting started early in the morning and continued until noon.

The same process was followed. Again, a big crowd had assembled.

"I don't know how you are controlling your emotions Gautam!"

"I think we should not stand here. I don't want people to keep reading your emotions every time updates are announced. So let's go to the mess and wait for the final results directly."

We went to the mess to sit and wait. We could hear the claps after every update that was announced, but could not figure out the trends. That was the intent. We didn't talk. We only kept track of how many rounds of updates have happened...1...2...3. Gautam was tracking and communicating the same through the count of fingers.

Soon, we heard a big hurrah from the reception area. We didn't move. We tried to identify the voices that were part of the celebration. I recognized and immediately my jaw dropped. It had the sounds of Jolly, Viru, Spidy and others.

I hesitantly walked towards the common room along with Gautam, who wore a smile on his face, while I tried to control my emotions.

Final results read:

Amitabh	225
Double A	213
Invalid votes	4

Marginally more students had participated in the voting today. Amitabh was maintaining the decorum. He was calm in the victory, which was appreciable.

Double A and his team slowly walked away to their respective rooms. I noticed TK and Double A congratulating Amitabh on his victory before leaving. TK looked more disappointed than Double A.

I think two factors which potentially helped Amitabh edge pass Double A in the re-elections were - majority of the people who had voted for the Ph.D. candidate last night would have voted for someone who they thought would be winning, thereby not letting their vote go waste. Also, the overnight wave supported by Spidy may have led a few B.Tech. voters change their mind.

One extra night turned out to be so crucial.

Amitabh was now the new House Secretary of Karakoram.

~ 39 ~

That same evening, we had the external elections – to elect club secretaries, and board general secretaries from second-year and third-year student nominations, respectively.

Soon, we noticed Amitabh joining the outgoing house secy Anirudh and Narayan in managing Kara's participation in the external politics. Apart from the apparent accountability, it was also Spidy's BRCA G Sec candidature that set Amitabh in action.

Beyond BRCA G Sec for Spidy, Kara was also gunning for Rocky for Indoor Sports Club Secretary. Voting for institute posts started in the evening in the SAC premises. Given the newly-elected club secretaries were to vote in the elections, the polling for the secy elections was completed first.

A large crowd was now awaiting the results. Soon the professor-in-charge of the elections started announcing the results. The whole of Kara was waiting for Indoor Sports Club announcement. Anirudh, Narayan, Amitabh, Rocky and others were standing right in front of the professor.

Professor announced, "The new Indoor Sports Club Secretary is Amod Gulati."

A shockwave passed through the Kara junta. Everyone was now looking at Anirudh and Narayan. Anirudh was completely shocked. Narayan couldn't believe and checked with the professor, "Are you sure, sir?"

Professor shot back, "What do you mean? It's based on the counting of polled votes."

Indoor Sports Club result now made everyone in Kara jittery before the BRCA general secretary voting. Narayan was immediately back to work with the other coalition leaders who were also present there. One could notice the urgency in his actions. In my whole year in Kara, this was for the first time that I had seen Narayan stressed. Although he was still focussing on the next most crucial agenda.

As the evening progressed, the temperature fell to bearable levels. But it was not helping anyone with the current anxiety levels, that too in the crowded setting.

Finally, we had the voting for general secretaries for all the boards. People waited for the results with bated breath.

Professor stepped out with results in hand. As part of sharing elected G secs for respective boards one after the other, he announced, "The BRCA G Sec for the next year is Sankalp Verma."

It took everyone from Kara a second to understand because Professor had just called Spidy by his original name. As it finally sunk in, "Kara ka enthu" cheering started. Spidy was the new BRCA G Sec of IITD. We had won the most powerful and sought after poltu position on campus.

Our celebration began in the SAC premises itself. House cheering, bumps to the seniors, anti-cheering – one followed the other. Narayan and Anirudh were tossed in the air multiple times by the large group cheering for the house.

Gautam and I were also a part of the celebration. During the cheering, Gautam whispered in my ears, "I guess Spidy's open support to Amitabh really helped."

"Going purely by the results, he surely gave Amitabh an edge," I agreed with him.

"By the way, our senior batches are quite fortunate!"

"What do you mean?" I couldn't understand his reference.

"Can you realize who is getting benefitted the most in the last 2 years on campus?" he asked.

I realized what he meant. "This year Kara organized the biggest Tryst ever in IITD history. The second and third-year folks were the activity heads and coordinators. Next year, Kara will organise Rendezvous, where the organizing team will comprise of the students from the third and the fourth years. So, again, the people from the same team will be the activity heads and coordinators."

Gautam smiled.

"There is another way to look at it. People from our batch are late by one year. And we are destined to be volunteers only, always!" I concluded. Both of us laughed out loud.

What was outstanding in the celebration was the participation of Double A and TK. They showed us a united face with Amitabh during the external elections. It was great to see people who went through a two-week battle, forgetting what all happened, and overcoming bitterness that possibly could have got accumulated.

One person who was expectedly disappointed in the whole affair was Rocky. He gave up the internal post with a hope of winning in the externals, but ended up winning neither. Though that did not hold him from joining the celebrations; he was still at his cheerful best.

Elections were followed by the 'BHM night' in the ground in front of the hostel area. The highlight of the night was the 'Awards ceremony' where trophies for all the boards were distributed to the winning houses.

Along with the BRCA trophy, Kumaon also won the Best House for Hostel Management. With two board trophies, it remained a formality for Kumaon to win the award of the Overall Best House.

It was followed by a big round of cheering *"Jai Kumaon"* spread across the ground.

Sadly, Kara had not won anything this time. We could only applaud for other hostels that were there to collect trophies.

"This is the night where all the effort through the year sums up." Kaushik joined us for dinner after the awards ceremony.

"Totally. It would have been such a matter of pride had we won something. Currently, I feel embarrassed as well as anguished." I couldn't resist.

"I understand. If you are part of the hostel enthu stream, if you have put in the effort and if you have tasted success at different points of time, you are bound to feel so," Kaushik consoled me.

"But I feel kicked for the next year. Action tonight gives you the extra motivation to understand what it's all about," I tried sounding positive.

"Wait until late night. You will realize it even further."

I was curious now.

After everything wrapped up and we were preparing to go to sleep, I could hear a light drumming sound. "Gautam, can you hear that? Seems like someone is playing the dhol."

"Yeah, and it's getting louder." It was only growing.

Like many others, we came down to the reception to check what was happening. We were astounded to find a large group of students from Kumaon dancing in front of our hostel around a hired professional Punjabi group playing dhol and nagadas. The group then went through the campus, dancing and cheering in front of all the hostels. It almost felt like they were making a statement in everyone's face.

It was an age-old tradition. I felt embarrassed. I was also kicked for future action, realising what Kaushik had referred to.

Soon, we had the House Day in Kara. where hostel residents across batches were awarded for their contribution to the hostel. These category of awards had been there for generations.

It started with the handover of all the roles to the new secretaries – house secy, mess secy, cultural secy, sports secy, and maintenance secy. Old secretaries passed on the symbolic baton to the new ones. It was followed by individual awards.

Bala was awarded the most talented person of the freshers batch - a natural choice.

TK and Shashi were awarded in the cultural category while Double A was awarded in the hostel management category. Rocky and Vatsal were awarded in the sports category.

TK got the most massive applause when he went to collect the award. It was marked with endless cheering and whistling. I was leading the same.

"It seemed like the end of an era when I saw TK collecting his award," I told Gautam.

"True. I was thinking about how today is so different from the day when we saw TK for the first time. From calling the shots to passing on the baton, we have witnessed a remarkable journey of an outstanding leader."

"I think it shows how hostel life is like a never-ending, continuous stage play with periodic handovers. Every year a set of characters exit after playing their role for three to four years. For TK this is virtually the end of his role in the stage play of hostel life while Amitabh still has another year to play his newfound role," I went a little philosophical.

"It is more heartfelt if you think that this stage has been there for ages and will continue to remain in the future. We will replace, to be eventually replaced."

"In the end, it just boils down to how you played your role when you were on the stage. And as the case with every stage play, it's the applause that matters. Nothing else. No one knows it better than TK, who won everyone's heart." I knew I would miss TK big time.

"Basis whatever I have witnessed in one year, I think this is *Mahabharat*, with every event and character playing a connected role. While the events, especially in the 'Even' semesters, set the ball rolling for the inter-linked events in the future, every character's entry and exit was determined by the events they governed and survived." Gautam summed it up well.

"We also see the 'survival of the fittest'. With reducing posts every year, only few remain relevant by remaining fit to survive."

~ 40 ~

Days following the elections were full of boredom. It was the lull before the academic storm. Soon, majors for the first even semester arrived. This time, I had applied the learning from the first term. Despite a hectic non-academic schedule in the house since Minor-II, I continued to maintain being regular in the classes. Overall, I felt I fared better than the last semester.

A certain level of academic regularity and performance was required at the IITs. It was quite evident, given the rigor that we went through, but its serious implications became more apparent to us post the results of the majors.

At IIT, every subject had pre-defined credit points, and everyone was expected to complete a certain number of credit points in the four years. If one failed in a course, he still had a chance to repeat the course and earn the credit anytime over the rest of the four years, thereby still eligible to complete the degree in time. In case one was unable to complete the required number of credits in four years, then his degree would be extended one semester at a time, depending upon the extra time needed to complete the credits.

Accordingly, there were a minimum threshold number of cumulative credits required at the end of every year to continue in the system.

Post the results of the first semester, Vivek was in the danger zone. Vivek had to complete a minimum number of credits by the second semester. Sid tried spending time with Vivek during this semester to ensure that he passed the courses. Once Sid had mentioned to me, “I don’t see Vivek taking it seriously. I don’t know what will follow.”

Post the results of the second semester, I immediately asked Sid about Vivek.

Sid responded in a shallow voice, “I’m afraid that my fears have come true. Vivek has not been able to make the cut.”

I was shocked and reached out to him directly. "Vivek, did you try reaching out to the professors?"

"I reached out to a few professors to explain my situation of being on the expulsion borderline, but they could not help me get passing marks. The bridge was too long to cross without breaking the rules. So I don't think there is any route left for me."

I didn't know what more to tell Vivek. It was going to be painful for him.

We were all leaving for our homes during the semester break after the exams, but it was so different for Vivek. He was going forever, never to return.

A day before Vivek was leaving, I checked with him, "All ok? Have you told your parents?"

"Yes, I am fine. I have not told my parents yet. I think it would be better to tell them when I meet them in person."

"Hmm, I think that's the right thing," Gautam was supportive.

"This system can sometimes be so cruel." Sid was visibly upset.

"No, Sid. Don't blame the system. They give you multiple chances. In fact, I would say that it can't be more student-friendly than this. But what I realized in the last one month is that if it is taking so much effort for me in the first year at such an early stage, then imagine the effort it would require going forward. If I found it difficult even after so many chances, there is no point in pushing myself for the next three years. As of now, I am only losing one year, but had I managed to stay back, I cannot tell how many years I would have lost. And with every year, the commitment would have leapfrogged." Vivek's clarity of thought and confidence made me happy for him.

"This is not the end of the world, man," I supported him.

"Absolutely. Let's see what to do next. Will keep you guys posted." Vivek concluded.

I told Sid about another student from my department who was leaving for the same reason. “That guy from my department was in the top 150 rank. He doesn’t know what he will do and looks visibly broken. I have to say it’s quite courageous of Vivek to deal with it this way.”

Sid was sadder than Vivek.

Vivek left for home the following day. I knew Vivek was leaving behind a huge gap in our lives. Gautam and I had no clue then about how we were going to miss Vivek in the future for a precise role, which only he could have served.

Year 2: Semester III

July – Dec 2003

Updated Index of characters: Semester III

Abhimanyu's batch (Second Year)

Abhimanyu Rishabh	Main protagonist of the Story
Prashant *Gautam*	Abhimanyu's room-mate and best friend; rare talent of Hindi poetry and debating; New Hindi Samiti Club Representative of Karakoram
Siddharth aka *Sid*	An innocent boy from a small town; perfect friend of Abhimanyu
Saurabh *Bansal*	Abhimanyu's room-mate and friend; Most diligent and logical individual in the group
Harshvardhan *Edison*	A good friend of Abhimanyu & Gautam; shared interests in Hindi literature; New BSP Hindi Representative for Karakoram
Rudra Rakesh	Dramatics (comedy) and Athletics talent; Insincere and insensitive in approach; New Dramatics Club Rep of Karakoram
Vishal Arora	Best friend of Rudra; known for his drinking abilities; Demonstrates limited respect for others in the batch
Pushkar	Expert in fine arts; ardent participant of house production team; Denied Fine Arts Club Representative post in the first year
Prabhat	Department mate and very good friend of Pushkar

Shubham	Swimming champion from a small town in Bihar; Unsuccessfully played the opportunist card for a political position in 1st year
Aditya *Sanghvi*	A very enthusiastic individual - shared an unsaid bond with Abhimanyu for the hostel work; New BSW Rep of Kara - kept his political ambition in place right from the start
Makhija	New Quizzing Club Representative of Karakoram; Emerged as the key political coordinator in the batch
Rahul	Sports talent - fastest cricket bowler in the institute; New BSW Rep of Kara along with Sanghvi
Utkarsh	Sports talent - expertise in TT, Baddy, Carom; New Indoor Sports Club Rep of Kara
Thomas	Rare English debating talent in the institute; respected individual in the batch; New EDLC Representative of Karakoram
Bala	Exceptional talent in Music - master of multiple musical instruments; New Music Club Rep of Kara – highly respected in the batch
Barnwal	Only person in the batch with prior theatre experience
Mridul	Fine Arts expert; rarely resided in the house consistently; New Fine Arts Club Representative for the house
Rachit	Abhimanyu's department mate; always a helping hand in studies

One year senior to Abhimanyu's batch (Third Year)

Shashi Ranjan Singh	Ex-Dramatics Club Representative, a major cultural club; immense theatre talent; Surprisingly didn't go for any political position at the end of his second year
Vikash *aka Guru*	Enthusiastic soul with a serious approach to hostel work; excellent friend of Shashi; Leveraged Tryst to become more visible and become new Mess Secretary of Kara
Rocky	Sports talent: Baddy, Squash, Hockey; Ex- Film Club, a minor club, Rep; Deserving individual who didn't end up with any position of responsibility at the end of the year
Vatsal	Sports (Cricket) and Dramatics (comedy) talent; famous for his sense of humour; No significant position of responsibility even by the end of his second year
Kaushik	Ex-Hindi Club Representative; Most charming and popular senior; Unexpectedly no major participation in politics
Kalra	Best athlete in the house; represented Kara in most of the sports; New Sports Secretary of Kara
Aniket	Ex-Music Club Representative; Surprisingly emerged as the new Cultural Secretary of Kara
Viks	A good friend of Guru; visible face in the batch; Gained out of the loss of Rocky to become the Maintenance Secretary of Kara

Two years senior to Abhimanyu's batch (Fourth Year)

Amitabh Gupta	New Karakoram House Secretary
Spidy	New BRCA General Secretary - responsible for organizing Rendezvous this year

One year junior to Abhimanyu's batch (First year)

Aryan	New drama talent in the house
Pratyush Prakash aka *PP*	Jharkhand boy; talent in multiple cultural activities - singer, dramatics
Aneesh	Super enthusiastic individual –passionate for house success
Sajid	Enthusiastic individual, tag team with Aneesh
Sikka	Music talent in the batch
Dixcy	Individual with more enthu than talent – fine arts, theatre, music
Thakkar	Alum from Gautam's school; not interested in hostel activities
Suresh	Low profile individual; only in touch with Gautam
Shanky	Humble, enthusiastic individual – more of enthu than talent
Charsi	Individual who showcased enthu across events; couldn't identify with any group

VI

New start: Bonding at its best

~ 41 ~

It was a new academic year – my second year in college. Every year, our wing and rooms were supposed to change. So, our batch was shifted and distributed between the second floor in the new wing and the third floor in the long wing.

Many people continued with their last year's roommate, while few chose new ones. Sid, who was with Vivek, had to settle with Barnwal. He no longer remained part of my wing. He belonged to the other wing that had Vishal, Rudra, Pushkar, Prabhat and Shubham. Beyond Gautam, Bansal and Edison, my wing had Sanghvi, Rahul, Makhija and Utkarsh, among others.

Meanwhile, a new batch of freshers had joined. And we were expected to play the same role that our seniors had played last year. Secretaries and representatives had a natural obligation, but few others like me had a genuine inclination.

"Gautam, I really enjoyed the process last year. So, I am going to be an integral part of the group involved in on-boarding the freshers," I told Gautam.

"You should. I will also try. But I don't think that I have as much patience and dedication as you."

"I know your style. You will not join the batch meetings. But you will soon have a huge fan following through personal connections." I knew Gautam's way of working.

"I don't have any such plans. What's your plan?"

"From my experience in the last year, I personally believe that 'healthy interaction' period is meant for both ragging for fun, as well as helping juniors understand hostel life, enthusiasm and facilitating their personal development. I will try to ensure that they understand the importance of the second one as much as they enjoy or react to the first."

"All the best, man! I am sure it will make a difference."

It was quite nostalgic to take the fachas through the early morning jogs, late night batch meetings in the mess and long cheering sessions. It was not long ago that we were on the other side, wondering what the hell was happening. All the characters in this stage play of hostel life had been replaced.

☆ ☆

One night at dinner, I saw this junior eating sheepishly in front of me. I started the conversation. "Give your intro."

"Sir, I am Aryan Parashar. My AIR is 1221. I am in the Industrial and Production department. I am from Lucknow. My room number is A14. I like painting and have tried dramatics in school days," it was a standard intro as taught in our long batch meetings.

Aryan's chubby look added to the innocence he carried while he spoke in a sluggish manner.

"Dramatics? Interesting," I found him quite chirpy.

"Yes, sir. Got few chances in school before class tenth." I was correct in identifying his buoyant spirits.

"Are you in touch with Rudra for the fresher's skit event?" I had to interrupt him. That was my way of showing seniority – crisp talking with the right set of actions for juniors.

"Yes. I gave my name on the first day." He tried being precise.

"You must follow up with him to find a place for yourself. He will not come looking for you." I was at my instructional best. "And why are you not eating? Talking to a senior doesn't mean that you need to stop. Keep eating, keep talking."

"Yes, sir." He replied with a smile.

"That doesn't mean you can smile at will. You will be doing the Smile Wipe act in tonight's batch meet. If I forget to call you out during the batch meet, do remind me." I had to act like a strict senior.

"Sorry, sir." Aryan was back to his obliged ways.

Aryan performed the first smile wipe for the batch. As always, it never stopped at one performance. We had smile wipes in eleven languages that night.

I knew the importance of maintaining batch discipline and not letting them take anything for granted. I had learned it from Double A.

On one Friday evening, when I came back from college, I saw a junior in Utkarsh's room. He seemed a physically fit person from a middle-class background.

I joined the gang.

"Give your intro." Utkarsh was at his authoritative best

"I am Aneesh Kumar. I qualified in the reserved category. I am in Mechanical department. I am from Ghaziabad. My room number is A11. My hobbies are biking, running and bird watching."

Everyone burst out laughing for his interest in bird watching.

"Okay, describe a hot girl for me in five sentences." Utkarsh was not going to leave him.

He tried his best to describe a girl in five sentences.

"Now, repeat the same lines. But this time instead of using 'A girl' use 'My sister'," Utkarsh caught him by the balls.

He tried, but by the third or the fourth sentence, he could not speak. He started stammering and was almost in tears. I had to intervene.

"Don't try to be over-smart. You can leave for your room." I directed him to leave.

"Ok, sir," Aneesh left.

Aneesh was visibly disturbed. I followed him in the wing. I put an arm around his shoulder and said, "It's ok. It's part and parcel of life. You can't get hurt all the time. You need to understand that you are no longer at home. And don't try to act over-smart with seniors."

"Ok, sir." He seemed better than before.

"And yes. If there is any problem, reach out to me. Don't go and complain against your seniors without consulting. You will learn and evolve personally during these early days." I tried calming him down so that it did not become a bigger issue.

I knew it was required to an extent to make them come out of their comfort zone. I had learned it from Shashi.

During one of the morning sessions before jogging, everyone was asked to cheer at the top of their voice. And there was this guy whose voice level was not encouraging.

"Shout...*Kara ka enthu high hai,*" Shubham was shouting at him.

He was still not able to take it to the next level.

I intervened, "Give your intro."

"I am Pratyush Prakash. My AIR is 934. I am in Electrical Power department. I am from Jamshedpur. My room number is B11. My hobbies are singing and theatre." Pratyush was a short, thin and fair guy who was short on confidence, which reflected in his way of talking.

"Your name sounds so old-fashioned. Let's call you PP." I rechristened Pratyush. "You are interested in theatre, and you cannot shout! You know, to sustain anywhere in this institute you need to have an echoing voice. In the classroom, at the hostel, in the ground, or the seminar hall, everywhere. You must make people listen to you, and for that to happen, you have to let go all inhibitions and shout. Otherwise, you will be lost in the crowd." I helped him open his voice for the next few days, especially when we cheered as a team.

I knew loudness played an essential role in inspiring confidence. I had learned it from Guru and Rocky.

I noticed a guy named Shirish Thakkar missing from most of the batch meets. His roomie always had the same reason, "Thakkar is not in the room, sir. I don't know where he is."

I asked Thakkar's roomie to ask him to meet me that night. Honestly, I was not expecting Thakkar to come on his own, but he surprised me.

"Hi, sir! You wanted to meet me." Thakkar was one of the tallest people in the batch. He had sharp features and wore specs.

"Hi, Thakkar. How are you? Heard you were not in the campus during the batch meet?"

"Yes, sir had gone to Jiya Sarai to meet my friend," Jiya Sarai was next to IIT Delhi campus.

"That's close by. You could have come back for the batch meet."

"Yes, sir. But after experiencing what happens in the batch meet for a few days, I thought I may not lose anything by not attending the batch meet."

"I don't think you know what you are missing out. Knowing your own cohort, making friends with your own batchmates as well as your seniors, understanding the house culture, identifying opportunities to participate and develop yourself."

"You may be correct, sir. But I would make friends as and when it happens. And I don't seriously believe in this culture and opportunity thing. If it must happen, it will happen. I am fine on my own."

"It's a choice you are making, and I can't force you for anything. But you would be missing on a large part of life in the campus. Good night."

"Good night, sir." Thakkar came across as a stubborn, but a humble person.

I knew he didn't have any clue what he was missing in campus life. I had learned it from TK.

One night, a thin, short and fair guy with a fair share of white hair at such an early age approached me after the batch meeting. "Sir, I am ..."

"...I know you Dixcy. If I remember correctly, you are Aneesh's roommate?" I didn't know how he got his nickname, but his new name was already famous in the house.

"Yes, sir." Dixcy was visibly now more comfortable talking with me. "Sir, I have a situation. Aneesh asked me I should reach you for this. You will solve it for me."

"I can try. Tell me!"

"Sir, we have a fine arts event on Sunday. And one needs to prepare the oil painting a day before. I had originally planned to be at home over the weekend, but given the event, I plan to be back on Sunday morning. I had told Mridul, our FAC rep that I would prepare Kara's entry on Saturday at home, but he is not comfortable taking Kara's entry directly to the event without his guidance or preview. Either he wants me here over the entire weekend, or he may ask someone else in the batch to represent." I could feel that Dixcy desperately wanted to represent Kara.

"Can't you avoid going back home?"

"Sir, it's my cousin's engagement on Saturday. I am leaving early Sunday morning to be here on time."

"Let me talk to Mridul. You will hear from him either way by tonight."

Kara won the third place in the event. Dixcy represented Kara in the competition after having a blast at his cousin's engagement.

I knew identifying passion for the house was more critical than anything else. I had learned it from TK.

On a Saturday afternoon, Shankar aka Shanky reached out to me. "Sir, wanted to check if you have the book for MA110?" Shanky was one of the most innocent guys in the first year. His physical appearance was like a teddy bear – massive and impeccant.

"No Shanky. I didn't have that course. I had MA111 in the first semester, and I am sure no one else would like to do that course."

"Why sir?"

"All those who join IIT think they are the best brains in Maths. And it takes you one lecture of MA 111 to break that myth. It's like an abstruse course which is beyond conventional mathematics. But about the book, let me check with Bansal."

I got the book from Bansal and gave it to Shanky. He was thankful both for the book and the story.

I knew a caring senior is always respected. I had learned it from Kaushik.

"Abhimanyu sir," Chandrak aka Charsi came running to me. Charsi was renamed during the first week itself. He was an enthusiast from the first year who had participated in most of the sports events. He was the fittest of the lot and could possibly give anyone a run for their money in stamina.

"Yeah, Charsi."

"Sid sir was telling me about all the action that happens as part of facha skit last year."

"Yeah, it's the most important event for the batch."

"Sir, I want to participate in our entry for the event. Sid told me you will play an important role in the preparation."

"Sid!"

"Sorry! Sid sir told me," Charsi stressed on 'sir' this time.

"We will have audition for the batch and then Rudra, being the dramatics rep, will decide about the cast. From my experience, I can tell you that the element that will matter most in the audition is the enthusiasm that you can bring. Am sure you will give your best."

"I will try my best sir, but it would really help if you could also recommend."

"Charsi, as I just mentioned, it will be an open audition. If you try honestly, you will make it." I did not like his approach now.

"Got it, sir. Will give my best."

I knew honesty was so critical in these early days. I had learned it from Vatsal.

"It seems you are doing a great job with juniors." Thomas met me at Wind T in the institute.

"I am trying what we got from our seniors."

"Looks like it's much beyond that. I think your attitude of making the freshers realize the importance of the true side of 'healthy interaction' makes you the most approachable and respected senior."

"Come on!"

"I am serious. I was talking to a couple of folks from the first year, as part of the EDLC event preparation. They told me how they reach out to you to discuss and get potential solutions to their problems. From studies to prioritization, to extra-curricular to day-to-day issues, I think you are helping them with all. And I could see genuine fondness for 'Abhimanyu bhai' in them."

"I guess, to an extent, Sanghvi is playing a similar role. Even he seems to be very approachable."

"Yes, he is. But you have stood out for them."

"It started as fun for me, but it's great to hear that the freshers are able to understand."

'Abhimanyu bhai' was now famous among juniors.

~ 42 ~

From second year onwards, we had a mix of compulsory and elective departmental courses. We also had few non-departmental electives.

The second year was the time to study different topics within the department and depending upon the topics of interest, choose right set of focussed electives going forward. It was now time to know the professors from the department more closely.

Interestingly, course curriculum and areas to be covered as part of the course was entirely in the hands of the individual professor taking the course. So we witnessed everyone's unique and refreshing approach to teaching. Some professors made every session very objective and mathematical in line with the engineering principles, while others would keep them subjective. Few had structured approach with a recommended book, marked chapters for references and quizzes spread through the semester, and others followed notes-based teaching with lots of assignments to carry along. I was learning to adapt to varying styles of teaching.

"It is completely possible that the same course will be taught in a very different manner to the different batches if taken by a different professor." We all arrived at this conclusion very soon.

"Our digital electronics professor is at a different level." I was talking to Sid and Bansal.

"What happened?" Sid asked.

"He is the best professor that we have in this semester. I am a fan of his ability to keep the conversation engaging. Many people wait for his dose of humour during lectures."

"Like?" Sid wanted to know the details.

"The other day he said electronics is way more impactful than power engineering. We deal with Milli-ampere and Milli-volts while those poor guys work at mega-amperes and mega-volts. Just imagine the accuracy we need to work with. On the other hand, for them, there is so much scope to make an error and still live with it!"

Sid and Bansal laughed out loud.

I continued, "In fact, last time he caught someone sleeping in the class. After that, he told the students 'You guys don't understand the importance of time that I am spending with you. If you cut my hand, you will not see any blood coming out of my veins. Rather you will witness a lot of knowledge and wisdom which is stored inside me, built through years of practice and application.'"

"I guess that keeps the class awake," Bansal said smiling.

'No wonder everyone likes the professor's style." Sid was impressed.

Every student who joins the campus is assigned an advisor, a professor from his own department, right at the start of the first year. The role of the advisors is to mentor the students while helping them decide the courses basis their interest, performance and progress in the institute. Students realize the importance of the advisor only by the second year, when they need to understand the elective courses in detail.

I barely connected with Neel Chandra, my advisor, during the first year. At the end of the first year, I spent more time with him, spread over a couple of sessions to discuss the course options and areas that I could think of exploring.

Neel sir had a lean and thin built, was identified with his thin moustache and big glasses which were difficult to ignore. I had found him very humble and approachable right from the beginning.

During our discussion, he mentioned, "Your course choices should depend upon what is your objective – it can be to learn and build your knowledge or to score marks and boost your grades or to balance out the load during the semester. As of now, I could see this is a relatively heavy semester for you and a couple of tough courses on your plate, which will not be the case next semester. Please decide and distribute course choices accordingly."

"Yes, sir. I get what you mean. We will go with first option for this semester and keep the second one for the next semester to balance it out," I confirmed my choices to him by pointing to the courses listed on the desktop screen.

"Sure. By the way, what is keeping you busy these days other than academics?"

"Nothing much, sir. The first years have recently joined. So, spending some time after class hours with them in the hostel."

"Are you any club rep?"

"No, sir!"

"Did you try?"

"Yes, but couldn't make it. But that doesn't stop me from participating and spending time with juniors."

"I like that. Keep up your spirit. Also, do share what's happening with you beyond the classroom. I can bet that there is more interesting stuff happening in the hostel. It will give me a chance to boast in front of my peers!" He laughed out loud.

I smiled back.

Neel sir was able to convert even the most subjective matters into objective outcomes. And it was evident to me that he was going to be more than an academic advisor for me.

~ 43 ~

Events for freshers were scheduled one after the other for different clubs and sports, just like the preceding year. Kara fachas were also participating with full enthusiasm.

As second-year seniors, our expectation from first years was based on what we had achieved during our facha period. Unfortunately, Kara fachas' performance was not anywhere near them.

"I don't want to take anything from our fachas, but in a way, it reflects the natural talent in the batch. There is some limitation, and we should just acknowledge the same." I once shared with Sanghvi.

As always, the facha skit was the last and the most significant event for freshers. I was keenly looking forward to the same. As the dramatics rep, Rudra was responsible for the competition. And Aniket, cultural secy, had to make sure that it happened the same way as we had experienced last year.

Rudra asked the juniors to assemble in the storage hall for the auditions on a Friday night. I also joined. As Rudra was yet to join, I started with the regular set up.

"Who all have done this before?"

"It's more about enthusiasm, energy and letting go your inhibitions."

"One should definitely try."

Rudra joined in late. He was accompanied by Vishal.

"Abhimanyu, you are also here?" He was not expecting me.

"Yeah! How can I miss the opportunity to be part of the facha skit preparation? It is so much fun."

"So, is there any talent in the batch for the skit?" Rudra started unexpectedly.

"Yeah, I am sure there will be many," I said, realising it was not the best start from him.

"Let's see what's in store for us." Rudra said.

Then we had auditions. Many people in the batch tried. Some voluntarily while others when put into the spot. Aryan and PP played their parts well. Shanky and Dixcy were decent. Charsi also tried multiple times. Eventually we were able to identify a team for the skit.

Rudra and Vishal were writing the script as a team.

"Please let me know if you need any help." I offered my assistance to Rudra.

Rudra said, "Will let you know if I need your help." He never came back to me.

I made a point to join practice sessions to help juniors in their role. In the practice sessions, I found Vishal and Rudra true to their style. They were improvising on the go. New scenes and acts were being added as and when required. First timers were finding it challenging to adapt.

I checked with Rudra. "Have you written the complete script?"

Rudra confirmed, "Yes, it's there. We are just implementing it accordingly."

Once Aryan was asked to come up with his own dialogues for his scene. He was able to pull it off. It turned out to be an excellent opportunity for someone like him. Shanky was failing miserably when asked to do the same. I had to spend some time separately with Shanky to make him write his own dialogues and practice delivery.

One day, team practice was scheduled in the evening. The team assembled. I also reached as per the schedule, but Rudra could not make it. Rudra sent the message through a first year to cancel the practice. Instead of cancelling the practice, I made the team do a full run, which had not happened yet. It gave everyone a chance to understand the complete picture of the skit. For the first time, they practiced without Rudra. There were fewer breaks. Also, there were no instances of public humour at the cost of personal humiliation.

Next day, PP told me, "We got a real scolding from Rudra for practicing without him yesterday."

"Did you guys tell him I was there?"

"Yes, we told him. But it didn't change his behaviour," PP said honestly.

I realized Rudra and Vishal did not like my interference. I knew situations of contrasting styles, and creative disagreements would always arise. But this looked beyond that.

I mentioned this to Gautam. "I think, there is an unsaid tension between Rudra and me. Both Rudra and Vishal don't like that juniors are finding my style of working more appealing."

"I am not surprised. Now, it depends on how you want to contribute. The choice is between trying to deliver to perfection, while having an ego-clash with Rudra and Vishal. Or maintaining a distance where ownership lies with Rudra, but you drive the enthusiasm of the juniors."

"It's better to avoid a situation where juniors are torn between different directions to opt for." I chose the latter.

☆ ☆

We did not end up in top three in the facha skit. Moreover, fachas felt disappointed after watching performances of other houses.

"Don't get disheartened. You all will have your moment of applause. We have a long way to go." There was no better way to cheer them up than what I had learned from TK. "Kara ka enthu high hai."

And soon the whole batch joined me.

Apart from Aryan and PP, who became the star of the batch post their performances in the skit, Aneesh was one person who stood out. He was the backbone of the overall performance. Though these were still early days for him, Aneesh took complete control of the production support. Rudra's habit of delegation gave him even better opportunity to take control. I could notice his ability to 'make it happen.' He had all the *jugaad* skills that were much needed for the role. Aneesh was well supported by Sajid and the 'deadly duo' established a reputation for themselves.

☆ ☆

Overall, it was the worst possible start to our chances of BRCA.

"We couldn't win a single point during the facha period. Such a shame!" Sanghvi pointed out.

"It's just the start. Am sure we will pull it back when the stars from the batch are in action," I was optimistic.

"I hope so. If all our cultural reps take their responsibility seriously, am sure we will be back on track." Sanghvi was also hoping for the best.

The real action for the year was expected to begin soon.

~ 44 ~

Though we had limited success in the facha events, most of us experienced the enthusiasm expressed by the new batch. We realised that it was perhaps a batch low on talent, but very high on spirits. I was impressed with their enthusiasm and told Gautam the same.

"Maybe it's the result of your efforts through the facha period," Gautam said.

"It would have helped for sure, but they have an unmatched spirit of their own."

Over time, Gautam and I developed a close friendship with a few fachas. Aryan and PP slowly became the core of our group. Theatre was a common reason for our friendship.

"Sid, Aneesh and Sajid are the two most enthusiastic and jugaadu people of the batch. They act as a team – you need props for any event to be made, explain it, and they will get it for you; you need people in the batch to assemble, they will go and get them; you need food to be arranged for late night practice, they will arrange; they will act almost before you tell them." I knew the importance of such people in the batch.

"Great! I guess you will get some leverage from them for your dramatics events." Sid was thinking about the helping hand for me.

"Yes, for sure." I was confident.

"What's your take on Charsi? He gives everything a try," Gautam asked.

"He is an enthusiast. I felt his spirit for the house at multiple occasions. I think he tried for your dumb charades team as well, right?" I asked Gautam.

"He tried, but with PP being so good with his knowledge of Bollywood and Shanky and Dixcy supporting him well, he couldn't make it." Gautam had witnessed Charsi's efforts. "How did he react when he did not make it to the core team of the skit?"

"Of course he didn't like it, but he supported Aneesh in the production eventually."

"Maybe he learned from his experience of dumb charades." That confused me, so he explained, "Charsi didn't take his rejection for dumb charades well. To me, he is an enthu guy, but seeks visibility. Once he understood he may not end up in the team, unlike others who couldn't make it, he stopped helping the trio during the practice. I felt that if he makes it to the team, his house enthusiasm is high, otherwise his spirit dampens. After the event, I did tell him how he should think about this. Maybe it helped." Gautam told me the complete story.

"Edison, do you know the secret behind Gautam's ability to develop friendship with relatively unknown people in the batch." I joined Edison and Gautam sitting in our room.

"Who are you talking about?" Edison was surprised.

"Suresh. He is one such protégé of yours whom I have never seen anywhere else other than our room."

"Oh, Suresh! He is just interested in poetry. He likes discussing different styles of writing with me." Gautam played it down.

"I should have guessed that."

"Gautam has a fan following across batches. And I am sure it will only grow going forward." Edison was impressed.

"But why is Suresh not seen anywhere else?" I asked Gautam.

"Suresh wants to concentrate on studies. He has come through the preparatory course and so wants to give his hundred percent to academics. And I think there is nothing wrong in his thinking."

"I think Suresh has got the right mentor in you." I had my answer.

"There are also people like Thakkar in the batch, who are never seen anywhere – neither in batch meets, nor otherwise. I don't know what to do with people like him. Despite multiple attempts, he just does not seem to participate." I had not figured out Thakkar's style yet.

"Leave him. He is that way." Gautam replied looking at his desktop.

"How do you know him?"

"He is from my school."

"Aha! He is from Patna. I didn't check his school. Maybe you should try once."

"Have tried it already. Thakkar hasn't changed a bit from school days."

"Thakkar always behaves courteously with me, though." I was unbiased in my opinion.

"He is a courteous guy. It's just that he has his own way of thinking, which is difficult to influence."

"He has also developed a group of his own to hang out with."

"I am not surprised. I remember Thakkar had a strong group in school as well," Gautam reminisced.

"Anyway, overall I feel that we have developed a good core team in the first year for the house."

"I would see that as a great start for the year." Gautam sounded optimistic.

We knew the importance of developing a working team for the house.

~ 45 ~

During the facha skit, every boys' hostel needs girls' clothing, both external as well internal. Sometimes people would reach out to friends in girl hostels to get the required set of outer clothes. But for the transformation, the most critical part is to get inner wear of the right size. For Kara, Rudra made a significant contribution by buying them in bulk so that they can be used for future, depending upon the role. It was a similar situation in all the hostels.

Someone in Jwala just took it to the next level this time. And who knew it better than Aryan. "My department mate, a facha from Jwala, called up the landline at the reception of Kailash hostel a day before the skit. He asked guard *Saab* to connect to any girl around reception citing an urgent request."

"And then?" I was interested.

"When the call was picked up by a girl, he made a straightforward request – 'we need two bras. One light and one dark in color. Can you please arrange? I can come and collect it from your hostel'"

"What!" I couldn't believe.

"Wait until you hear the reply which was even better. The first thing that the girl asked the boy in return - are you from the Jwalamukhi hostel?"

I couldn't control my laughter.

"My department-mate was surprised that how could she know about his hostel and so he checked with her. Her reply was epic."

"What was her reply?"

"It's easy to guess because it's the hostel of ICs.' She was an old timer. My department-mate from Jwala, being new to the campus, didn't stop and checked what she meant by IC."

"OMG!"

"She was direct. 'You are an Institute Chutiya. And you have already added to your hostel's tradition."

"That's unbelievable. What made this 'special' facha pull off an act like this?"

"Quite predictable! A senior asked him to do this as part of the 'healthy interaction'! And he told us the complete story citing it as such a fun experience."

"Great to see the Jwala facha taking it in right spirit. Am sure he would be famous among his seniors."

"Not only in Jwala, am sure he will be famous in the whole institute."

The story was told and re-told in hostels, in the institute, everywhere.

Amid all the fun that we had with juniors as part of the 'healthy interaction,' there were always people in the first year who would take it to heart. I knew this and so spent a lot of time on calming down individuals where I felt the danger. I also made a point to make them realize the side of ragging, which is essential.

But there was a significant fallout that happened in Aravalli aka Ara. It was a case of 'healthy interaction' not taken in the right spirit and therefore going south.

"I don't know who is at fault. But it's serious this time." Sid brought the news to all of us. "This time one of the top AIRs in IITD, belonged to Ara. For the last few days, he had refused to come to hostel citing mental agony. Yesterday his parents informed Ara Warden about his hospitalization."

"Am hoping he is back to campus soon. Otherwise, you never know how things will turn out for seniors in Ara." I was hoping for the best.

Slowly this news reached the media, and it became a hot topic on the campus. Initially, everyone thought it would pass. But things took an ugly turn when there was news of police looking into the matter.

"I heard the institute team was collecting the photos of all the seniors from Ara. The top ranker fellow presumably identified people from the pics showed to him and Dean, Student Affairs has been informed about the same." Sid always knew the campus news.

"Given the media coverage of this top ranker in the hospital, Dean is under tremendous pressure to take action. There is a rumour that owing to media pressure central HRD minister is looking into the matter as well." Edison had his share of information as well.

Within a couple of days, news of four people from Ara being asked to drop a semester spread in the campus. It was a far stricter action by the authorities that anyone expected. One of those four was a close friend of Gautam from his department.

"Am sure he got into trouble because he was one of the visible guys in the batch. He is a sporty fellow who used to take the batch for morning jogs and so was easily identifiable. He is a fallout of all the drama that happened." Gautam could not believe the news.

"Gautam, I personally always believed that 'healthy interaction' on our campus is healthy for students, and it helps one make lifelong friends at the end of it. There is always a need to carefully deal with instances which have the potential to go out of control. But I never felt that 'healthy interaction' could lead to such outcomes for seniors." I was shocked too. Everyone thinks about the impact of extreme ragging on juniors, but this time people were witnessing the result of a severe reaction to the honest effort by someone. "I think one needs someone in the seniors to play the role of moderator. So that things never go out of control on either side."

"You are correct." Gautam agreed.

"It has made me realize that 'healthy interaction' needs to be communicated in the right way. It is also equally important to discard people who don't want to understand and can react extremely. One gets to realize the importance of 'healthy interaction' only when all the three essential behavioural impacts are communicated well – breaking your boundaries to try everything you wish to do without, multi-tasking from day zero, and bonding with best people of your batch and seniors. My personal experience taught me there is no substitute for bonding that happens because of interaction between the seniors and juniors. No other medium can make it happen. And I believe it even when I know that I can't tell everything that happened to me as part of 'healthy interaction' to everyone." I felt strongly for Gautam's department mate.

"It's ok Abhimanyu. You can't control everything. Thankfully we have people like you and Sanghvi in the batch to take care of the same. I hope authorities also take note of this best practice."

I ended up talking about it with Neel sir who heard my arguments patiently.

"But you need to think about the freshers as well. You can't expect them to deal with both the positive and negative sides of ragging in the same way. I am sure a few seniors crossed the line."

"I do not deny that sir. Everyone has the right to question the wrong actions, especially if it is crossing the line. But one needs to be aware of the implications of the same. Given the situation today, there is a possibility of implications far more drawn than the underlying actions. At least for one of the victims, it's true." I made my last point. "At the end of the day, the line is purely defined basis one's comfort which can vary from individual to individual."

"If you feel so strongly about it, why don't you write to the Dean to what could be the potential solution to avoid these situations in the future?"

"Is it possible? Can I do that?"

"You can. But make sure that you are logical and not emotional!"

"Will you review it once?"

"I can." He agreed after giving it a thought.

I ended up writing a letter to Dean requesting for a more formal way of handling the reactions to the 'healthy interaction' in the hostels. I suggested a few options for this precise mechanism. I even cited personal experience as a fresher and as a student from the second year to bolster my suggestion – key point being that both the juniors and seniors are equal stakeholders. I got a prompt short reply from the Dean on this matter – "Principally I am in alignment with your thinking and approach. I promise to take up the possible suggested solutions for effective communication between the batches so that we don't end up like this in the future."

I shared the same with Neel sir and thanked him for the encouragement.

~ 46 ~

Post the facha skit and the freshers night, Minor-I arrived. As always, it hit the first year hard. It also provided the chance to identify people whose sole priority in life was going to be academics with a limited interest in extra-curricular.

In many of my subsequent discussions with the freshers, the discomfort caused by the results was evident. And to all of them, my only submission was - "It's still very early days. This gives you a chance to understand where you stand. So learn from the mistakes and be prepared for the next of the many battles you are going to experience!"

Gautam had bought a new mobile phone at the start of the semester, still a luxury for many.

One night, Gautam got a call from a girl who was looking for me. “Someone looking for you. Is there anything I am not aware of?” I could notice mischief in his eyes.

“I don’t have anything to hide. Give me your mobile.”

“Hi, Abhimanyu! Bhavna here. Am a first-year Ph.D. student in the Maths department.”

“Sorry, I am not sure if I know you. Why are you calling me?”

“Don’t tell anyone, but can you come to the Block II terrace.”

“But why?”

“PP is completely drunk here. And I need someone to take him back to the hostel.”

“PP? Oh, I will come!” I disconnected the call.

“Where are you going?” Gautam was surprised.

“To Institute. Will come and explain it to you. Am not sure.” I was shocked that a Ph.D. girl was calling on behalf of a B.Tech. boy.

As I reached there, I could see PP sitting with his back against the wall. This girl was sitting next to him. As I reached closer, I could identify the girl. She used to take the tutorial for MA120 course for other groups.

“What happened?’

“He is drunk. Has puked also. I don’t think he will ve able to walk to the house on his own. So, I called you.”

“And why the hell are you guys here?”

“Ask PP when he is back to normal.”

“Sorry, I shouldn’t have asked you so rudely. Let’s take him downstairs. I will take care from there.”

I brought PP back to his room. He was not in any position to talk that night.

Next day, PP came to my room. "Abhimanyu bhai, sorry about yesterday."

"Hmm. You don't have to explain anything."

"I think I should tell you. Bhavna is my girlfriend."

"I was able to guess from what I saw."

"I don't know how it happened. But in the last two months, we have come quite close to each other."

"How did you end up on the terrace of Block II?"

"It was Bhavna's birthday. So I planned this cake cutting and drinking on the rooftop. I don't know how I ended up so drunk."

"You seem to be going fast in this case. How did it all start?"

"It started when I reached out to her to help me with one of my assignments." PP's department was clearly helping in his cause. He scratched his head and added, "By the way, Bhavna wanted to meet you in a better way. She is embarrassed."

"Why should she be embarrassed? *You* should be embarrassed. We should meet soon. How come she called on Gautam's number and asked for me?"

"I had told her once that she should reach out to Abhimanyu bhai for help if there was any mess. I had given her Gautam's number."

"I respect your trust in me. But "Abhimanyu bhai" for her as well? That's not fair!" I chuckled. "What is the age gap between both of you?"

"Am not going to tell you that! Will soon plan a catch-up for all three of us together. You can check it with Bhavna then. Bye." PP left in a hurry.

"I can do the calculation on my own even if you don't tell me."

~ 47 ~

During Tryst last year, I had worked with Guru. It helped me in developing a close friendship as well as rapport with him.

I was drafted by Guru, Mess Secretary this year, in the Mess Committee at the start of the semester. Fixing and revising mess menu, conducting mess surveys, distribution of coupons during house events, organizing mess day and managing extra time during the exam days were few of the responsibilities of the committee.

"Going by last years' experience, most of the people in Mess Committee are not very visible. But it should be a good experience for you, Abhimanyu." Sid was encouraging.

Within a few weeks, it helped me understand mess operations completely. More than that, it became a source of continuous interaction with Guru. Soon, for every housework, Mess or otherwise, I was the first-person Guru used to reach out to.

"Abhimanyu, let's get coupons printed for the facha night."

"Abhimanyu, can you create the next mess survey?"

"Abhimanyu, can you please take care of the duty roster for the extra night mess?"

I was increasingly becoming visible in mess activities as well as close to the mess secretary.

"You friendship with Guru seems to have grown recently," Sid stated what he was observing.

"Work has become the obvious connect."

"Hmm, you need to be careful. Otherwise, you seem to be leaning more towards the group of Guru, Shashi and others. You can't stop people from cooking things up, you know!" Bansal was cautious.

"I don't know about the group, but yes the friendship has surely grown with both Guru and Shashi because of Mess and dramatics." I was honest.

Hostel work was still the common link for my friendship with them. Gautam listened to the conversation but didn't say anything.

VII
Passion driving Ambition

~ 48 ~

Other than Amitabh, the house secy, and few of his close friends, fourth-year people were not much visible since the start of the semester. Expectedly, TK was not in action since the beginning of the year. After witnessing a year of election, I could now understand why beyond Anirudh no one from the final year was visible last year. There was limited motivation for everyone. The group which had lost the elections was understandably no longer part of the mainstream. And the people from the winning group spent most of the time among themselves and left it to the house secy to take care of the regular proceedings.

"No one in the first year can guess who was running the show last year!" I told Gautam.

"Agree! Exactly the case when we joined the house last year. Everyone moves on and thinks about the future," Gautam added.

"This year Shashi has taken responsibility for the Hindi play."

"Makes sense. Even though Shashi is not the cult secy, he is the most experienced person in the house."

I was eagerly waiting for the action to start.

On a Saturday afternoon, Shashi came to my room. I was sleeping, so he woke me up. "Abhimanyu, I want you to play the role of Panditji in the play. It's an important role. Here is your script copy. If you have any questions, let me know?" He surprised me.

"Sorry." I was still trying to make sense of what Shashi meant.

"Did you get it?" Shashi was louder this time. His approach was similar to when he had offered cigarettes to me in the first year.

"Is there no reading, testing involved?" I had to understand his style of working.

"No, I don't think that's required. Let's assemble tonight at 8 in the TV Room, and you will get to know the other people in the play."

Shashi had picked up a philosophical script, decided cast on his own and then directly informed the relevant people to assemble.

When I reached the TV room that night, I found a group of 8 people – Vatsal from Shashi's batch, three from our batch and four from the first year. Makhija and Barnwal were the other people from our batch. Aryan, PP, Dixcy and Shanky were from the first year. Shashi then explained the roles played by each one of us. Vatsal and I were given the lead roles.

Rudra being the dramatics rep was expected to handle the production. I was surprised that Shashi didn't pick him for any role in the play.

In the next week, we understood Shashi's style of working. He would come prepared with explicit instructions to everyone and minimal chances for the participants to improvise. Getting the right cast without biases, clarity in his thought process and single focus to deliver the best possible scenes in the play were quite evident. Shashi spent time with all the participants individually, explaining what was expected from them before making it public.

Slowly, I understood he was quite blunt with people in his expectations and judgement of their limitations. During these discussions, Shashi himself told me, "Rudra was the best suited for the role Makhija is playing, but I changed my mind after talking to him. I felt it may not be fruitful for the first years; we need only one person calling the shots."

Shashi gave more than his hundred percent in practice sessions. He spent considerable time with people, training them how to maintain intensity over a long period of time. "You guys need to use your stomach more while delivering long, high-pitched dialogues. You can't keep using your throat." It was difficult initially, but slowly I realized the importance of leveraging stomach for high-intensity dialogues.

On a few occasions, Shashi used to leave us to ourselves to practice without him. But it showed below par performances and I asked Vatsal to explain this to Shashi. But it was Shashi's style, and no one could get him to change his mind.

Shashi was able to pass on his energy to everyone else in the team. Sometimes he used to get overboard on criticism, resulting in participants taking it to their heart. I got scolded multiple times. But slowly, we all adjusted.

One night at the end of practice, Shashi asked everyone, "Let us sit together in a circle and give open feedback related to scenes, changeovers, direction, acting and beyond." He soon started this practice every other night.

Initially this unique style of feedback became a driver to keep people engaged, even when others were practicing as everyone had to contribute during the feedback session at the end of the day. But over a period of time, I feel the open criticisms became a platform to push their view.

"Rudra had requested Pushkar to help with the production support. But he refused." I was discussing play preparations with Gautam.

"Who told you?"

"Rudra himself."

"Why did Pushkar refuse?" Minor I just got over." Gautam was in think-mode.

"I was also surprised. Pushkar would have been an asset to the team, given his experience from the last year." I didn't have any clue.

"Is it in any way related to missing the FAC Rep opportunity?"

"Possible! I have not seen Pushkar visible at all this semester."

"So? Is Rudra going to take the complete responsibility? Am sure it will be hard on him." Gautam said.

"Yeah. So, I have recommended Aneesh's name to Shashi. We all saw his dedication during the facha skit."

Shashi asked Rudra to take Aneesh's help for production. As expected, Aneesh was there from day one once he was informed about his role of providing production support for the play.

Shashi got his usual trusted hands, Guru, to manage the lights. Aneesh, therefore, also got the opportunity to learn the tricks of lighting for the stage play from Guru.

Since I was playing one of the two lead roles in the play this time, it resulted in more stage time and opportunity to gain serious theatre experience. I told Vatsal it was a great learning experience.

"It must have been. I think you have been associated with some great house productions till date," he said.

"It is also learning to adapt to different working styles. TK and Shashi are so different. I am getting to know pros and cons of each style. It will help develop my own style."

"Aha! That's a nice way to approach this." Vatsal liked my thinking.

It also gave me a chance to spend more time with Vatsal and juniors in the house.

Vatsal was a great natural actor. He was soft spoken, had a great stage presence and an infectious sense of humour. Feedback discussions were pure fun with Vatsal.

Once Makhija was giving feedback to PP, "I think your voice projection needs to improve. You are still not using your stomach."

Vatsal immediately replied, "Yes. And you are using your stomach so beautifully that some of us believe you have taken a step ahead and started using your ass now for louder voice. No doubt you are as energetic as you ass." It winded up the session that night for all of us.

From that day, every time Makhija's intensity went down during practice sessions, everyone used to start shouting, "Why are you not using your ass, Makhija?" Makhija never gave feedback to anyone after that.

We as a team were almost inseparable entities for a couple of weeks, and it led to a new level of bonding among all of us.

The night before the final performance, we went through the rigor of spending time in the seminar hall to plan our positions and movements. First-year were expectedly more excited.

We delivered a smooth performance which was applauded by the large crowd present at the event. When results were announced, judges made an exception. "Guys, we had many strong performances today. Let this be the day to celebrate the team spirit which helped deliver such performances. And so we will not have awards for individual performances today."

Judges then went ahead to announce the results. We ended up second in the event. And given the enthusiasm from the first years, we had a large Kara team cheering for us when the results were announced. Kumaon was the winner.

As soon as I got out of the seminar hall, I heard Neel sir's voice from behind. "Hey Abhimanyu!' He was standing in the Wind T. I had invited Neel sir to watch the stage play, but wasn't sure he would join.

I went running to him to find him smiling. "I've never watched a stage play in the campus before, but from now on, I will try to watch whenever possible. It's a nice experience. Thanks for introducing me to this. You are a fine actor man! Keep up the good work."

"It was a great success experience, but it showed that there were things we could still change. We were in the top two, but not the best." I told Gautam. He agreed with me.

"By the way, with the experience of politics in the first year behind us, I think I could find the rationale behind Shashi's enthusiasm so far in the year." I added.

"Interesting! Some learning for you basis the past experience!" Gautam winked at me.

"Surprisingly, it also brought me closer to a senior whose own aspiration I could not have figured out otherwise. I could feel Vatsal is going to play a longer stint in the house politics."

"Are you not stretching it this time?" Gautam was doubtful.

"Only time will tell. I can only guess basis what I felt."

I had learned this ability to evaluate people's political ambition as much from Gautam as from the experience of the first year.

~ 49 ~

"One thing which I have slowly started liking about exams is the stillness they bring to our fast-paced hostel life. We get a break from our routine which is otherwise always fragmented with multiple areas to focus on. It's a relief from our daily multi-tasking!" I was telling Bansal. Minor-II was starting from the next day.

"But it also brings three-four really stressful days," Sid, who had joined us, was also correct.

The three of us reached the mess. We took our paranthas and went ahead to join PP and other first years.

"So PP, looks like you have completed your syllabus for tomorrow's exam?" I patted PP's back.

"No Abhimanyu bhai! Not at all. But I don't think it will matter in the end. Like Minor-I, Minor-II results are not going to be any better! We will know how bad we are!" PP had decided his fate in advance.

I didn't like PP's way of thinking at all. "No PP. Not at all. Nothing is decided. It all depends on where you *want* to stand. I agree that academics in the campus are competitive and it's not easy at all. But letting one exam decide your fate in the future is foolish. I know many people think like this and they only end up achieving much lower than what they possibly could have. If you start believing what you just said, you will only end up finding excuses to not perform better. You should think one step at a time. Better than last time!" I told them what TK had told me in the early days of campus life.

PP and others were looking at me without blinking. I had to break the silence.

"Ok. You can have your parathas."

"I think we should go back to studies." All of them hurriedly completed their meal and left.

"That was cool," Bansal told me while we were coming back.

"Sometimes you need someone to make you believe in yourself."

Drinking was an inherent part of our hostel life. Few pick it up early in the first year itself, while others catch on by the second year. I belonged to the other half.

Our wing was close to the students of final year, and their daily living was very different from ours. They had far few classes to attend. It was also time for their campus placements. Depending upon the date of interviews and someone from

Kara getting placed, there were parties planned in the wing. We were frequently invited to these parties marked with crazy drinking. Multiple buckets filled with different types of alcohol were arranged in the wing, and people were expected to drink from them.

One night we had a big party hosted by a couple of seniors – they had bagged one of the most coveted jobs offered on the campus. And we second years were pulled out of our rooms for it. It gave me a chance to experience alcohol for the first time in my life. I ended up experimenting with multiple varieties. I didn't like it at first go, and didn't realize when I lost my senses.

Next day, I ended up waking up in Gautam's bed.

"You had a long night Abhimanyu." Gautam left for the classes making this statement. I was not in the position to go for classes.

Then the full evening was spent listening from Gautam what I did the night before. "You seem to have huge ambitions in life!"

"What ambitions?" I was surprised.

"After two shots of Vodka, you only talked about becoming the Prime Minister of the country! And how you are ready to do whatever it takes to make it possible. I think you repeated the same thing a thousand times until I brought you and dumped you on my bed."

"PM of the country? Am not sure what you are saying."

"But am sure what you want in life, especially in hostel life!"

I couldn't make out if Gautam was making fun of me or trying to make sense of what I did yesterday.

~ 50 ~

This year was celebratory for Kara as we had the BRCA G Sec, Spidy from the house. Kara was the house organizing Rendezvous, the annual cultural festival. The scale and success of the fest were always associated with the hostel that held it.

"Given Kara has got Rendezvous after a long gap, it's on us to make up for all these years. It needs to be the best among the ones organized in recent years," Guru and Rocky shared the same emotions.

Preparation for Rendezvous started at the start of the semester, but the effort was limited to finding sponsors for the fest. Thomas and Gautam were involved in writing the brochure and creating other materials which could be leveraged to reach out to potential sponsors.

Soon, dates of the fest, and the organizing team of coordinators (cordis) and activity heads (ac heads) were announced. From Kara fourth year, everyone who belonged to Amitabh's group was made coordinator. Lakhan was the only one from TK's gang who got a place.

Ac heads were also the usual suspects from the third year – Shashi, Rocky, Vatsal, Kaushik and others. Hostel secys were not given any position of responsibility in the Rendezvous though they were expected to share the workload. It was a matrix structure with people either allocated to a particular event, e.g. rock show or to a vertical with requirement across events, e.g. Infrastructure or publicity and presentation.

As per Guru, basis his last years' Tryst experience, "Publicity is the area which requires mobilizing a lot of junta from the house. Right from inviting people from across the country and managing their participation in creating the buzz in Delhi and other relevant cities, it requires maximum effort. And to pull off the same, it requires leveraging the fachas in the best possible way. Accordingly, it offers the opportunity to develop long-lasting relations with them."

Shashi was picked as the activity head for publicity in the Rendezvous team.

"Maybe Guru's learning from his Tryst days made Shashi take up this responsibility or maybe it was a good pick, considering Shashi's abilities. But I am sure people who are close to house politics will never fall short in connecting the dots from here onwards." Gautam summed up his understanding of the matter.

Rocky and Vatsal were chosen as the infrastructure activity heads. Given the scale of the events in Rendezvous, this vertical required multiple heads to be able to coordinate and pull off numerous large events on the same day. It was another critical post with large scale requirement of fachas during the fest time.

Sanghvi was aligned with Rocky and Vatsal to work as part of the infrastructure team during the fest.

Shashi picked me to work alongside him for his piece. Designing posters, printing relevant materials on a large scale, handling packaging of the publicity materials, mailing the couriers to relevant recipients across the country, taking teams of fachas to DU colleges and campus, following up with multiple schools – it required multi-tasking on different fronts. It gave me a chance to connect to first years even further.

"I have made a point to personally meet as many college cultural secretaries as possible," I told Sid.

"It means your evenings and weekends will be spent travelling through the city." Sid was concerned.

"Yeah! But I am sure it will drive participation."

I also contacted all my friends from school days studying in different parts of the country to reach out to the respective cultural secys. Publicity material was sent to them with clear follow-ups on acknowledgment.

Shashi and I used to meet the right college representatives to brief and invite them for the fest while fachas used to spread around public places in the campus, putting up posters and distributing pamphlets to the residents.

A funny incident happened during one of our trips to a leading girl's college in Delhi University which soon became famous.

I told Sanghvi about it. "So when we reached this girls' college in the south campus, a large group of our fachas entered the college through the main gate with posters, bags and stationery in hands. Since there was no security guard at the main gate, fachas spread around in different directions. I walked up into the main building to meet the college representative. Apparently, we didn't notice the rules for entry into the college."

"Then?"

"As soon I reached the first floor, I saw so many security guards whistling, shouting and running across from different corners of the campus towards our fachas. It felt as if they were going to beat them up for whatever they were doing. It started a chain reaction of fachas also running away from them towards the main gate.."

"Oh my god!" Sanghvi said, concerned.

"Every facha was then held at the gate with a group of guards surrounding them. Guards were not ready to listen to them and wanted to hand them over to the police. I had to eventually request the college secretary to sort this out for us. She got them released by talking to the administration, but not before the group apologized to the college authorities. It was embarrassing. I am going to check a thousand times before entering a girl's college."

Sanghvi laughed out loud. "I am sure you are enjoying your stint in the publicity team".

"At least there is some comic relief!" I signed off.

I knew it sounded comic now, but then, all of us were afraid of the possibility of bringing a bad reputation to the institute.

During one of these city trips with a large facha group to north campus, Shanky surprised me with his query. "Abhimanyu bhai, you seem to be there for the hostel all the time. Your enthu is so genuine and infectious – no one can say no to you. Am sure you will go for some position of responsibility in the house next year?"

"How do you know who all will run for the positions of responsibility in the house?"

"I don't know. But naturally, someone doing so much for the house should take over a position of responsibility."

"Better you don't get into politics so early in life Shanky!" I navigated the discussion, but it left me with a thought somewhere in my mind.

Close to the fest, Spidy reached out to Shashi and his team. "You guys have made us so proud. It has made efforts of marketing team also easier as sponsors are ready to increase their sponsorship. The number of participants for the fest is overwhelming. You guys deserve special thanks." It was the result of an intensive effort by the volunteers of the publicity team.

The night before the first day of the fest, Amitabh called me. "You need to be part of the security team for the fest as well."

"Why me?" I was dead tired to take up this new thing during the fest.

Amitabh explained. "Few events in the fest like the dance event in the convocation hall require passes for entry, given limited seating capacity. Given it's a Kara fest, no one from Kara should face any issue in getting entry to such events, especially the first years as they are witnessing it for the first time. There is no one better than you who can make sure that it's taken care of at all the events."

I ensured all the entry points for every event were suitably managed for Kara junta. The first year junta from Kara was especially taken care of!

During the fest, the effort put in by the Kara team was clearly visible. The rise in sponsorship money led to high priced musical bands for both the Indian night as well as the rock show. The prize money was raised for most of the events. We had the dance floor with DJs at multiple locations. The poolside setting for RDX was completely revamped. A large fun arena with numerous latest outdoor activities was set up near the SAC. Given the large crowd attending the fest, the scale of fest infrastructure – performance stages, dance floors, outdoor activity area, open-air buses to ferry crowd from one location to another and many other infrastructure elements – was beyond what people had witnessed before.

While I was returning from the SAC along with TK on the last night of the fest, a comment from a group of the fifth year students sealed it for the Kara team. "The scale at which Rendezvous was organized this year was the best we have seen in the last five years. Great job guys!"

We responded back with, *"Zor se bolo jai Kara ki!"*

The day the fest ended, the final years and seniors at Kara planned a huge party. Only two people from our batch were eventually asked to join the party – Sanghvi and I. Sanghvi had also worked extensively with Rocky and Vatsal for all these days.

During dinner, Kaushik made a point. "Did you guys notice how both Sanghvi and Abhimanyu are preparing to play a larger role in the upcoming house politics?"

I denied. "It was an honest effort from my side so that we have the best fest organized by Kara. Don't think there is any point reading much into it."

People made fun of me. Sanghvi remained silent. Next day, people in the batch pulled our leg on being given so much importance by the seniors.

"House runs because of you two guys only!"

"After Amitabh, Kara has Sanghvi and Abhimanyu!"

"Are you guys already declared the next king of the hostel?"

And my only reply was, "I don't care about anything. I just want to sleep for the next whole week."

Overall, it was a hell of a last three weeks for me.

"It feels as if there is so much time in life now, after what we went through in the last three weeks." I was talking to Sanghvi.

"Agree. It was so tiring!"

"But worth the effort."

"Absolutely." Sanghvi couldn't agree more.

"You didn't say anything when Kaushik raised the question during the celebratory drinking night?" I checked with Sanghvi.

"No point in reading too much into it." Sanghvi avoided explaining. "Even if he was correct, how does it matter?"

"What do you mean?" I was curious.

"See, even in case am planning, I don't have to defend anything out there. So I didn't respond." Sanghvi was honest.

~ 51 ~

Even Gautam and Edison didn't hold themselves from taking my case. "So, how was it? Now you belong to them more than us?" Gautam started.

"It was a good dinner. That's it. Can you stop making fun of me now?" I was tired both physically and mentally. I just wanted to sleep.

"Ok! Don't get pissed. You must be tired."

"Yes, Gautam. It will take a week of sleep at least to get me back to normal. But more than that, there is one thing which is troubling me."

"What?" Gautam was surprised.

"Everyone is linking my effort, hostel spirit, and enthusiasm to political ambitions. I ended up having separate conversations with the first year as well as third year on the same topic. I feel like am being judged for my actions." I came clean.

"That's a wrong way to look at it. In fact, you should be happy that people are automatically linking it to ambition. As such, you don't have to make any effort for the same."

"But it's a wrong linkage." I did not like it.

"So what? I completely understand that you always put your effort honestly. But there is no harm in now linking the same efforts to the potential ambition. There is nothing wrong in having ambition and then working towards it." Gautam's words hit me hard. All this while, I was taking it as an accusation. He was converting it into an opportunity.

"Am listening."

"You need to realize that it's not bad to have ambition for power. There can be three types of motivation to have power – either enjoy power wherein you have control of everything happening around you or have and abuse power for personal gains belittling other's cause. The third and most important reason can be to use power for change, creating impact or create an environment better than what is existing today. And it's always in the best interest of everyone to have a leader who wants to use power for change." Gautam was making me think better.

I was starting to get clarity.

"In fact, you should treat that as a motivator to raise your ambitions. Power in itself can be bad. Power with responsibility always balances out. And there can be no one better than you whose sense of responsibility and accountability is acknowledged across the batches. This very quality of yours will never let power get to your head."

I felt much better after I looked at it this way.

~ 52 ~

While I had met Bhavna multiple times post the embarrassing event on her birthday, I had never got such an urgent request from her to meet.

PP had eventually introduced Bhavna to his close friends. She was part of most of my catch ups with PP and Aryan in the institute area during class hours. She used to join us for our dinners in the canteens close to the girls' hostel.

Before meeting Bhavna, I had expected her to be more mature than PP. But she was as carefree and impulsive as PP, if not more. Maybe that's what connected them so naturally. Slowly I could realize how difficult it must be for PP to plan for another element in our multi-tasking life given I never saw PP cutting down on any hostel activities.

Bhavna called to meet in the afternoon. Since I had tutorials in the afternoon, I promised to meet her in the evening. I was surprised that she asked me to not inform PP about this.

When I reached Barista in front of the IIT Gate, I found Bhavna sitting with Aryan. It only added to the suspense.

"Hi Bhavna!"

"Hi Abhimanyu!" Bhavna was as cheerful as always.

"Aryan, if you were going to join us here, we could have walked together from the hostel. You know it's such a long walk." I was serious.

"Abhimanyu bhai, I just wanted to avoid any questions on why we are meeting like this. I wanted you to hear from Bhavna." Aryan didn't look into my eyes.

"Ok, enough of this suspense. What are you guys cooking?" I was getting frustrated.

"Not yet Abhimanyu. We would need your help to cook it in your mess," Bhavna had some plans.

"Cook in the mess?"

"Aryan told me you are one of the Kara mess committee members who has good relations with mess staff."

"Seriously! you guys have called me to talk about Kara mess?" I was angry now.

"Abhimanyu bhai, don't get angry!" Aryan chipped in. "Let me explain. We have PP's birthday this Sunday and madam came up with this idea of surprising him in the night by celebrating his birthday in Kara."

"Okay! She can join us in the common room. Not a big deal!"

"That's where the surprise comes in. I want to be in the hostel room," Bhavna came in immediately.

"That's not possible. As per hostel rules, girls can't come to our rooms in the hostel."

"That's why it's fun. And Aryan told me that the only person to make this possible is you through the mess's back door." Bhavna had done some homework.

I turned towards Aryan. He immediately retorted, "That's why I said I wanted you to hear this from Bhavna and not me."

"Guys, this can't be done. You guys are dreaming." I was vehemently against the idea.

"Come on, Abhimanyu! Can't you do it for your friends? I will remember this for my life. And you can ask me anything in return whenever you want." Bhavna was persistent.

"Don't get so senti, madam. You are just putting me in a difficult situation." I could see they were not going to leave me. Plus, I started to feel privileged to play a significant role in this revolutionary event in the history of Karakoram.

"No one else will come to know of this." Bhavna was pleading.

"One needs to pass a full lawn, then cross the full parallel wing and two levels of staircases. And repeat the same task while going back. How will no one come to know?" I was thinking.

"So, you have already planned the entry in the lawn through the mess?" Aryan jumped from his seat.

"That means I am getting into the boy's hostel to make this surprise real! Thank you, Abhimanyu." Bhavna was beaming. "I will leave you guys to plan. I need to get back to hostel before the gates are closed. We can catch up tomorrow." Bhavna immediately rushed out of the café.

"Wow. She can't take a risk with the girls' hostel rules, but wants us to take the maximum risk with our hostel." Aryan was laughing.

"This will need one hell of a plan to execute." I had already started thinking.

Mess staff in IIT Delhi hostels are all referred to as *'butler saab'*. One of the senior butler saabs heading the operations was responsible for getting the stocks uploaded in the mess through the back door, shifting it to the cold room and maintaining the inventories. He carried the keys to the cold room, stock room, kitchen room and, most importantly, the back door.

I had been a part of multiple decisions related to menu changes, incoming inventory quality checks and back-end operations. I had spent a lot of time with the mess staff which helped them understand and address the feedback that mess comm regularly received from the hostel residents.

"Butler saab, when do you come in the morning to start the breakfast preparations?"

"5:30 a.m."

"You will find me with the keys in front of the stock room when you come."

"Saab, you are not even telling me why you need the keys. If you want, I can come and open the back-door in the night in front of you."

"Butler saab, you need to trust me on this. None of your schedule will get impacted. No one will even know that I had the keys. Give me the keys when you are leaving for the day post dinner and you will have it back once you arrive in the morning." I was almost pleading.

"Ok saab. Please don't tell anyone. Please collect it from me by 10 p.m. We would have completed the cleaning by then."

Aryan and I met Bhavna in SAC at 11 p.m. I had collected the keys from butler saab for the night.

"You need to wear this sweatshirt with hoodie over the Top you are already wearing." I gave Bhavna my Karakoram House sweatshirt. All the residents of the hostel had one.

"Why?" she was surprised.

"We have the easy part sorted. You will get an entry into the mess from the back-door."

"And then?"

"From there, you will get through the open window on the lawns, cross the same, enter the residential building and then walk through the parallel wing. Parallel wing on the ground floor has Ph.D folks only. They are the most boring people who stay inside closed rooms. So that's a safe passage to the end wing." I explained the plan.

"What do you mean by Ph.D folks are boring?" Bhavna surely didn't like the last part.

"What Abhimanyu bhai meant was 'most' of the folks and not 'all'." Aryan came to my rescue.

"You don't have to defend Aryan. I understand the sentiments you guys carry! Anyway, you haven't told me why the sweatshirt?"

"When we cross the lawns and walk through the wing, even if someone crosses us, no one will notice a Kara sweatshirt. The hoodie gives you extra protection from getting recognized." I explained.

"That's some planning! I told you, Abhimanyu bhai will make it happen," Aryan appreciated the thought. "If we are heading towards the End wing, am guessing we are doing this celebration in your room then?"

"Yes. It's the first room after we climb the stairs to the second floor. If we plan to go to your and PP's room at the end of the long wing, by the time we reach there, the whole institute will come to know that a girl is in the boy's hostel."

"So, we need to inform Gautam bhai in that case?"

"No! Gautam has gone to Faridabad for the weekend to meet his sister." I never knew how the absence of Gautam was going to play out over the rest of the night.

The three of us walked from SAC to the back-door of the Kara mess. Kara sweatshirt with hoodie made it easier to cross the main hostel entry without being noticed by the guard saab.

Leaving Aryan and Bhavna outside, I came back, entered the mess and opened the back door. With mess lights completely off, we walked in the darkness from the kitchen to the mess window opening into the lawn. Aryan recapped the route to Bhavna from the lawn to my room, explaining the directions we were going to take.

We took a deep breath and jumped into the lawn. As soon as we crossed the lawn and entered the residential building, I noticed a couple of first years coming from the long wing.

"Speed up," I whispered. I wanted to turn into the parallel wing before they come face to face with us.

As soon as we turned, one of them shouted from behind, "Hi Abhimanyu Bhai!"

"Hi guys!" I replied raising my hand without turning back. I was almost thinking of running.

With no reply from them, I looked back to see their backs walking off. No one had noticed.

We rushed past the Parallel wing of Ph.D. on the ground floor. As expected, most of the doors were closed. "This is what I was referring to," I said as soon as we were on the staircase.

"Not the right time Abhimanyu bhai!" Aryan wanted to get this run over. Bhavna tried to ignore.

Reaching the second floor, we turned left to enter the first room in the wing, my room. As we turned, I saw Edison coming out of the room at the end of the wing. I almost pushed Bhavna inside my room before he could notice. Aryan followed her, while I waited at the door.

"Hey Abhimanyu! Where are you coming from?" Edison was walking towards me.

"Was in the common room with Aryan."

"Is Gautam also with you?"

"No! He has gone to Faridabad."

"Oh! So, who else is there with you two?" Edison was being inquisitive.

"PP. We were thinking of discussing the plot of the upcoming dramatics event." I said the name that came to mind. Maybe Edison had noticed the first person entering the room.

"Then am not going to join you guys. Am going to the canteen. Anything you want from there?" Edison headed towards the staircase.

I was relieved, "Nothing for me!"

We had accomplished the historical task of getting a girl into the room of a boys' hostel.

After we settled down in the room, Aryan went to get the cake from his room. I called PP asking him to join us in my room for a surprise birthday party.

"PP is coming along with Aryan. PP was telling me he needs to leave immediately after midnight to the library to meet you!" I told Bhavna.

"I told him that! Now am here! This is so unreal." Bhavna was excited.

"You will have to keep your voice low."

Soon we heard a knock at the door.

"Abhimanyu bhai! Open the door." It was Aryan.

As soon as PP entered, he sounded agitated. "What are you guys up to? Aryan isn't letting me call anyone from the hostel for the birthday. I am sure I am missing something."

"You were missing me PP!" Before I could say anything, Bhavna responded from behind the door.

"Oh my god!" PP almost shouted. I had to keep my hand on his mouth to keep the voice low.

"Control your emotions, PP! No one other than Abhimanyu bhai and I know that there is a girl in Karakoram." Aryan pulled PP in and shut the door.

"All this for my birthday! Such a surprise Bhavna. I love you." PP went ahead and hugged her.

"Oh boy! No one cares for the two of us who did all the hard work." Aryan didn't leave the chance to tease them.

"You are my jaan, Aryan!" PP now hugged Aryan.

"Okay! It's midnight now - let's cut the cake. Then we need to take her out as well." I was planning the return.

We huddled to cut the cake, sing the birthday song in a low voice and gave bumps to PP.

"Let's go back now!" I got up.

"Abhimanyu bhai! Can we speak for a minute before we plan the exit?" PP pulled me outside the room and took me to the bathroom.

"What happened?" I checked.

"Abhimanyu bhai, don't you think what you guys pulled off is something really crazy?" PP started.

"Yes! So?"

"And so, it deserves better respect?"

"What do you mean?'

"You also know how difficult it is for a boyfriend and girlfriend to spend some private time anywhere in the campus. You have taken so much risk to get Bhavna here. Can't I get some more time to spend with here alone?"

"PP, we are stretching this to an extreme now. Every extra minute she spends here increase our chances of getting caught."

"I understand that. But don't you think the late it gets, the easier it will be to get her out."

"Hmm, fine! I give you some-time. We should start from the room at 2:30 a.m. I will go and stay in your room with Aryan until then."

I saw a slow revolving fan which looked unfamiliar. Why was I sleeping with the light on? Whose pillow cover and bed sheet was this! I was sleeping on PP's bed. I immediately jumped and wore my specs to see the table clock. It was showing 5:10 a.m. Shit!

I shouted, "Aryan!"

"Yes, Abhimanyu bhai!" He was still sleeping on the other side.

"Why didn't you wake me up?"

"Why should I wake you up?" Aryan was still in the bed.

"Because I need to return the keys by 5:30 and we are still sleeping here. We are short on time. Let's run!" I dragged Aryan from the bed, and he fell on the ground.

I am waking up PP and Bhavna. You come there, and quick!

I knocked at my room door. There was no reply. After the third time, PP spoke "Who is it?"

"Open the door, PP! We are late." I knew we had to rush.

PP opened the door. He didn't intend to open the door fully. He was wearing shorts only. I could see Bhavna draped in a bed sheet. There were clothes on the floor, including my sweatshirt.

"Sorry bhai. Give us two minutes!" PP assured.

PP locked the door. I was getting impatient, thinking that if I don't get her out of the back door and then be in front of the stock room in the next ten minutes, I could be suspended.

Aryan also came running "Why are you waiting outside?"

"Because our friends are still wearing clothes! I should not have agreed to PP." I was angry with myself.

"We will get it through. Let me go down and check if ground is clear."

PP and Bhavna finally stepped out. I looked down through the staircase, and saw Aryan waving his hand for us to come down. We rushed through the stairs and parallel wing on the ground floor. Then we make a dash through the lawns. The window to enter the mess was locked from inside.

"Looks like guard saab closed it during his late-night rounds. Let me get in the mess and open it. You guys wait in the cycle stand until then."

I went through the main door of the mess and got them in. As they entered, I noticed butler saab entering the house, having a chat with guard saab.

"Aryan, take them through the kitchen to the back door. Lock it and meet me in front of the stock room."

As soon as butler saab entered, I engaged him in chit chat. "You are dot on time!"

"If am not on time, how will saab log get breakfast. I knew you will be there before me. Give me the keys, I need to get stock out."

"Yes, let's go to the stock room," I said, hoping Aryan was there.

We handed over the keys and walked back to our rooms.

"Where is PP?"

"He has gone with Bhavna to walk her back to the girls' hostel," Aryan said.

"In his shorts?

"I think so. Actually, I don't care what he is wearing, now that Bhavna has gone outside Kara. I was so scared when you woke me up in the morning."

"All is well that ends well."

Both of us needed some sleep before we could get on with our classes.

~ 53 ~

In sports, Kara had the best chance in hockey this year, given the combination of Rocky and Kalra in the forward and Rahul and Vatsal's presence in the defence. One match of the inter-hostel hockey tournament that stood out was the semi-final where Kara was playing Ara – the best team in the institute. Ara's team had seven players in the Institute team.

At the end of the first half, Ara was leading 1-0, which was still a good position for us. It was not easy to hold Ara's forwards for so long. As soon the halftime score was communicated back to the hostel, a strong cheering team from Kara, mostly comprising of folks from the first year, descended on the ground which clearly outnumbered the people from Aravali. And soon, the stadium was echoing with *"Kara ka enthu high hai"* and *"Zor se bolo jai Kara ki."*

In the second half, it fuelled a new life into the team. Rocky and Kalra started creating back to back chances for the team. And soon, we had the first goal for the team by Kalra. It almost brought down the roof of the stadium, thanks to the Kara cheering. Ara became more aggressive. Multiple chances were created by their forwards, but Rahul, Vatsal and crew were on their toes. Every time the ball went close to Kara's goal post, it felt as if there was a huge team defending from outside the ground.

The match was coming close to full time. Barely a couple of minutes were left when Vatsal served a long pass, from the deep to Rocky, who was in Ara's half. As soon as Rocky received the ball, cheering team was back in action. Rocky was able to dribble through a couple of Ara defenders on his own. With every passing second that he was getting closer to Ara's goalpost, the crowd was becoming hyper. With last ten seconds of the match left, Rocky passed through the last defender and took the final shot at the goal. The ball hit the right hand of Ara's goalkeeper and got deflected. It went ahead hitting the left top corner of the goalpost before finally settling inside the goalpost. At that very moment, we heard the final whistle for the match.

It took a second for everyone to realize what Kara had achieved. And then the cheering started afresh. We all tossed the champions in our arms.

The usual suspects comprising of Rocky, Kalra and Vatsal from third year and Utkarsh, Rudra, Shubham, and Rahul from the second year were playing the significant role in the inter-hostel sports events.

We ended up in the top three in hockey, baddy and water polo. In hockey, we ended up runners-up after losing out in the finals, but that semi-final match left lifelong memories for most of us. In baddy, Rocky and Utkarsh were able to win bronze for the house, which was a bit of a disappointment.

Vatsal had his heroic moments in the cricket tournament, but his bowling effort was alone not enough to help the house qualify for the semi-finals. Similarly, Kalra, Rudra and Amitabh's heroics in football were not enough to take Kara to the semi-finals.

In swimming, we lost our semi-finals but were able to win the bronze medal match. Shubham and Viru were the star players of the team.

Though we were not anywhere close to winning the trophy, it seemed we would end up better in BSA compared to the previous year.

~ 54 ~

The street play was the next big event of the semester. After last years' experience with TK, Gautam wanted to completely own and write the whole script.

"I already have an idea for this year's Kara's entry. I now need to spend the time to develop the same."

"If you own it end-to-end, the final product is bound to be excellent," I encouraged him.

After understanding Rudra's way of working during the fresher's skit, I wanted to on-board him as soon as possible, as one could never be sure with his plan.

So, I suggested Gautam. "Let's loop in Rudra for his view on the way forward. I am confident that he would be fine with you taking the lead this time."

Rudra didn't give us the expected response. "Give me more time to mull over the topic and let's close this over the weekend."

The next day, Rudra called Gautam to meet and discuss the street play. I joined him. We were pleasantly surprised to find that Rudra had a very different idea. He seemed interested in putting a fight for the event. But Rudra added a twist, "Gautam, I want you to write couplets for some parts of my play. I would be able to give you a better idea in the next few days."

Gautam found it strange. Still, he offered to contribute to Rudra's script depending upon whenever Rudra needed his inputs.

When we came back, Gautam shared his opinion with me. "I learned it well the last time that the script needs to be written by one person, otherwise it's difficult to get the tempo and flow right. I can contribute in bits and pieces, but it will not help. To tell you the truth, I don't like his concept at all. It will look kiddish."

Rudra's working style was entirely different from Gautam's and I could see some challenges here. But I took Rudra's side, "Gautam, I don't think his idea is that bad. If he puts in effort, am sure he can pull it off. Let him write the script and then you can see?"

Gautam said thoughtfully, "Ok. Let me not be biased. Will help him whenever he needs me." It seemed a forced decision.

"Gautam, I don't want you to do this under pressure. Tell him your feedback frankly."

"Maybe Rudra wants to prove himself this time. In the Hindi play, he didn't get a chance, so he wants to make street play his baby. Am not worried about whether he can write a street play; am sure he is. But he is just so insincere and inconsistent! I don't know whether he will dedicate time. And then, no couplets will be of help. Anyway, let's see."

Gautam waited for a week to get update from Rudra on the progress. And when Rudra explained it to him, it turned out to be too vague for Gautam to attempt anything meaningful.

Gautam kept me in the loop. "Rudra himself is not sure about what he wants, but still, I have promised to come up with something."

When Gautam shared the couplets with Rudra, he didn't like all of them. They brainstormed together, but with limited output.

It was already less than a week till the day of the performance. Finally, Rudra called up the first years five days before the day of the event, distributed scripts and started practice. Gautam asked me to join the practice session in the lawn on the second day to witness the "new style".

"What I found most appalling is that many participants have been asked to fill in their dialogues on their own. That too, live while practicing." I shared my unhappiness with Gautam.

While the practice session was going on, I couldn't restrain myself and called PP out to help with his part. "Let's sit and fix your dialogues. Have you thought about anything yet?"

Rudra noticed it from a distance. He walked across the lawn to join us. It clearly looked from his face that he didn't like my interference.

Rudra asked, "What are we trying to achieve here?"

I was surprised by his question "I am helping PP complete his dialogues. I don't think everyone can achieve the same on their own so—"

Rudra cut me short. "I can take care of it. You don't have to get into this."

I didn't like Rudra's approach. I asked him, "No point in having an argument here. Why don't we sort this out in private?"

Gautam and Vishal were observing us from a distance. As Rudra and I walked inside the mess, they also joined us.

When we were far from the first year, Rudra started shouting. "You need not join the practice sessions."

"Firstly, don't shout! Secondly, whatever issues you have with me, sort it out in private, not in front of juniors. Don't think you are building any of our reputations by doing the same."

Rudra continued at a lower voice this time, "Your presence always leads to multiple instructions to participants. It's not helpful for people who are new to this kind of activity."

"Fair point on multiple instructions. But you can't ask people who are new to write their own lines. I was hoping you would have learned from the experience of facha skit. Even if it takes a day extra, we should plan completing the script first." I was trying hard to make the situation better.

"I know what I am doing. In street play, participants should at least be able to improvise to this extent. These first-year fellows have not been of any use in the year so far."

I lost my temper at Rudra's last comment, "How can you say that?"

Gautam realized the gravity of the situation and immediately intervened, "Abhimanyu, let it be! Let Rudra manage the whole street play if he wants to do it on his own. I have given Rudra all the couplets he wanted. Vishal is also helping him. If they require our help, they will let us know."

Gautam was pulling me away, while Vishal was only observing.

We walked out from the practice that night. During the next four days, I got updates from Aryan and PP on the progress being made.

Finally, on the day of the event, I asked Gautam. "We should join the team in the ground. It will not take much of your time." Gautam was not in the mood, but I dragged him.

Within few minutes into the Kara performance, we realized that we were going to witness precisely what Gautam was always afraid of.

"Looks like a piece prepared in a hurry." I was angry. There were killer punches, few from Gautam and others from Rudra's inventory, but overall coordination, lack of practice was quite visible.

Nonetheless, we complimented the first years on their enthusiastic participation. We didn't meet Rudra and Vishal.

We returned to the hostel before the results were announced. As expected, Kumaon won first prize, and we were nowhere near the top three.

~ 55 ~

After the street play experience, I felt let down. I was furious.

"Gautam, I should have listened to you earlier. I could have navigated our actions better, even if it meant taking on a few people head on." I was repenting.

"It's ok. Not that we didn't try."

"It's not okay. We can't leave it for the next time every time. Last year, we didn't have control and we were learning. Last year, there was so much effort. This year, the way we have progressed so far, I think the results will only be worse. We need to raise our thinking. We need to think beyond the event. We need a larger vision so that all effort and resources are put in the right direction for the larger trophy. As of now, no one seems to have any clue where we are heading."

Gautam nodded empathetically.

"The way we are progressing, before we realize it, our time in the house will be up." As I said the last line, I felt terrible.

"So?" Gautam was in the listening mode.

"We need to do something about it."

"How? Do you have a plan?"

"Yes! You remember we talked about the accountability at all positions and how difficult it is to cultivate this culture. The only way this could work is to drive it from the top. One needs to leverage authority to build and drive this culture of accountability among the junior batches.

"If we again leave it to chance next year, I don't think we will be able to win the trophy."

"What do you mean by next year? What do you want to do?" Gautam was pushing me.

"I promise you – we will bring the BRCA trophy to Karakoram. I can't tell you how, but we have a heady mix of talent in our batch and enthusiasm in our juniors. Now, we need to plan for the trophy and not just for the events."

"So?"

"So we need to use the right mix of leveraging power from the top while manoeuvring people at the bottom for the best interest of the house."

Gautam finally broke his silence. "Abhimanyu, your passion reminds me of TK. It's infectious. Your thinking seems to be so logical and strategic. We need to create more Abhimanyu-infected people in the batch and juniors, and then I am sure BRCA won't be far from us."

"Gautam, now I understand that aspiring for power to bring about a change can never be a cause for an accusation. Rather, one who aspires to change without an effort for change is a right case for accusation. After spending four years here, I would not like to go believing that I cheated myself by not giving my best." I looked at him in the eye as I said, "We need to plan to gain power to be able to use it to drive growth. To win BRCA trophy - a dream for us."

"I am so proud of you, Abhimanyu. I bond with very few people, respect even fewer. I made a strong bond with you, and now I respect you." Gautam hugged me while completing his sentence. I felt elevated.

✩ ✩

The semester was drawing to a close, and with it came the majors. With the decision and promise to play an active role in the politics in the next semester, I could visualize how the next 'even semester' was going to pan out. It would require a lot of investment of both time and energy. Balancing out political activism and academics was going to be challenging.

Accordingly, I realized the importance of making this semester count significantly.

My hard work and planning reflected in my results of the semester. There was a steep jump, primarily because of my performance in the major. In most of the courses, I ended up a grade higher than I was trending at the end of Minor-II.

I had the personal best results in all semesters till date and shared the happiness with Sid, my study partner.

He replied, "Actually, I am jealous of you. Despite spending so much time in the extra-curricular activities, you pulled off such a CGPA. Barring Bansal, whose only priority in life is academics, you have the best CGPA in the group. You are now in the top twenty percentile in your department as well."

"Come on, Sid!" I was embarrassed.

"What next?" Sid was curious.

"Nothing! Now it's the time to focus on the next item on the agenda." I was ready.

Soon enough, we all left for our homes. Next even semester eagerly awaited us. The priorities were already set and defined.

Year 2: Semester IV

Jan – May 2004

Updated Index of characters: Semester IV

Abhimanyu's batch (Second Year)

Abhimanyu Rishabh	Main protagonist of the Story
Prashant *Gautam*	Abhimanyu's room-mate and best friend; rare talent of Hindi poetry and debating; Hindi Samiti Club Representative of Kara
Siddharth aka *Sid*	An innocent boy from a small town; perfect friend of Abhimanyu
Saurabh *Bansal*	Abhimanyu's room-mate and friend; Most diligent and logical individual in the group
Harshvardhan *Edison*	A good friend of Abhimanyu & Gautam; shared interests in Hindi literature BSP Hindi Rep of Kara
Rudra Rakesh	Dramatics (comedy) and Athletics talent Dramatics Club Rep of Karakoram; Insincere and insensitive in approach
Vishal Arora	Best friend of Rudra; known for his drinking abilities; Demonstrates limited respect for others in the batch - supports Rudra throughout
Pushkar	Expert in fine arts; ardent participant of house production team; Denied Fine Arts Club Representative post in the first year

Prabhat	Department mate and very good friend of Pushkar; Unexpectedly becoming active in the House through Pushkar
Shubham	Swimming champion; small town boy from Bihar; Unsuccessfully played the opportunist card for a political position in 1st year
Aditya *Sanghvi*	A very enthusiastic individual - shared an unsaid bond with Abhimanyu; Tag team with Abhimanyu; BSW Rep of Kara - kept his political ambition in place right from the start
Makhija	Quizzing Club Representative of Karakoram; Emerged as the key political coordinator in the batch
Rahul	Sports talent - fastest cricket bowler in the institute; Ended up becoming BSW Rep along with Sanghvi; Took his rivalry in Hindi Samiti with Gautam to politics
Utkarsh	Sports talent - expertise in TT, Baddy, Carom; Indoor Sports Club Rep - unbeaten in his political ambitions
Thomas	English debating talent in the institute; respected individual in the batch; EDLC Representative of Karakoram
Bala	Exceptional talent in Music - master of multiple musical instruments; Music Club Rep of Kara – highly respected in the batch
Barnwal	Only person in the batch with prior theatre experience

Mridul	Fine Arts expert; rarely resided in the house consistently; Ended up becoming Fine Arts Club Representative for the house
Rachit	Abhimanyu's department mate; always a helping hand in studies

One year senior to Abhimanyu's batch (Third Year)

Shashi Ranjan Singh	Ex-Dramatics Club Representative, a major cultural club; immense theatre talent; Surprisingly didn't go for any political position at the end of last year
Vikash *aka Guru*	Enthusiastic soul with a serious approach to housework; excellent friend of Shashi; Mess Secretary of Kara
Rocky	Sports talent -Baddy, Squash, Hockey; Ex- Film Club Representative; Deserving individual who didn't end up with any position of responsibility at the end of the year
Vatsal	Sports (Cricket) and Theatre (comedy) talent; famous for hi. sense of humour; No significant position of responsibility even by the end of his second year
Kaushik	Ex-Hindi Samiti Club Representative; most charming and popular senior; Unexpectedly no major participation in politics; New Common Room Secretary
Kalra	Best Athlete in the house; represented Kara in most of the sports; Sports Secretary of Kara

Aniket	Surprisingly emerged as the Cultural Secretary of Kara
Viks	A good friend of Guru; visible face in the batch; Gained out of the loss of Rocky to become the Maintenance Secretary of Kara

Two years senior to Abhimanyu's batch (Fourth Year)

Amitabh Gupta	Karakoram House Secretary
Spidy	BRCA General Secretary from Karakoram - organized Rendezvous this year

One year junior to Abhimanyu's batch (First year)

Aryan	New drama talent in the House
Pratyush Prakash aka *PP*	Jharkhand boy; talented in multiple cultural activities - singer, dramatics
Aneesh	Super enthusiastic individual –passionate for house success
Sajid	Enthusiastic individual, tag team with Aneesh
Sikka	Music talent in the batch
Dixcy	Individual with more enthu than talent – fine arts, theatre, music
Thakkar	Alum from Gautam's School; not interested in hostel activities
Suresh	Low profile individual; only in touch with Gautam
Shanky	Soft, genuine, enthusiastic individual – more of enthu than talent
Charsi	Individual who showcased enthu across events; couldn't identify with any group

Key people holding different positions of responsibilities

	Positions Internal to the House	*People*
4th year positions	House Secretary	*Amitabh*
3rd year positions	Mess Secretary	*Guru*
	Maintenance Secretary	*Viks*
	Sports Secretary	*Kalra*
	Cultural Secretary	*Aniket*
2nd year positions	BRCA Representatives for respective clubs	*Thomas (EDLC), Bala (Music), Makhija (Quizzing), Utkarsh (ISC), Gautam (HS), Rudra (Drama), Mridul (FAC)*
	BSW Representatives	*Sanghvi, Rahul*
	BSP Representatives (Hindi, English)	*Edison (Hindi), Srini (English)*

VIII
The Lost opportunity

~ 56 ~

Given the experience of the first even semester, people knew what to expect. Two types of people became active and visible during this time – those who had earned respect from the batch or juniors; and those who wanted to play an essential role in the house politics. Two people who fell in both the categories were – Sanghvi and I.

"Sanghvi is the only person who I genuinely respect for his contribution to hostel despite limited capabilities," I was honest with Gautam.

"I am sure this respect is not one-sided. It is high time that you guys sit together and find a common way to leverage this 'unsaid' relationship." Gautam was already planning.

"Got it."

"But make sure, it happens over a series of discussions. It will help you read Sanghvi's mind better," Gautam sounded prescriptive.

I knew how crucial it was going to be.

When I met Neel sir at the start of the semester to finalize the course electives, he congratulated me for my results of the last semester. "Great, Abhimanyu! There is a positive trend in your results over the last three semesters. I think with time, you have understood what it takes to excel in the academics, especially given that the last semester was academically the heaviest semester."

"Thank you, sir. I think I have learnt to multi-task."

"Great! By the way, I could see a shift in the courses that you have chosen this semester. You are planning for a lesser number of credits and lighter courses. Is this to make up for the heavy last semester?"

"Yes sir, to an extent! But this is also to avoid any dip in my overall cumulative grades if I don't do as well in academics as the last semester."

"And why exactly do you think that will happen? Are you planning to smoke all through this semester?" Neel sir was laughing while making the last statement.

"No sir!" I then explained to Neel sir about my plan to stay invested in the hostel politics this term to bring about the change for my goal of winning the BRCA trophy. "I know you will find this weird, given that we are here to focus on studies. But as of now, that's what I have decided." I was feeling embarrassed to talk about this with him.

Neel sir replied in his natural style, "I don't find that weird at all. You are in the campus for a broader reason - to learn, to be able to make your own decisions and to develop as an individual. And I am happy to see you on this path. It's not easy to have a vision complemented by a long-term work-plan. If I don't judge you by your focus area, it's commendable that you are able to think through your vision. So, I will stick with your plan."

"Thank you, sir!" I was happy to hear it from Neel sir.

"But, while you are lowering the academic load with lesser number of credit and courses, just make sure the grades don't dip," Neel sir advised objectively.

It was still the first fortnight of the semester. We were planning to go out of the campus on a Friday night when Edison started the favourite topic "Am sure Abhimanyu, you must have decided about joining poltu this time?"

"Why only me! Everyone is invited. Am sure Gautam will play as important a role as me if not more," I replied to Edison.

"Am sure Gautam will play a much bigger role. It will not do justice to the quality of poltu in Kara if Gautam is not part of it," Sid added.

Gautam was maintaining his silence.

"Gautam, are you also thinking to contest for any post?" Edison wanted to be sure.

"No no. I am not," Gautam came clean.

"Gautam is way above all the *moh maya*. He is the kingmaker and not a king himself," Sid quipped.

"Sid, what did you have in dinner?" I couldn't resist myself.

"Same what you had." After a pause, Sid checked with Edison, "Tell us if you want to contest for anything, I am sure these two will find a way for you!"

"Actually, I was thinking to contest. Not sure which post I should go after." Edison surprised us.

I exchanged a smile with Gautam who looked equally surprised.

"Any post you have in mind, Edison?" Gautam checked.

"If I talk about options, either I go externally for BSP Hindi secy or go internally for maintenance, given I was part of maintenance committee. Internal option is primarily driven by limited contribution I could have for cultural or sports." It seemed Edison had thought through his strategy.

"For externals, I think you should talk to Amitabh. There is no one as close to him as you in the batch. Amitabh will definitely let you know his plans and therefore any possibility of fitting you in the same. Internally, we will support you for your ambitions. Rest we will have to leave to the batch." Gautam was now talking like a friend.

When we were back to our rooms later in the night, Gautam told me, "I was not totally surprised with Edison. He is a strong individual. But now, the whole play would require careful deliberation, given this new twist that our friend had brought in."

"How realistic are his chances for the externals?"

"I don't know. Hopefully, Amitabh's plans and Edison's ambition overlap somewhere."

"Otherwise, we will have to figure out something in the internals."

"Absolutely! It will require some thinking, else it could get messy."

~ 57 ~

Even semester is always marked with English play and Music Manoranjan (MM). The two events were again scheduled close to each other.

English play is dramatics rep's responsibility, so Rudra was in-charge. He gave complete control of the play to the first year. They were all excited about the responsibility. Their effort soon became visible to all of us.

MM was music rep's responsibility, so Bala took it on with his collaborative approach. He called me, Rudra and Vishal for conceptualization and execution. We came up with a few good ideas.

Bala pushed Vishal to contribute, "Vishal, You will be the right person to write songs this time."

Vishal was also optimistic. "Between Rudra and me, we will definitely take care of songs."

Bala said, "Great. Let's connect by the end of this week to take stock."

"I think we should meet before that." I wanted to push the preparation.

"No! Give me some time so that we are prepared well," Rudra said.

At the end of the week, I checked with Bala for our next meeting. He was not sure. "Rudra has asked me to connect after a couple of days."

We eventually met after ten days. Vishal came prepared with a few songs and mentioned, "Rudra is taking care of others. We will soon have the complete version." I could sense early signs of withdrawal from him.

After a couple of days, Bala called me to explain the situation. "Vishal came for the next discussion with a version which was still not completely baked. Rudra didn't care to even join. Doesn't look like Rudra is interested anymore. I hope you are still there. Otherwise, would be difficult to pull off even a decent performance."

I promised Bala that we will make a good show. "Let's start getting a bigger team on-boarded to deliver. Is Vishal still eager to contribute?"

"Am not sure." Bala had given up already.

PP informed me the next day that, "Rudra is interested in playing one of the roles in the English play that we have chosen to execute. I don't think we can keep him away even if we want to. To be fair to Rudra, he suits the role he has picked up. And with him around, it would also provide us with a senior cover in case some critical calls need to be made." The first year clearly lacked experience, and they didn't mind a senior in the team.

I explained the situation to Gautam and Sid. "I can never understand Rudra's way of thinking. If he wanted to do the English play, he should have been a part of it since the beginning. Why did he commit himself to MM and then back off?"

"What about Vishal?" Sid was worried.

"I don't think Vishal will spend time alone with us anymore without Rudra."

"May be after understanding the task at hand for MM, Rudra decided to choose a relatively easier option. I hope he does justice to his role in the English play," Gautam said basis the street play experience.

"What will you do now?" Sid checked.

"Just focus on executing the MM. The biggest challenge would be to get the skit team in place. The first-year junta has chosen an English play with many characters. So, many of the potential MM lead players are now part of the English play. Now I can understand why TK planned English play with Jolly. He knew that for MM, he needed a larger team – mostly from the first year and few from the second year. We could have planned this similarly by involving Shashi and Vatsal in the English play or MM from the start. Now it's too late. Let me see what we can do." I knew the task was uphill.

We didn't have time to start afresh and had to remodel the current idea to be able to deliver in time. Bala was a complete talent in music, but had limited creativity for what was required in MM. I could use my experience from the last time to come up with something which was respectful as an entry.

I soon got Aniket, cultural secy on board, who got the music team in place. From first year, I drafted Sikka as one of the lead singers. I couldn't get PP in music team as he was part of the English play team.

I convinced Barnwal to play an important role, but Makhija refused to play any part, citing time constraints. Vatsal was not in town during the weekend MM was scheduled.

I reached out to Shashi. "I know it's not right on my part to ask your help at this stage of preparation, but still, please let me know if you would." I felt ashamed in reaching out to Shashi. It was like asking a master of art to start afresh.

"I would have helped you, Abhimanyu, but Rudra reached out to me to help the team in the English play. They have prepared a version. Rudra brought some experience to the act, but they now want me to oversee the whole preparation and help them polish the whole act."

In the end, it felt as if a group of substitutes were taking care of the house in the absence of the lead players.

Since we were short on time, we didn't have the luxury to let both the music and skit team perfect their art separately and then integrate. Only after a couple of days of practice, we had to combine both the groups.

MM gave me a chance to completely own an event. Unconsciously, it helped me learn so many tricks of the trade – visualization, coaching newbies, time management, pushing the bar, being prepared for the contingencies, and driving a large team, among many others. It was a steep learning for me.

~ 58 ~

I requested Pushkar to take care of the MM production. He couldn't commit immediately.

When he did not come back even after two days, I went to his room after one of the late night practice sessions.

"Pushkar, you didn't come back to me on my request." I took a chair kept close to Pushkar's desktop. I felt too tired to stand and talk.

"Sorry Abhimanyu, I couldn't come back as I got busy with my assignment. I don't think I will have enough time." Pushkar was apparently not interested.

"For your support, I will get Aneesh and Sajid from the first year. They will provide good leverage. You will have to spend limited time." I was trying to convince him.

"Why don't you directly work with them if they could execute? I can't—" Pushkar was getting irritated now.

"Can I know what this is about?" Prabhat, Pushkar's roommate, got up from his bed and joined us in the discussion.

"I need Pushkar to help me with production support for MM. But it seems he is short on time."

"Pushkar, is it because of the CX210 assignment?" Prabhat checked with Pushkar.

"Yes!"

"Don't worry about that. I will take care of it. You should help Abhimanyu."

"But—" Pushkar was very hesitant.

"Am telling you, Pushkar. If you had told me this before, you could have started taking care of production support much earlier. Anyway, join now and lead the team."

Pushkar finally agreed. "Will come to storage hall for practice from tomorrow night."

"Also, get Aneesh and Sajid with you." Prabhat sounded particular about this.

"Thanks, Pushkar. See you tomorrow." I was surprised to find unexpected support in the room.

When I returned to my room, Gautam, Edison and Sid were watching a French movie, for obvious reasons. I told them about the whole conversation.

"Was Pushkar active during the Hindi play last semester?" Edison checked with me.

"No! Rudra could manage with limited production support from Aneesh, who did a good job."

"Could you not manage with Aneesh alone?" Sid had his own idea.

"I could have, but then I would also have to spend significant time with them. Given production support for MM is at a much larger scale, I thought Pushkar would be the right choice."

"I don't remember Pushkar being visible this year, which may be partly by chance and partly by choice." Gautam had his mind already running.

"What do you mean?" Sid was curious.

"Pushkar partly gave up on house activities after being ignored for fine arts club rep."

"Do you think this is a chance for him to gain back his visibility?" I could also connect the dots.

"Absolutely! I would not have been sure had Pushkar agreed on his own. But the way you described that Prabhat pushed for it, I am more than sure who is playing behind the scene now."

"The only dot left is what they are aiming for." I took it a step ahead.

~ 59 ~

Basis the running point tally for BRCA, I knew that we didn't stand any chance for the top two in BRCA anymore. For MM, my motivation was to have a respectful entry from Kara. So, the whole team, especially the first-year rookies, put in the maximum effort during the last few days.

On the day of the event, we had a full house of the first year in the seminar hall cheering for the hostel's performance. We all enthusiastically went through the rituals of dressing up the skit participants, arranging music instruments in the wings, testing the lights and setting the stage with the props. All the characters gave their best.

We delivered a decent performance. I made sure that Aryan, PP, Sikka, Shanky, Dixcy, Aneesh and Sajid watch all other performances to understand the standard we were competing against.

Expectedly, we didn't end up in top three in MM.

In English play also, we didn't end up winning anything. Fachas tried everything they possibly could with some support from Shashi during the last days. Rudra did eventually play the role he wanted to and was appreciated for his performance. He was apparently the best actor from Kara participating in the play.

"To win any event, you need a right mix of talent as well as enthusiasm and hard work. But with English play and MM so close to each other, the role of planning was far more important. We didn't end up having the right talent for any of the events which hampered the enthusiasm and hard work. The way TK handed it last year was such a better solution." I was talking to Kaushik a few days after both the events concluded.

"You guys should have involved Shashi and Vatsal from the starting." Kaushik was correct.

"Rudra should have planned it better. But I will not blame him completely here. Aniket could have played a bigger role, especially when he knows about Rudra's style of working."

"I guess Aniket lacked motivation. We didn't do well in BRCA, and the results in these two events would not have changed anything. I don't think he is planning any role for himself in the hostel in the future." Kaushik was pragmatic.

"But that doesn't justify the actions completely."

Kaushik nodded and asked me, "But you should be happy?"

"Happy? Why?"

"It gave you a chance to completely own and deliver for the house. Given the circumstances, we didn't end up doing well, but am sure you have grown as a leader. Doesn't that make you happy?"

"That way, it was satisfying. I definitely learned a lot." After a pause, I added, "Also, I guess now I would be able to aim for the results better. I forced the juniors to watch the other performances to prepare them for the future. Fresh out of the poor planning for this year, maybe I am unconsciously planning for the next year already."

"You have two more years to get better results." Kaushik mentioned it in passing.

I reminded myself that I have *only* two years left now.

In sports, we couldn't continue the success we had in the last semester. Kalra was the sole person who added points in this semester to Kara's overall score.

Rocky was not able to replicate the baddy success in squash. Kara lost their bronze medal match to Ara. Similarly, Utkarsh was not able to repeat his baddy's success in TT. Vatsal and Rahul's efforts were not enough to get any position in basketball. In athletics, Kalra and Rudra were the only hope for Kara. Kalra was able to win bronze in the 800m race. Rudra qualified for finals in 100 m, but didn't end up in top three. Kara didn't qualify for the final in others.

"So, another year, we didn't end up winning anything." Sanghvi was as disappointed as me the day after all events were over.

"Yeah, we could only manage success in bits and pieces." I knew internally that post the street play debacle, Gautam had lost steam in the even semester. Otherwise, he would have done better.

There was an intense discussion of various events and what all went wrong from our side.

"I think we need to have the right set of powerful individuals to drive the larger team – someone in power who is able to drive accountability at all levels. So that we can have a TK at all levels, in all fields."

"Maybe you are right. But I don't know how to make that happen." Sanghvi was not sure.

"For that, we need to talk to make sure we have the right leadership team in power next year." I had to bring it up.

"I understand. So, what you are going to go after?" Sanghvi was talking.

"Not decided about the post, but will participate actively. Will let you know at the right time. What about you?"

"I am in the same boat as you. Am surely in, but will decide at the right time."

"Hopefully, we will be able to pull it off together in the best interest of Karakoram."

As I walked into the canteen, I could see some animated conversation happening between Bhavna and PP.

"What's up guys?" I took the chair and settled in.

"Nothing much. Anyway, I was leaving, have some work. So, you guys carry on." Bhavna was in a rush.

"What happened? Doesn't seem to be in a good mood today." I checked with PP.

"Bhavna wants me to meet her parents. I told her we can't rush it this way. This is still my first year of engineering!"

"This seems to be more complex than *Dil Chahta Hai*. At least there was no parental pressure there!"

PP had a severe look on his face.

"I was just joking. Sorry." I hadn't understood the seriousness of the matter yet.

"No no. It's absolutely fine. I think you are correct."

"Tell me one thing – why this, all of a sudden?"

"Because her parents have got some hint about us."

"Did Bhavna tell them?"

"No. Bhavna has a cousin sister in the campus."

"And her sister went ahead and complained to her parents?"

"No no. They both are quite close. It just came up in the conversation in the family. That's why it's a hint only."

"Have you met her sister?"

"Not really. Maybe she has seen me with her or something."

"Do you know her?"

"Yes, she is the maintenance secy of Himadri."

"Oh! I though she is also a Ph.D like Bhavna! She turns out to be B.Tech. Am sure Bhavna gets all these crazy ideas from her only!"

"Do you have to bring this Ph.D thing in the conversation?" PP sounded frustrated.

"Sorry yaar! I didn't mean it that way."

After a pause, PP asked me. "What should I do, Abhimanyu bhai?"

"I don't know. I don't have any experience in love."

"Still... if you were in my position?"

"I don't know. But one thing that I would suggest – be honest to everyone, especially Bhavna and her parents. No point in fooling around. It will make things worse for both of you. More for her. Think about it."

"Hmm, thanks bhai."

IX
The deceitful games

~ 60 ~

As soon all the events for the year were over, campus weather was ready for the expected change. It was time for the new poltu season to set in with our internal batch poltu for starters.

Within our batch, all the expected four fractions started working in some form or other.

- Vishal & Rudra
- Sanghvi & Makhija
- Prabhat & Pushkar
- Gautam & I

One could classify three types of of people in the batch. Firstly, whose loyalties to either of the four groups was already defined. It included Sid, Edison and Bansal whose reliability was established for our group. Similarly, there were some for the other groups too.

Secondly, whose loyalty was not known until recently, but had started to emerge.

And then there were others who never resonated with any group and were expected to vote for the right deserving candidate.

Also, while it was still early days for the season to show true colours, the batch's expectation from people like me and Sanghvi became evident in my conversation with Bansal.

"The batch is now clearly divided into distinct groups." Bansal had apparently observed the divide in the batch.

"Yeah, the season is here now. So it's high time for the same."

"I hope a few people in the batch rise above such groups," Bansal was talking true to his style.

"Definitely. There are people like Thomas and Rachit." I knew them well.

"Am talking of those who need to rise above their respective identified groups and vote for the right cause. Many people in our batch will expect that at least from you and Sanghvi. And I am telling you this basis my discussion with a few others." Bansal was giving me an impartial logical opinion.

"It will depend upon how the season eventually pans out. But I don't see any reason why that would not be possible."

As the group position started becoming clear, I had to decide for myself. Gautam shared, "Abhimanyu, am assuming you are gunning for cultural secretary."

"You are also thinking like others."

"I didn't understand," Gautam was surprised.

"Everyone believes I will go for cultural because I have participated in a lot of dramatics events for the house and tried for dramatics rep previously."

"Yes! You have delivered in the events and your enthusiasm makes you a perfect choice."

"So if you believe that I have 'unmatched' enthusiasm for the cultural activities, then why do I need to hold the position for execution? I can do without a post and still be able to get the best out of people around me." I had my rationale ready.

"Okay! Though am not completely aligned with this theory, I can understand. So, how are you so confident of execution given the struggle we faced when power was in hand of someone else and that restricted our say? Secondly, does that mean you are going to remain external motivator without any power even this year?" Gautam was curious as well as worried.

"Gautam, last year was different. It was about taking Rudra or Vishal, our batch mates who didn't share a similar motivation as mine, head on. But next year, execution of power will be with the new reps. With them, my power of influence will be much more than others, given the spirit we have been able to instil within the group. Hopefully, the new cultural secretary, whoever it may be among Bala, Rudra, Makhija or even Vishal, will work for the best interest of the house. In case he is not as responsible as we want him to be, he will still not be able to hijack our plan. You can trust me on that."

"I agree, if it's Bala, Makhija or Vishal, but am not sure about Rudra."

"For your second question, in this semester, I am going after power. But it will be in line with what is best for the hostel. I am going to try for the mess secretary. Along with BRCA, we should give ourselves a strong chance for the house management trophy. With Sanghvi as the potential maintenance secretary, we could aim for the same." I explained my thoughts.

"Aha! Brilliant thinking. Personal ambition linked to the hostel enthusiasm – it can't get better than that. Am sure you already had a word with Sanghvi on this." Gautam was visibly excited now.

"Sanghvi didn't tell me explicitly. But he told me that he will participate in poltu. And I don't see any better position than maintenance secretary for him to go after. In principle, we had alignment on creating a leadership team which will be the best for Kara."

"You could not have started better. Though to me, mess will be a tougher battle. As a result, cultural will become easy for others to go after. If you win Mess and Rudra doesn't become cultural secy, that would be best for Kara. Then we are set with the plan you just described."

"So are you with me on my decision to go after mess?" I wanted to confirm.

"Totally. In fact, I respect you for that. We will have to figure out the game and crack it this time. Let's guess the potential candidates against you. Everyone would be thinking that you will go for cultural secretary and so every group would be planning for mess. Who all are going after the other three posts will decide your opponent as well as coalitions." Gautam was already getting into the planning phase.

"It's going to be exciting. I am loving it!" I couldn't hide my excitement.

"It's just the beginning. We will have to manipulate many variables to make this possible. I hope you remember Edison's plan. In case Amitabh is not thinking about him, it has the potential to mess many equations."

The stage for the battle in the batch was set. Only the disclosure of the key players for this battle was awaited now.

~ 61 ~

I got talking to Rahul and Makhija one night. Makhija had done his homework and had a set plan in mind.

He updated, "To me, everything fits so well if we all plan well. If our groups stay together, we can easily have the best candidates for each of the four major posts."

"Who all do you have in mind?" I wanted to understand their plan.

"Let Sanghvi be the maintenance secy, you can be the cultural secretary. So, Dipesh and Rahul can be the mess and sports secretary, respectively." Dipesh was a close friend of Sanghvi and Rahul from their department.

Gautam was right in his thinking. They had planned someone for mess, thinking I will go for cultural. Rahul's candidature for sports was kind of expected.

"It seems we are distributing posts among the people in this and the next room," I said.

"I am just trying for both of us to come together. If the majority of the batch supports what I just said, then we can pull this off." I was surprised at Makhija's clarity.

"What about Rudra and Vishal? Are you discounting them? And there is always Prabhat-Pushkar to pull off surprises."

"Many people would vote for the candidates, not groups."

"I don't agree. It will all depend on who all are contesting elections. For example, if Bala stands for cultural secy, your assumption will hold true and no doubt people will vote for him. But if Dipesh stands for mess secy, am not sure if the batch will vote for him." I was realistic.

"So who do you think should stand for mess?"

"I don't know as of now, but if Dipesh stands for mess, am not even sure that all the people in this wing will vote for Dipesh or not!"

"Okay. What do you want to stand for?" Rahul spoke for the first time and directly.

"I am sure I will contest. Maybe cult, maybe mess. If I just go by what will be in the best interest of the hostel, mess would be better."

"Why?" Both Rahul and Makhija asked at the same time. They were caught on the wrong foot.

"Because for cultural activities, I will continue to contribute. I feel Sanghvi and I will be a strong team to pull off Board for Hostel Management (BHM) Trophy. And then the best house is not far." I was frank with them.

"So you are fine with Sanghvi being maintenance secretary?" Makhija wanted an agreement.

"Maintenance would be perfect for him, but then again we need to have a discussion in a larger group to decide that. We can't do that in this room. By the way, where is Sanghvi?" I was expecting him to play an active role after whatever we discussed a few days back.

"Talking to Sanghvi or me is same Abhimanyu. To avoid any confusion, we have decided that I will talk or communicate decisions on behalf of our group." Makhija had indeed done most of the talking today.

"Also, what about Gautam?" Rahul's question surprised me.

"Didn't understand. Gautam will always be with me."

"You never know. Somehow, I don't trust Gautam," Rahul was blunt. This was surprising. I knew Rahul's rivalry with Gautam since our facha days, which had converted into an unexpected battle for the Hindi Samiti rep last year.

"Not trust him for what?"

"Which side he will take?"

"He will take the same side as me, if that is your question. And in that way, you may not trust me as well." I didn't like whatever was going through Rahul's mind.

"No, I didn't mean that."

"I hope so. We need to trust everyone who we want to vote for us."

"Abhimanyu, if you want to go for mess, it will be better if we clear it as a team as soon as possible. So that we think for other posts accordingly." Makhija tried keeping the discussion focussed.

"What about Dipesh? He is a good friend." I didn't want someone to get pissed at this stage.

"I can talk to him," Makhija offered.

"Let's talk to more people and then decide," I concluded.

The discussion clarified few candidates for a larger group. But it raised trust issues between Makhija and us and team.

One night I was working on a practical report due for submission next day. Gautam was also awake, browsing on his recently-bought desktop. An unexpected guest arrived late at night.

"Gautam, Abhimanyu! Are you awake?" It sounded like Shubham.

Gautam opened the door.

After some small talk, he asked straight away, "Are you going for mess or cultural secy?"

"Don't know if I am even contesting." There was no point in telling him yet.

"Come on! Everyone knows you will contest."

"Am sure you are not here to discuss what Abhimanyu will contest for," Gautam intervened.

Shubham responded with loud laughter, "Gautam, you are a difficult one to get through."

"I have someone to take care of me!" I never let go a chance to express my fondness for Gautam.

"Who are you guys supporting for sports secy?" Shubham came to the point.

"Oh ho! So here comes the true story," Gautam said.

"Don't know. There are so many contenders – Rahul, Utkarsh, Rudra," I laid down all options.

"Am surprised that you didn't take my name in the long list," Shubham was severe.

"Because we didn't know yet," Gautam took over.

"Gautam, I will be direct with you. I will run for sports secretary this time. And Prabhat, Pushkar and our gang are serious about it."

"Great! But 'our gang' sounded very offensive," Gautam kept it short.

"I want you guys to support me." Shubham didn't care about anything else.

"We are with you Shubham," Gautam sounded supportive.

"That is what you said last year too. And I don't want the results to be repeated." Shubham had a changed expression.

"I also don't want that. This time Abhimanyu is again deserving, and I will make sure he wins." Gautam was at his offensive best.

"That would be difficult without my support," Shubham was overconfident.

"So we should support each other." Gautam wanted to conclude.

"That is what I want." Shubham toned down now.

"Great! So now let's go to sleep!"

After Shubham left, Gautam had an analysis ready. "Two things are obvious. Firstly, Shubham is determined and so must have been working for long on this agenda. Secondly, he has not forgotten last year and has a feeling that we didn't support him enough. So he will not vote for us."

"So, one post that Prabhat's group is aiming is clear for us."

~ 62 ~

It was time for Minor II. Unlike last year, this time it was difficult to switch off entirely from politics and concentrate on studies. The participation, involvement, tension, pace of events and stakes were much higher.

Sid and I were talking about multi-tasking when I confessed, "I always thought I mastered multi-tasking. But the excitement and anxiety is holding me back. My mind keeps slipping away to poltu from the equally important task at hand."

"I don't think you have a choice. Let's not talk about politics for the next four days while we have exams." Sid suggested, "I am also going to make sure that you practice another recommendation of mine."

"What?" I also got curious.

"Come with me." Sid took me back to my room.

Gautam looked at both of us surprisingly and checked, "What happened?"

Sid replied, "Both of you need to get poltu out of your minds for the next few days. And for that to happen you guys need to avoid talking as much as possible during the exam days." After a pause, Sid continued, "I understand politics is important and you guys are invested into it, but both of you need to avoid each other for a few days. Abhimanyu can shift into my room and I can take his bed for the time being." Sid was not asking us. He was telling us what to do.

For the next four days, I went to my room only to change clothes. I ended up faring poorly compared to the other minor exams I had taken. Had Sid not taken that call, maybe Gautam and I would have fared even worse in the Minor-II exams of this 'even semester'.

It was the weekend after a long week of exams. It was expected to be full of action.

"Edison, did you get chance to talk to Amitabh?" Sid asked Edison.

"What is this about?" Bansal wanted to know.

"Has Edison not told you about his poltu plan?" Sid checked.

"Yes, he told me briefly. I don't know about any recent developments." Bansal had a faint idea.

"I had a word with Amitabh. He told me very clearly that currently in his plans for externals, BSP Hindi secretary doesn't fit."

"So?" Bansal asked Edison.

"Should we talk once we reach our rooms?" I wanted this to be a closed-door discussion.

We all got into Bansal and Edison's room.

"So, Edison, what's next?" Bansal restarted from where we had paused.

"I don't think there is any option other than going for an internal post of maintenance secy." Edison was clear about his next step.

"Abhimanyu has decided to go after mess." Gautam opened his mouth for the first time.

"Is it?" Edison was surprised. Bansal and Sid also looked at me.

Gautam than went on to explain the rationale behind going after the post of mess secretary.

"Great. In that case, we both can aim for the same trophy." Edison was thinking about the future.

"I like your spirit Edison." I knew it was getting complex. Bansal looked at me for my response.

"You may have to run against Sanghvi, which will be a difficult battle," Gautam was testing Edison.

"Am sure we can fight him as a team." Edison was mentally preparing himself.

"We will have to plan it out well. It will be much more difficult than you may be thinking." Gautam looked visibly stressed.

Both Gautam and I knew the situation was getting complicated with every passing day. Bansal could understand our position.

Bansal asked me to make the right choice when he met me alone later, and I knew he meant every word about getting over the politics for larger good.

In the same spirit, Gautam and I had decided to start evaluating and clarifying things. One agenda at hand was to convince Bala for the post of cultural secy.

Bala was far from all politics. I raised the topic with him, "Why don't you try for cult? Am sure the whole batch will support you."

"I am not interested in participating in any way."

"Why?"

"It's a difficult job and will require a lot of commitment. One MM was enough for me to test my commitment. Why don't you go for it?"

"I am thinking for mess." Then I explained to Bala my rationale. He was impressed.

"You are a deserving candidate, Abhimanyu. I'm sure you will win." It was a confidence booster.

With Bala not contesting for cult, we understood this was a going to be an even trickier affair.

Prabhat and Pushkar caught up with me next day in the mess.

Prabhat started the conversation "Abhimanyu, so have you decided?"

"For?" I couldn't get his drift.

"What are you running for?" Prabhat wanted a direct conversation.

"Yeah. I will go for mess."

"What?" clearly Prabhat was not expecting my choice.

"Yeah, mess!"

"Why not cult?" It seemed Prabhat was caught off guard.

"Because I can contribute to BRCA even without any post. But if we can grab BHM along with BRCA, Best House is not going anywhere."

"Seriously. Is that your plan?"

"Why are you so surprised?" I could feel Prabhat's discomfort.

"Because you decide posts to go after basis what's the equation and not basis what you will do after you get the post."

"True! But unlike you, there is always a cause that serves me as the motivation to go for power. It's never about absolute power for me."

"Ok. But that will unsettle a lot of equations."

"Like?"

"Like we may end up on opposite sides because Pushkar will also go for mess," Prabhat disclosed his target post.

"And why will he exactly go for that? What has he contributed there?"

"He has done enough for the hostel. And he can go for anything which can make up for it."

"Agree that he did a lot during the first semester in the first year and was not rewarded for that. But that was the case with Abhimanyu as well. Though unlike Pushkar, it didn't change anything for him. In fact, he was more dedicated to the house than the first year – everyone witnessed that." Surprisingly, Gautam joined the conversation. He had just walked into the mess and had overheard our discussion.

"So what? That doesn't make any case against Pushkar. He was involved in Kara's entry for MM this year. Everyone saw that." Prabhat was now on the back foot.

"I knew poltu was the only reason for you to make Pushkar work during the MM. At least you will have something to talk about during the next few days. We are now set for a big match. Hopefully, we all just be the way we are now." I set the record straight.

"Only time will tell," Prabhat swiftly replied and moved ahead.

My direct opponent was clear to us now. It was now going to serve as an anchor for our future set of actions.

~ 63 ~

The names of the potential house secretary candidates were the talk of the town. We also belonged to the same town.

"Looks like three or four people are in the race this time." Gautam had done his calculations.

"I can predict one." I knew part of the story as well. "Shashi will definitely go after it. It's evident now why Shashi didn't go for the cultural secretary last year. Shashi and Guru as Secretaries would have dented their chance to project one of them as house secretary this year. To me, Shashi is in the race for sure."

"I agree. It must be one between Guru and Shashi. Guru was quite visible as the mess secretary, but then everything that Shashi did through the year is set up nicely. In fact, I would say Guru helped Shashi set it up by working as the Rendezvous publicity coordinator to be able to reach out to even larger group beyond the dramatics team." Gautam agreed.

"Hmm. What about the other options?" Sid wanted the discussion to move ahead.

"Everyone knows what happened to Rocky last year. Then we have a talent like Vatsal who has not played any large secretary role yet, which is the biggest surprise for me till date. Rocky and Vatsal were active through the year. I think both are going to play a significant role this year." Gautam had identified the most visible people from the senior batch.

"If both of them go for it, it will be killer." I didn't want that to happen honestly.

"What do you think about Kaushik?" Gautam checked with me. Kaushik was a genuine, sweet, soft-spoken, down to earth person who was liked by everyone in the house.

"Kaushik is a very genuine person, but I don't think we should link his friendship across batches, especially with first-year people, with his political ambition." Many people had thought that till now, but I didn't believe in this theory yet.

"Politics is always a game of surprises. I don't think you can ignore Kaushik so easily," Gautam was expecting Kaushik to play an important role.

"I am not ignoring him. It will be critical to see who will have his support eventually. Shashi is his department mate and close friend, but his room is next to Vatsal."

"I think you forget, Rocky is also from the same department." Sid corrected me.

"Oh yes! It looks like all three of them have equal chances to get Kaushik's support. I think it's going to be super interesting. Sid, why don't you check with Kaushik? Am sure he will surely share with you." I knew Sid could get some insider information from Kaushik.

"Okay! But if he is himself planning for the house secretary, then I don't know what kind of equation will remain in their batch," Sid pointed out.

~ 64 ~

For the post of house Secretary, Rocky, Vatsal and Shashi were in the game right from the start. But an unexpected entry happened close to the dates of final elections.

"Do you know the latest entrant to the party?" I wanted to share which I witnessed on the way to our room.

"Who?" Gautam left his desktop, listening.

"Kalra! He has started campaigning in the wings of first years."

"What! Kalra?" Gautam was surprised too.

"Yes. I was shocked too. In fact, he has openly disclosed his candidature while others are still waiting." None of Rocky, Vatsal and Shashi had openly disclosed the candidature yet.

"Am not sure of his support in the B. Tech batches." Edison was also perplexed.

"He is going to count on his support from the M. Tech junta," Sid joined us.

"M. Tech. support?" Gautam and I asked the same question.

"Yes, I met Kaushik today at dinner. He told me about Kalra. He has made friends among the M. Tech junta. And so, unlike last year, there will be no M. Tech candidate this time." Sid had his own sources.

"That's an interesting way of getting the numbers. We still have a significant number of M. Tech guys in the hostel. And if you get a large chunk of them along with a critical mass of B. Tech guys, you are through." Gautam was now thinking.

"I am sure he will have critical mass, given Rudra and Vishal will surely back him up. In fact, I will not be surprised if they have a role in convincing Kalra to go for house secretary." Gautam made me think about the equations now.

"And why only Rudra and Vishal? Why not Prabhat and Pushkar – even they would be closer to Kalra than other possible candidates." Gautam was right.

"Talking about other candidates – Declaration of Shashi's candidature is also a formality now. Both mess and maintenance as a team will be behind him. Guru himself told me that they are the just waiting for the right time." I had a word with Guru during the last mess committee meeting that he had called for.

"Kaushik also confirmed to me that he is not in the race. He doesn't want to ruin any relation because of poltu and so will not take the front seat." Sid confirmed what I had always believed.

"So then, all eyes would be on Rocky and Vatsal now," Edison said.

"I guess Kalra's step would force them to declare sooner than later." I was still not clear about their strategy.

"House secy elections with four candidates would be just killer – no one will be a clear favourite." Gautam's anxiety was right, especially in the context of Kalra joining the fight.

~ 65 ~

Shashi's candidature was declared the next day with his first round of campaigning across batches and wings of the house. Shashi was expectedly joined by mess secretary, Guru and maintenance secretary, Viks. Many others from their wing also joined him.

Shashi's team looked strong, as we had expected. It had the right mix of talent as well as visible and famous faces in the batch. The single important person missing from this group was Kaushik.

"Shashi and Guru can give anyone a run for their money in the field of their choice," Viks observed.

"Also, given our *bakaiti* standards, you guys would have found many of us very approachable to solve any of your problems through these two years." With Kaushik not in the team, it was undoubtedly an attempt to ride on Shashi's strength.

Sid didn't hesitate in raising an honest query. "Shashi, since we are still awaiting disclosure of all the house secy candidates, just wanted to check if there is someone in your team who has not come along today as part of your team, but we should know about." Most of us knew that Sid was hinting at Kaushik.

Shashi answered, "Sid, thanks for asking this question. Everyone here plays an important role in my team. And none of them need any introduction. Kara has been represented by each of them multiple times in the last two years. We have always been a transparent team without hiding our passion for the house as well as ambition at the same time. Maybe you are referring to Kaushik. Kaushik is a terrific friend of mine and will always remain the same way. But he has chosen not to be part of this team. It's his personal choice, and I respect him for the same. For the house secretary post, I think Kara needs a team of efficient, effective and experienced individuals led by an enthusiastic leader who has personal relations with housemates and is directly approachable. The team that I have with me will serve that well." Shashi stressed on 'the last two years'. It was indeed an attempt to make us consider everything that we would have witnessed over the complete two year period spent in the house till date.

He had played safe by saying that Kaushik was and will be a good friend, alongside highlighting his own strengths.

With every passing day and without any declaration from either Rocky or Vatsal, it was clear that there was a game happening behind the curtains. And it was only visible to the third year people belonging to the D-Parallel Wing – that is where all three Vatsal, Rocky and Kaushik lived. Kaushik was, therefore, our only hope, but he had already told Sid, "This should remain within our batch and I would prefer that you guys come to know about it only when it is made public."

"Rocky is a sports enthusiast. He is quite popular and has been very approachable to everyone," Sid stated.

"Most of us know that he was unlucky last year. That could be a big factor in driving him home. I think Aniket may support him. Don't know if Kaushik will support him or Vatsal," I was thinking of the equation in the batch.

"Vatsal also has great respect across batches. Am sure Kaushik and Vatsal together can get many votes, just basis the relationship they share with the housemates across batches." Gautam was right in evaluating Vatsal' position of strength.

"Kalra would definitely benefit if Shashi, Rocky and Vatsal are in the race because it will divide the votes that will go against him." I was thinking in the best interest of the house.

As we were discussing the potential candidates in my room, we heard voices from a group outside who were asking all of us to join them in the corridor.

"Abhimanyu, Gautam, Rahul, Sanghvi – can you guys come out?" This was Aniket.

"Utkarsh, , Edison, Bansal – come out guys!" This was Kaushik.

"Looks like they are going to end all surprises," I said as soon as I recognized Kaushik's voice.

As we came out, we saw a large crowd. Much larger than we expected. And surprisingly, we saw Vatsal, Rocky, Kaushik, Aniket and many more from the third year standing as part of the group.

Makhija tried to act smart. "Aha! Seems like tonight we will have complete clarity on all the candidates for the Karakoram house secretary."

Vatsal as always didn't miss a chance, "Don't worry Makhija. It will not impact any of your chances, if you have any! By the way, are you gunning for any post in your batch?" It was enough for everyone to burst out laughing.

Kaushik intervened, "Leave him for now, Vatsal! And let this be about why we are here!" Kaushik was as calm as he always was.

It seemed Vatsal and Kaushik were going to do most of the talking today.

"Guys, we know there have been a lot of rumours. So, I thought it's high time for us to get it clear." Everyone was waiting eagerly. "Rocky is going to contest the house secy elections. And he has complete support from our side in full confidence. And by everyone, I mean everyone that you see out here with us." Vatsal announced Rocky's candidature.

Gautam and I exchanged smiles at this announcement. Vatsal announcing Rocky's name was perhaps the best way to tell everyone that they are one team and Vatsal is not going to contest on his own.

"We all thought Kaushik will also contest!" Sid tried pulling Kaushik's leg in between all of this.

"We all know that Rocky would be more capable than him," Vatsal defended.

Finally, Rocky spoke, "Guys, between all the fun that we are having here, just wanted to appeal to you guys for your support so that we can have the best team for the house going forward. The one that has worked hard for the house."

Sanghvi asked honestly, "What about Shashi? I think he also has a team which had worked tirelessly for the house."

Vatsal took that question. "Totally agree with you, Sanghvi. But we also need a leader who can take everyone along, who has a consistent track record and who never takes things for granted. Rest I will leave you guys to decide." It was a simple attack on Shashi's habit of either giving hundred percent like in the Hindi play or nothing, like in the MM.

After regular questions, answers and discussions, Rocky's team went on to the next wing, and all of us went back to our rooms.

~ 66 ~

Next day, Sid entered our room with a purposeful walk. "Did Bansal tell you guys how Rocky has started playing an emotional angle?"

"No. What happened?" I was inquisitive.

"Rocky met Bansal and me while we were walking back from the institute. While making his case for the post of house secy, Rocky played a sentimental card about how he left maintenance secretary last time for the good of the house despite no clarity in externals. And so for all the work he has done for the house, he deserves a position this time."

"So?" Gautam asked.

"I think he is taking it too far. Though, I believe Bansal was impressed with the argument." Sid clearly didn't like Rocky's argument.

"So what? I don't find anything wrong with that. Rocky is just stating what happened to him. He is just trying to make his candidature stronger. It's now for people to decide." Gautam was right.

Vatsal announcing Rocky's candidature was indeed a surprise. And no one would know the background story better than Kaushik. It took Sid a couple of days to get back to us on the story that happened behind the visible scenes.

"So Sid, we hope your charm worked this time with Kaushik?" Gautam was inquisitive.

"Not completely. Kaushik is a good friend, but he knows where to draw the line. After all, it's about his batch, and he definitely wants to guard the secret."

"Okay, you don't have all the information?" I was curious.

"Kaushik told me about the role he had to play to bring both Rocky and Vatsal together. Initially, both were hell bent on contesting. But their team wanted only one of them to contest. And Kaushik himself didn't want to support one against the other. Finally, post Kalra's declaration, Kaushik got the job to convince them. Now it's not an easy job to convince two strong individuals.

But given that both have a lot of respect for each other, there was still a chance. What I could pick was there is a compromise backed by a kind of deal, but Kaushik didn't say much. He is of the opinion that it will automatically become public at the right time. He doesn't want to talk about something which will neither be beneficial for his batch nor ours." Sid told us everything that Kaushik had shared with him.

"Both of them coming together is in the interest for the house. And thanks to Kaushik that he was able to pull it off." I knew this was the best possible outcome for the house.

"I could understand that it would not be beneficial for their batch. Didn't understand why it would not be beneficial for our batch." Gautam was perplexed.

"Because Gautam, it will divide our batch even further, basis their loyalties." Sid was still a novice.

"As if our batch is not divided already! And I am sure there is no loyalty divided between Rocky and Vatsal. They would get respect from same set of people in our batch." I was also confused.

"Exactly!" Gautam agreed with me.

Poltu was showing its colour across batches. But, as it always happens, when the stakes are high, it came along with unanswered questions.

X
'Poltu' at its best

~ 67 ~

It was already late, and both Gautam and I were on our respective beds.

"Abhimanyu, Are you awake?" Gautam started.

"Am trying!" I was not able to sleep.

"Good, then we can talk! So what options do we have now, given candidates are pretty much decided?"

"Ok. Let's recap what we have on the plate. Mess – Pushkar and I, maint – Sanghvi and Edison, cultural – Rudra and Makhija given Bala backed out and sports – Shubham, Utkarsh or Rahul and maybe Rudra. We need to talk to Vishal directly to get clarity." I summarized the current situation.

"Given we are pitted against Prabhat and Pushkar for mess. So, the only two options available for us to form a coalition are Sanghvi and Vishal. Now, if we go with Sanghvi, Edison will have to back out because that's a direct conflict." Gautam laid out the clear option for us.

"That leaves Vishal and Rudra as the current best option for us. But Gautam, my conscience is not allowing me to support someone knowing well that they are not the right people for power in the long run." I raised my genuine concern.

"See, we need to make the best of the situation for the hostel. Best bet for us would be Rudra targeting sports because in that case, he can't go with Prabhat. And Sanghvi will never support Rudra and Vishal." Gautam was calculating Rudra and Vishal's future action.

"Am still trying to make up my mind for creating a coalition with Vishal and Rudra."

"Should we talk to Edison? That's the other way to deal with the situation. I can manage the conversation with him," Gautam gave an option.

"I think at this stage, making him change his mind would be difficult. Moreover, that would be like compromising some within our team. Let's avoid that."

"Agree. In case we go along with Vishal and Rudra, we should be less bothered if Rudra contests. Even if we support him, I know it will be difficult for him to win, given his antics with everyone in the batch. So in a way, we will be sorted. My real worry is Vishal. Let's decide this finally after talking to him." Gautam concluded.

"Gautam, it's high time to have a clear plan." I was hinting to Gautam.

As we were having this conversation, my mobile rang. "And there it comes. Vishal is calling."

"Great that he is calling and not Rudra. Let's meet him." Clearly, Gautam did not want to talk to Rudra on this matter.

Vishal told me he will come to my room in five minutes.

"I hope he doesn't bring Rudra," Gautam said.

Within a couple of minutes, Vishal was at our room.

"Great that Gautam is also here," Vishal wasn't expecting him.

"So tell me. Am sure it's about poltu only!" I started the topic.

"Yes. Nothing else to discuss these days. Tell me, what are you standing for?" Vishal was also not in the mood to waste time.

"I will go for mess."

"And that's because you can oversee cultural activities anyway?" Vishal surprised me.

"Yes. So you have all the info!"

"No, because that will make my life easy."

"So, you are going for cult?" I was surprised.

"Yes!" Vishal kept it short.

"Aha. That's a twist. We were expecting Rudra to go for cult," Gautam joined in.

"No, he will go for sports."

"Aren't there too many candidates for sports?"

"Who all?"

"I thought one between Utkarsh and Rahul and then Shubham is anyway talking to everyone."

"Shubham? Where did he come from?"

"Good that we also have some info which you don't have," I was surprised that he didn't know.

"And great that you are not gunning for cult. Wanted to clear that out between us rather than hearing from others. But now, sports will be competitive."

"Have you already discussed with Prabhat?"

"Yeah briefly. But Prabhat didn't mention about Shubham."

"So I think equation would be you supporting us for mess and maint, we covering you for cult and sports." Gautam declared it without any hesitation.

"Maint am guessing it's Edison. For cult, who all will stand?"

"Someone from Sanghvi's group will be there for sure. Rahul, Makhija and others in their group will not want people from your team as secretaries. They can't leave it to go easily, given there is no one else from our or Prabhat's side who will stand."

"What will be our chances?" Vishal was trying to calculate the numbers.

"Am sure about Abhimanyu and you. Not about other posts." Gautam made it clear. "But that is the best option we have."

Vishal came thinking he had the upper hand, but was caught otherwise. "Ok. Seems like a plan."

"Great. Let's stack up against the numbers and meet once again tomorrow." I summed up.

"Maybe we stick to this small group only. Let's keep Edison and Rudra out of this now." Gautam was particular.

"Ok. Let's meet tomorrow."

Once Vishal was gone, I shared my understanding with Gautam. "Am sure Rudra is not contesting for cultural given his insincerity through the year as the dramatics rep."

"True. And so sports was his natural choice. That would have encouraged Vishal to try for cultural."

I checked with Gautam, "Why are you keeping Edison out of this discussion?"

"I had to keep Rudra out of this discussion. Vishal is more straightforward. Rudra has all the capability to break this alliance between Vishal and us. Vishal can keep Rudra aligned at an individual level, given he knows this is the best chance for him and Rudra combined. I had to give Edison in exchange of keeping out Rudra. Don't worry I will manage Edison. Though, for him, it would be next to impossible to defeat Sanghvi." Gautam was correct.

So we had to give and take with Vishal, knowing well that we were helping someone who was fundamentally wrong to get power. We had chosen to support our friend Edison and make the best out of the current situation.

~ 68 ~

Next few days were spent in discussions between all the four groups confirming the coalitions and final candidates. Also, every potential candidate would have reached out to individuals in the batch at a personal level to get votes, irrespective of the alliances.

There were few surprises even there. Shubham reached out to Gautam, Edison and myself. "Can you guys please vote for me? I promise to vote in return."

Gautam, as always, showed commitment to everyone.

"Do you believe him?" I checked with Gautam.

"Shubham is acting in desperation. Sports secy is the only post which may end up having a three-way fight. I don't know if

Pushkar and Prabhat would be aware of Shubham's desperate act. But am sure we can't trust him."

For me, the most challenging part was to team against Sanghvi. But I didn't discuss it with Gautam. It was one battle which I had to fight internally. On a Friday night, Amitabh called the batch to assemble in the TV room for the batch elections. He was accompanied by Spidy.

Amitabh addressed the whole batch, "Guys, am sure you know why we are here tonight. Am going to start by reiterating the unsaid rule in Kara. All the 3rd year secys will be elected by the batch among themselves and only the elected people will then file the nominations at the house level. There will never be an election for Cultural, Sports, Mess, and Maintenance at the house level within B. Tech. So, without any delay, I would encourage people from your batch who want to run for the different posts to come forward."

As expected, for the secretaries we had the following line up.

Mess	Pushkar and Abhimanyu,
Maintenance	Sanghvi and Edison,
Cultural	Vishal and Makhija,
Sports	Shubham, Rudra and Utkarsh

"So Makhija and Sanghvi have decided for Utkarsh over Rahul," I whispered to Gautam.

Gautam spoke in my ears, "Both Shubham and Utkarsh are going after sports. It shows there is a coalition between Makhija and Prabhat only for mess and maintenance. Sports has been left for individuals to decide as both the groups are contesting the same. This explains the reason for Shubham's desperate effort to barter his personal vote with our vote." Gautam summed up his observation.

As per the standard procedure, everyone in the batch wrote his preferences on a piece of paper and gave it to Amitabh.

For sports, people provided two choices with clearly marked preference order.

After the counting, Amitabh was back to take control. "Guys, results clearly indicate a pattern in the voting. Great to see that there are clear winners and all of them have won by some margin."

There was pin-drop silence. Amitabh continued, "I will only tell you the name of new secretaries for the house. And will not tell you the margin of votes. You can trust me, as I told you before, that margins do not matter, given there are clear winners."

"So here are the new Secretaries for the Karakoram House."

Sports	Shubham
Cultural	Vishal
Maintenance	Sanghvi
Mess	Abhimanyu

"You four should file the nomination papers tomorrow. If there are no nominations from the M.Tech junta, you guys will be declared elected unopposed. Also, a suggestion from my side to the batch – none of these four should be spared from bumps and batch treat!" Amitabh concluded and went.

Not to our surprise, there were no celebrations, no bumps and no treat. Everyone left the room in silence. Every group ended up with a reason to celebrate as well as a reason to contemplate.

Our group also left the room with mixed emotions. All five of us – Gautam, Sid, Edison, Bansal and I – headed to the college canteen.

Bansal broke the silence. "I think we can call it the most expected results."

"How come everyone won with large margins if people were elected from different groups?" Edison was still in the phase of accepting the results.

"Because politics doesn't always go with the rules of the coalition. Every candidate has an individual existence. He is individually evaluated by the voters as well. Am sure Abhimanyu and Sanghvi would have got maximum votes in the batch. They would have got votes from all the four groups and so the results." Gautam was trying to explain the rationale behind results.

"So, Gautam you mean, Pushkar and I would not have got the expected votes from the respective coalition?" Edison was analysing the results in his own way.

"I would rather put it the other way. Sanghvi and Abhimanyu would have got votes from the people in the batch beyond the coalition," Gautam was trying to control the discussion.

"It means the same thing."

"No Edison. It doesn't. You need to understand this. It means one can have a chance in politics if one rightly chooses his or her opposition. In your case, the opposition had very high equity in the batch which was difficult to overcome. It was not the case with Vishal. He had a weaker opposition. And so he won."

"What about Shubham?" this time it was Sid.

"I think it was the case of divided votes. Second preferences of the votes polled for both Utkarsh and Rudra would have gone to Shubham."

"Makes sense." Edison nodded slowly.

"Anyways, we tried our best for both the posts." Sid wanted to conclude.

"True, Sid! But we ended up winning only one of them." Edison required more time to accept.

"We should rather think we ended up winning a key position within the group. Should we not celebrate?" Sid was looking at the positive side of it.

"Why don't you guys go ahead? I will go back." Edison didn't want to join the celebration.

"No point in celebrating without you, Edison. We all will walk back to the hostel." I looked at Gautam, Bansal and Sid for affirmation.

"Sure Abhimanyu. Let's go back." All three of them said in unison.

~ 69 ~

House reps among the first years were also decided the same weekend. Most of the enthu people were expectedly elected – Aryan for dramatics, Sikka for music, Sajid for FAC, Rohit for ISC and Shanky for BSW. Aneesh was given the responsibility for Kara Forum.

The only surprise was that Dixcy didn't end up becoming any house rep, neither Cultural Club rep nor BSW rep.

PP didn't want to take any responsibility, so he didn't try. He later told me, "Most of the reps were decided by consensus." I liked this excellent news for the house, given collective courage and enthusiasm of everyone was needed to drive house aspirations next year.

"What about Dixcy?" I asked PP.

He replied, "Dixcy also wanted to become dramatics rep, but batch decided to back Aryan. We all know what Dixcy is capable of and so suggested him to take BSW rep or something like FAC rep that interests him. He didn't budge and refused to take up anything else. The batch didn't find his action in line with the spirit for the house."

"Let me talk to him. We all will need him in the next year."

"Absolutely, Abhimanyu bhai."

"What about Charsi?"

"He threw in his hat for many – ISC, Hindi Samiti, BSW and BSP Hindi rep. But he didn't have many people to support him. Batch always had the choice of a better candidate for each of these positions of responsibility. So, he didn't end up winning anything."

"So much like Charsi. I like his attitude to try for anything possible." I was smiling. "Did Thakkar try for anything?"

"No no. Thakkar and Suresh were the last two to join the batch meet. They didn't play any role other than casting their preference for each position of responsibility."

"I hope the enthusiasm of the batch for the house didn't take a hit. To me, it seems batch unity is very much intact." I was optimistic.

"I didn't feel anything has changed in the batch post the elections. The team of reps and others are looking forward to the next year with similar enthusiasm, if not more." PP sounded optimistic.

I met Dixcy at the dinner table next night. "So Dixcy, how is it going?"

"Nothing like what I was expecting." Dixcy was not happy and didn't try to hide it.

"Why?"

"Abhimanyu bhai, tell me one thing. Didn't I deserve to be the dramatics rep for my contributions?"

"Yes, and no!"

"What do you mean?"

"You deserved a post for your contribution. But the post is decided by the batch and not individuals. In fact, you had so many options on the table."

"So you mean Aryan was more deserving for dramatics?"

"I am no one to decide, Dixcy. It's always your batch which decides. You had a passion for the hostel, which is most important. Positions of responsibility are an outcome which has become important for you now. Please do not let your ambitions drive your spirit for the house. In fact, it should be the other way."

"It's easy for someone to give gyaan, Abhimanyu bhai. Had you been in my position, you would have understood."

I could only laugh internally at his comment. "I will only say one thing Dixcy. Hostel needs you. Just try to be there for the house the same way you were there for her on the first day. I know what you are capable of Dixcy."

"See you later Abhimanyu bhai. I need to run to Ara to take notes." Dixcy hurriedly left. He was no longer the same Dixcy I knew a few weeks back during the MM practice.

"Gautam, internally I hope if there is any negative feeling within the batch of first year, it goes away by the time they return next year after the break."

"I think you are too optimistic." Gautam was trying to be practical.

"Why? We have discussed how this batch has been different from us. Low on talent, low on ego, but high on innocence and enthusiasm."

"I am just hoping that the innocence of this batch, which you are considering as a strength, is not exploited going forward. I know from experience that there are people in our batch who are potentially capable of playing a bigger role in the future." Gautam shared his own evaluation.

"I want you to be wrong this time."

"Anyway, all that doesn't stop us from our agenda." Gautam turned optimistic now.

"Yes, it is so important to leverage this batch for creating a culture of accountability."

"Absolutely. Exactly the way we discussed it before. They are the best chance for us to be able to build this culture."

"Especially when we have *enough* power to control the same," I reminded myself.

"I liked when you said 'enough'. We know we now have two people with power in the batch who will help build this culture, and the other two, who will not care for the same."

"Agree. And that's why this batch is so critical."

~ 70 ~

While batch poltu and elections in first and second year were concluding, campaigning by the third years also reached its peak at the same time.

Both groups were concentrating on communicating themselves as the best bet for the house.

The respective pitches of all the three candidates on the night – where they took questions from hostel mates – and the way the dynamics were unfolding, made it impossible to predict the results.

"Kaushik, it's interesting to see how you guys brought together your team. But Aniket, cultural secretary's support for you guys was surprising to me." I met Kaushik in the institute and hostel talk was expected to happen.

"Why did you find it surprising?" Kaushik was amused.

"If I understand it correctly, Shashi was in the race for cultural secy last year. But he left it for Aniket, who was eventually elected unopposed."

"So?"

"So I was expecting that he would be supporting Shashi this time, given Shashi in a way made it possible for him."

"But that happened in the past. Aniket is doing what he believes is the future. See, Shashi made that choice in the past for his future. Now Aniket believes that there is no gain in the future by supporting a losing group. He would rather stay in the winning group. To me, it's not always a situation of 'give and take'. Shashi would have expected that Aniket will stay the course, but Guru would have definitely prepared for Aniket applying his own mind as an individual." Kaushik explained the rationale.

"Interesting. But you would have convinced Aniket for his support." I thought Kaushik would have played a role here.

"To tell you the truth, I didn't have to do anything. Once we had the clarity on the house secy candidate, Aniket himself went and talked to Rocky," Kaushik clarified.

"Don't know if it is completely fair." I felt bad for Shashi.

"See, Shashi didn't leave the cultural secy post for Aniket in just good spirit. He was thinking of his own future. Now Aniket is just thinking of his own future."

I could understand now that there was nothing predictable in the final phase.

"To me, it looks like a battle between a right-spirited team versus visible experienced faces of the batch." I was talking to Gautam, Sid and Bansal the night before the day of voting. Post the elections in out batch, Edison no longer joined us for such discussions.

"No one is giving Kalra a chance." Sid developed his view basis what he heard from like-minded people in the batch.

"Let's see. You never know." Bansal was keeping his finger crossed.

"Other than the support of different people in the third year for respective candidates, one thing stood out for me during this campaigning," Gautam shared his opinion. "If I compare this campaign with the one we witnessed last year, I could see one major difference. Last year Double A and Amitabh talked about their respective strengths, what they bring to the table and how they can contribute to the house. They rarely talked about the opposition. They never anchored their campaign on the weaknesses of the other group. But if you see this time, both the sides didn't miss an opportunity to identify and talk at length about the other candidates' weaknesses. There was a definite shift from utterly positive campaigning to a fair share of negative campaigning." Gautam had a point.

"Interesting way to look at it Gautam. But it's also possible that the campaigning style depends upon the batch in which campaigning is happening. Maybe the current first year batch found it the way we experienced it last year. Maybe Shashi, Rocky and Kalra's batch would have experienced last year what we are experiencing now. Though to be fair to your observation, standing today I can never think of Double A and Amitabh trying to attempt the style of campaigning that we witnessed this year." I had my own way to look at it.

"That's also possible Abhimanyu." Gautam was smiling at my observation.

"I found a key element missing in the campaigning of all the three candidates." Bansal, as always, had something unique to share.

"What?" Sid asked.

"Everyone talks about the previous work they have done for the house and their team's passion for continuing to work for the house in the future as well. But no one ever made a promise or shared a vision for something more tangible like winning a BRCA trophy or winning a BSA or BHM trophy. I found that unsatisfactory." Bansal continued to surprise us.

"That's such a nuanced observation, Bansal!" I was impressed.

"Something to make a note of Abhimanyu!" Gautam was smiling.

Then, Edison walked into the room half asleep, "If you guys are done with talking and noting down stuff, can we go to Nescafe? I am feeling hungry." We all joined Edison for his dose of Maggi.

The D-day was now eagerly awaited.

~ 71 ~

It was the D-day. As expected, there were M. Tech nominations for mess and maintenance. So, Sanghvi and I had to wait for the voting at the hostel level before finally getting elected. Shubham and Vishal, being the sole nominations for the sports and cultural secretary respectively, were elected unopposed.

In the morning, an unwanted drama happened. Amitabh called for an urgent batch meet in the TV room for our batch. When we reached there, we found all the three house secretary candidates, as well as outgoing secretaries in the meeting.

Amitabh was visibly irritated and stressed. He started the batch meet informing everyone, "Guys, wanted to share with all of you that something which was never ever heard in the history of Karakoram has happened today. Pushkar, backed by Prabhat, has filed the nominations for the post of mess secretary."

Not many of us could believe that it was a possibility. *"What?" "Really?" "Why?"*

Amitabh was aware of the brain behind this unwanted action and so tried to convince Prabhat in front of everyone. "You are well aware of this, Prabhat. It is an unsaid rule that the third year secretaries are elected by the batch and only the ones elected by the batch will file nominations. This has been the tradition in Kara, and you can't go against the Kara spirit for your personal ego. If your batch doesn't want you or your friend to become secretary, you can't do anything about it." Amitabh wanted to use the batch influence and force Pushkar to withdraw from the elections.

"But it's not a formal rule Amitabh. Everyone has the right to file nominations." Prabhat was trying to defend his action. He was correct technically.

Thomas started, "So Prabhat, you think we all voted in the batch elections without any purpose? This is not fair. You are not maintaining the sanctity of the wishes of the batch."

Next person to pull Prabhat for this action was a surprise for everyone. Rudra was visibly angry. "Batch has decided something, and we are all a part of the same. You will have to withdraw Pushkar's nomination for sure. This is not a joke."

It was followed by many people in the batch showcasing their unhappiness over their actions.

Shubham didn't say anything and was maintaining silence.

All house secretary candidates – Kalra, Rocky and Shashi – opposed this univocally. "This has never happened in Kara, and it should never happen. You will have to withdraw the nominations. Show some respect to your batch." Everyone knew this would start a practice which would only become worse going forward.

After a fifteen-minute discussion in such a large group, Prabhat realized that he was fighting a lonely battle. Finally, he gave up and agreed to withdraw Pushkar's nomination. Pushkar hardly talked during this whole discussion. It was clear that he was doing what Prabhat was asking him to do and he never looked comfortable during the entire batch meet.

Immediately after the batch meet, Pushkar withdrew his nomination for the mess secretary.

~ 72 ~

In the evening, during the house secretary elections, as expected, there were tense faces around.

I asked Gautam before voting. "We are sure who we are voting for?"

"Yes, as always."

Voting continued for over three hours. Shashi, Rocky and Kalra stuck around the common room during the voting. They were accompanied by crucial people of their respective groups – Vatsal, Kaushik, Guru and Viks.

At 8 p.m. sharp, voting was closed. Post voting, the counting process started.

As it had been in the last year, results for the first preferences were displayed in phases after counting of every hundred votes. No one cared for the outcome of maintenance and mess secretaries elections as Sanghvi and I were leading comfortably for the respective positions.

There was a surprise start when the result of the first hundred votes of the house secretary was disclosed. Rocky was leading among three while Kalra and Shashi were head to head. This surprise soon started becoming a reality. After counting of all the first preferences, when the results were displayed, everyone waiting outside the common room had accepted the shock built over the five rounds of counting. Not that no one predicted it, but surely majority didn't expect it.

Post the counting of the first preferences, Rocky emerged first, followed by Kalra. Shashi was shockingly knocked out in the first preference itself. Rocky maintained the lead from the first round. The difference between Kalra and Shashi kept increasing after every round of counting.

"The sole possible reason for this must have been a large concentration of the M.Tech votes for a B.Tech candidate. Don't think anyone would have predicted this," I told Gautam.

"Everyone underestimated Kalra. He has pulled off a surprise." Sid was equally surprised.

Post the counting of first preferences, second preference of all the votes polled for Shashi was supposed to be counted. But now it was only a formality. So within minutes, final results were announced. There was an enormous roar of Vatsal and Aniket. Kaushik was also present, but he maintained the decorum.

Rocky was the new house secretary of Karakoram. He maintained his composure and thanked everyone who was around.

I could notice Shashi and Guru leaving the house swiftly after the announcement of first preferences. And they were not seen the entire night.

~ 73 ~

Next day, we had external elections.

Kara and Kumaon were the hostels who continued their tradition of being 1.0 in externals. Everyone in these two hostels, who were part of the electoral college and therefore eligible to vote in the externals, were expected to vote in a union as per the instructions of the outgoing house secretary. I also did exactly what Amitabh asked me to do. Unlike other houses, no divided groups from Kara or Kumaon were sitting in different coalitions.

This time interestingly both Kara and Kumaon were in the same coalition. With two 1.0 hostels together, everyone expected Kara to do well in the externals.

By the end of the day, results started emerging. To everyone's surprise, Kara didn't win anything we aimed for in the externals.

In-spite of being 1.0, Amitabh couldn't bring anything for the house. It was a significant setback for the batch because being 1.0 in externals usually guaranteed winning coalitions. Within the alliance, Kumaon was able to win the posts of a cultural club secy and a G Sec.

"Kaushik was telling me the other day that our external coalition was a bit shaky. It was touch and go for most of the posts that coalition was fighting for. As it turned out, the coalition lost out on all the posts that Kara was fighting for, while winning a few others that our partners were aiming for. In fact, we had an offer from the other coalition to join them without any compromise on the posts that we were aiming for. With a 1.0 hostel joining them, it would have made the other coalition a clear winning one. But Amitabh decided to stick with Kumaon in the first coalition, knowing well that it would go very close for the posts that we were fighting for." I told whatever information I had.

"Amitabh would have planned to play it safe and not change anything at the last moment. He would not have expected that we will lose everything that we were aiming for. Am sure Amitabh would have done his calculations. Post elections, there will always be rumours. But who knows what would have happened had Amitabh joined the other coalition?" Gautam was not taking the rumour seriously.

"Agree. But in either case, when I look back, it's such a paradox that the one who was able to win house secy elections last year, leveraging his relationship with Spidy, who was going to be an important figure in externals, couldn't himself win anything for the house in the externals this year. Don't know if Amitabh was able to leverage Spidy this year for externals or not. But now he will always be remembered as the house secy who couldn't bring anything for Kara in the externals." I was looking at the last two years in unison.

"You sometimes surprise me with your way of thinking Abhimanyu. I would not have been able to see this side of the complete two-year story on my own." Gautam was impressed.

Post the election, most of us who were engaged during the season, felt a vacuum. It was like the feeling post a big festival.

Aryan asked me if I wanted to join him, PP and Bhavna for dinner at *Mezbaan*, the most frequented restaurant for IIT junta. With all the time at hand now, I agreed.

PP and Bhavna had already taken a table at the restaurant when we reached. PP got surprised to see me. "Abhimanyu bhai! Aryan, you should have told me you are bringing him along."

"Why? You would have asked him to not join us?" Aryan didn't like the reaction.

"No, nothing like that. We could have planned better." PP looked uncomfortable.

I looked at Aryan, checking if he was able to read the situation. He didn't.

"What are you saying PP! Come guys! Am feeling hungry. Let's order some food," Bhavna tried to compensate.

We joined them.

"It must be long since we all went out last time." Aryan was elated.

"Yeah, priority for last few weeks was different." I was settling in after an abrupt start.

"Congratulations Abhimanyu for becoming the mess secy!" Bhavna seemed updated.

"Thank you, Bhavna!"

"PP told me about the stories through the season," Bhavna said with a smile.

I looked at PP questioningly. PP immediately defended, "She gets more dope from her sister than me."

"My sister told me more on the externals. For internals, it's fascinating to hear stories from PP," Bhavna seemed quite informed.

"Are you so interested in poltu?" I was surprised.

"I told you, not all Ph.Ds in the institute are boring!" She clearly remembered my judgement.

"Yeah, not all of them will have the guts to celebrate birthdays in a forbidden area!" Aryan was quick-witted.

"Are you judging me?" Bhavna didn't like the joke.

"Don't get senti! It was just a joke. We know who got us into that situation!" Aryan looked at PP.

"I should not have asked you guys for dinner tonight. Now that poltu season is over, you have all the time to spend pulling my leg." PP was smiling.

"By the way Bhavna, PP told me that your sister was running for one of the Institute positions." Aryan tried to change the topic.

"Was she? Didn't know about that!" I became interested.

"You didn't know about it?" Bhavna sounded surprised

"Should we order food instead of talking of poltu again," PP hurriedly wanted to change the topic. He called the waiter, checked for everyone's preferences, and ordered food.

Once the waiter was gone, Bhavna continued the conversation. "Really, you didn't know about it?"

"Yeah, I didn't know. Actually, I didn't have much idea about the institute elections other than for couple of posts where Kara was contesting."

"So, how did you vote for one of the G Sec posts that you were eligible to vote for?" Bhavna continued to press me.

"Seems like you are quite aware about the process. Not even all the B.Tech. will know the process."

"Answer my question Abhimanyu. How did you vote?"

"Do we really need to talk about it now? Elections are done, results are out. Can't we have a dinner without talking about it? We can talk about it later." PP was stammering. He seemed disturbed.

"Yeah, let's have dinner. We can talk about all this later." I felt something wasn't fitting in.

"Why are they not bringing food!" Aryan said.

I looked at PP. He was looking pale by now.

"No, we need to talk about it right now. Tell me how you voted?" Bhavna had something in mind.

I didn't have any choice. I started hesitatingly, "In Kara, for externals, we vote as one entity as recommended by house secy, basis the coalition he would have formed. No questions asked. I didn't even care who all were standing for the post. Just knew who I need to vote for and so did the needful."

There was silence as soon as I finished. Bhavna turned and shouted at PP, "You couldn't even ask him! And you call this friendship. But you have the guts to lie to me."

Aryan and I were looking at each other, surprised.

"There is a reason. I can explain." PP tried to take control of the situation.

"No, you need not explain now. I am done with this. You think because I am from Ph.D. I am boring and will not understand the games you guys can play. You guys do things as per your convenience. And I can see that now clearly." Bhavna got up, pulled her bag from the corner, and got up to leave.

"Bhavna, I don't know what's happening. I am sure we can talk to sort this out." I tried my best.

Bhavna didn't bother to respond. She was angry and left without saying anything. PP went after her, but retuned within a minute. He looked miserable.

"What is happening PP?" Aryan immediately asked.

"It's all my fault!" PP retorted.

"How?" I had to ask PP.

"I never thought it would end like this. Bhavna's sister is one of the secys from Himadri. She was running after one of the G Sec positions. And electoral college for that post include incoming mess secys."

"Ok. So, I voted for someone against her sister?" I could connect the dots.

"Yes. But the problem is bigger. Given her sister, Bhavna knew about the electoral college for the post her sister was running. Before the elections, I had told Bhavna that Abhimanyu bhai may become mess secy. So she requested if I could ask you to vote for her sister in case you become the mess secy." PP helped us ramp up.

"So, why didn't you ask me?"

"Because I never wanted to put you in a dilemma, Abhimanyu bhai. You have your priorities and your conscience is clear; stacking up to Kara 1.0. If I had told you, you would have gotten stretched between hostel loyalty and our friendship. And I didn't want you to make any such choice."

"That's so thoughtful of you PP. Then what did you tell her?"

"I told Bhavna that I have asked you and you will vote for her sister. And told her not to reach out to you directly because it's a sensitive issue for you. Yesterday, in elections, I think her sister lost by a narrow margin."

"Yes, her opponent from Kumaon who we voted for won by 1 vote. And that means if I had voted for her, Bhavna's sister would have won!" I knew the results.

"Oh my god! So, all the time, she thought Abhimanyu bhai voted for her sister while you didn't even ask Abhimanyu bhai to vote for her in the first place. No wonder she got so pissed!" Aryan was right.

"I had thought once the external elections are over, I will tell you guys about this, so that we can all play along the script. I never thought we all would be having dinner together less than twenty hours after the external election. Thanks to Aryan. I didn't get time to brief you guys." PP looked angrily at Aryan.

"Sorry PP. None of us wanted it to end it like this." Aryan was disappointed.

"Hiding all this from Bhavna was not a good idea PP. But how it got unfolded today was also clearly not the best way." I wasn't sure if the choice PP had made was correct.

~ 74 ~

We soon had the BHM night for the annual awards where we again watched other houses picking up the trophies basis their yearly performance.

Ara picked up BSA. Surprisingly, Vindy leap-frogged Kumaon for the BRCA trophy. Kumaon had to satisfy with the second position in BRCA. BSP and BSW trophies were won by Kailash and Jwala, respectively. More surprisingly, Vindy won the Hostel Management trophy as well for the year. And so they ended up winning the Best House trophy. It showed us that Kumaon was dispensable.

BHM night was followed by the house days of the respective hotels.

House day is the first complete responsibility of the new mess secy. As always, it's the day to celebrate the year gone by and passing on the baton to the new batch. It involved setting a stage for the evening in the Kara lawns, arranging for an elaborate menu for the evening and inviting deans and all professors associated with Karakoram in the past. Unlike freshers' night, this time fachas were able to savour their own ice creams.

As part of the celebrations, I started with my first big decision as the mess secretary of Karakoram. Inspired by Neel sir, this time, all first-year people were encouraged to invite their respective advisors to the House Day.

"I think house day can serve a better setting outside the formal institute set up to build up the mentor-mentee relation. Hopefully, professors agree with me after attending the same!" I explained my underlying logic to Bansal.

Warden sir welcomed the professors, who joined us in their capacity as advisors to Kara first-year students, in his opening speech. He also thanked me publicly for coming up with this idea.

As always, house awards for the year was the most important event of the day along with the skit performed by the first years.

"So, Mess Secretary of Karakoram, how are you feeling?" Sid was in a jovial mood after an eventful night. Gautam was sitting alongside Sid.

"To tell you the truth, I didn't get enough time to think about it. It has been a tiring couple of days. As far as House Day is concerned, I found first year's skit funny. I liked it."

"Yeah, we all enjoyed. It was nicely set up. It seemed today that you have settled into your new job. By the way, when is the treat?" Sid had not forgotten the promise yet.

"Tomorrow definitely Sid! Let's go to Mezbaan."

We got chit chatting about the new responsibilities coming up. After a pause, Gautam checked with me. "By the way, I didn't see much of Guru and Shashi during the evening."

"Yeah, both came late and were not there during the award ceremony." I had noticed the same.

"It was odd when warden sir kept waiting with the trophy in his hand when both Guru and Shashi's names were announced for the hostel management and cultural award categories. Eventually, none of them turned up." Gautam didn't like it.

"I was not expecting this from them."

"Ignoring hostel awards for your contribution because of what happened in the house politics is not a matured way of thinking." Sid was correct.

"I don't know if that was the reason or something else." I was trying to ignore.

Guru and Shashi's action required an open discussion with Guru.

It was a lazy Saturday afternoon. The weekend was very dull after all the action.

"Sure sir, let's sit together and revise the mess menu tomorrow." I was closing a meeting with the mess supervisor. Responsibilities of the mess had come down to me for whatever few days were left in the semester.

As I stepped out of his office, I saw Guru entering the hostel. He noticed me exiting the mess supervisor's office. He chuckled. "So looks like someone is taking the job seriously from day one."

"Obviously, given I have big shoes to fill in! Anyway, what are you doing these days? You are hardly visible."

"Nothing like that. Just trying to prepare for majors." Guru didn't sound convincing.

We walked together to Guru's room. It was as messy as always.

"Didn't get a chance to catch up with you to post the election results, all ok?" I realized that I started it a bit hurriedly.

"Yeah, all ok. Not everything went as per plan. But at the end of the day, the house has a deserving house secy." Guru responded very calmly.

"Great to know that you believe we have a deserving person on the post."

"Obviously Rocky was as deserving as Shashi. They are very different people, but both are equally good for the house. Had Kalra won the elections, I would have been pissed."

"Why?"

"Because Kalra started something which had never happened before in Kara. Getting M.tech junta involved in mainstream politics – it's not done. Our whole batch is pissed with him." Guru sounded like old Guru from the Tryst days. Right attitude with the right motivation.

"Why did you not stand? Why did you guys choose Shashi?"

"Because he was more deserving."

"Did you guys decide last year itself and that's why Shashi didn't stand for cultural secy?"

"That was indeed the plan. But it was only discussed among three of us – Shashi, Viks and I."

"I thought Kaushik knew it.'

"Kaushik may have known this. Shashi and Kaushik have been very close since the first year – thanks to their common department."

"But I guess Kaushik is close to Rocky as well."

"Yes, he is – again thanks to their common department."

"Kaushik played a big role in bringing Rocky and Vatsal together."

"Actually Kaushik played a bigger role by supporting Rocky instead of Shashi. That turned around the overall equation. Rocky and Vatsal coming together was just an outcome of Kaushik joining Rocky."

"Why did he chose Rocky?"

"Because Kaushik is a person who is very good at heart. He has the largest close friend circle across the batches in the house. And I am not talking about acquaintances here. Rocky leveraged a sentimental pitch that eventually worked with Kaushik."

"What pitch?'

"The pitch was that both Shashi and Rocky are equally deserving. Both of them have done their bit for the house in separate fields. But Rocky had a chance last year for maintenance secy which he happily gave away for the hostel and the batch when he was asked by the seniors. So this year batch should support him for getting something which he couldn't get last year. It was a pitch which was completely pro-Rocky and not anti-Shashi. Kaushik being Kaushik made his mind accordingly. I was expecting Rocky to do something anti-Shashi to piss off Kaushik, but Rocky played well. I can't tell you how much we tried to convince Kaushik after that, but we met with limited success only."

"Limited? I would say zero success."

"No, it was not zero. Now don't tell this to anyone." Guru had taken the suspense to the next level. "Kaushik is a good friend of Shashi. So, he promised his personal vote to Shashi, but campaigned for Rocky."

"What?"

"Yes. That's Kaushik for you."

"I don't know what would have happened had Kaushik stood for house secy."

"Do you think we didn't try to convince him? Shashi offered him his own support. But Kaushik was never interested."

"Interesting." I asked him then, "You guys look cool after the results. Then why didn't you turn up for the House Day awards?"

"I am so pissed with myself for that shameful act. Abhimanyu, the frame of my mind last week was not like what I have today. Every defeat brings along bitterness. That's a universal truth. Now it's up to you to decide how much time you will take to start living with the defeat." The feeling of bitterness was still there with me when you organized the House Day last week. I pulled Shashi along with me. We went outside the campus and returned late. But if you ask me today, it was awful on my part.

I regret what I did that day. I went to Warden sir to apologize. Thankfully, he was not bothered."

"How do you feel now?"

"As fresh as possible. You may not find me hanging out with Rocky, but that was the case even before all the politics began. Today for most of us, it's very much like the way it was in the first year. No agenda, no game, no bitterness – a completely blank slate."

"Great to know that Guru. And this conversation makes me so happy for you and Shashi."

I left his room thanking him for all the gyaan – after all, he was not named Guru without reason. This conversation with Guru was at such a personal level that I didn't discuss it with Gautam in detail.

Soon, we had the majors for the 'even semester'. It felt like every day of the exam week was passing so slowly after a month of power packed action.

Elections had taken my focus away from academics to a certain extent, and I knew that my performance in this semester would be relatively mediocre compared to the last semester.

~ 75 ~

Soon after the exams, people started leaving for their homes to spend the year break.

"Gautam, coming for a walk?" It was our last night in the house for the year.

"Was thinking to go to Gossip & Bite with Edison and Sid. But let's go out for a walk. Will ask them to join us directly at the canteen." Gossip and Bite canteen was in the Institute area.

We took our usual route circling the ground, in front of the house, towards the SAC.

"So another year over!" I started the conversation.

"Yes. And it didn't disappoint. So much of action." Gautam was right.

"Absolutely! We had such an exciting year. New batch, new friends, new talent, new experiences, new learnings, unwanted new sour relations and of course the poltu which was one level up compared to the last time."

"Am sure you can write a book on what all we went through." Gautam always had his pick on things.

"I would have done that for sure if I could write even half as well as you."

"Am sure you can. Tell me Abhimanyu, among all the unpredictable events that happened in the last two years, which one surprised you the most?"

"That's a difficult question Gautam. You will have to give me a minute to think." After a pause, I continued, "I learned that surprises in poltu could be of three types. One which has a valid rationale behind it. TK's pulling off from the final hurdle belonged to this category. He had lost energy. Even Kalra's decision to fight house secy elections, notably when he was able to pull off second in the polls, belongs to this category. Amitabh being unable to get anything in the externals this year because he was not invested enough in the process. For such surprises, you get to understand the underlying reason sooner or later.

"Then come surprises where one can predict an associated agenda for the future. Shashi not going for the post of cultural secretary came with a prediction of him gunning for the house secy. Similarly, in hindsight, one can believe that Rocky willingly did not push for his ambition last year to gain people sympathy which in turn provided him the upper hand in this year's house secretary election.

"And then finally the surprises which are difficult to comprehend, which are beyond any logic. Amitabh wining over Double A just because Spidy supported Amitabh is not an acceptable logic. Vatsal and Rocky joining forces for this year elections again fall in this category. Here we know there is something in the store for future, but it's still not clear."

"Interesting way to categorize so many events of the last two years." Gautam was listening.

We took the left turn, at the end of the ground, towards the SAC.

"Though for me, the biggest surprise was Rudra scolding Prabhat and Pushkar in the batch meet when Amitabh told us about Pushkar's nomination. Until then, to me, he was the last person who could react in such a way." I had identified my surprise for the year.

"Rudra scolding Pushkar and Prabhat is as cool as Kaushik not running for the house secy." Gautam was right.

"What was the biggest surprise for you?" I checked with Gautam.

"To me, the biggest surprise was Pushkar, backed by Prabhat, filing nomination even after losing the batch elections. I could never predict that they were willing to put everything at stake to try to gain power, even going against their batch."

"It shows what Prabhat and Pushkar are capable of." I was expecting more action in the future. "Even in the case of house secretary election, the politics this year was so different compared to what we witnessed in our first year. Unlike last year, this time it was beyond the underlying candidate's principles and agenda. It became a fight between talented individuals. For the first time in Kara, house witnessed how to leverage M.Tech votes. If this trend of worsened elections continues, am not sure if we can even predict what is in store for us in the next year, given the talent our batch has already showcased. I am sure I can wait for two more years before writing the book because there is so much more to witness going forward."

"Why do you feel there is so much going to happen in the future?" Gautam was smiling.

"Because results ensured that all the four groups in our batch remain active next year as well." I could feel a future marked with intense actions.

"Are you happy with this year?"

"Yes, but Edison?" I knew Edison had not moved on yet.

"I hope you were not expecting him to win."

"Not really."

"So who did you vote for the post of maintenance secretary finally, Sanghvi or Edison?"

"You only taught me that post-election one need not share the choices that one made. I will stick to the same."

"I am proud of you!" Gautam smiled at the act of refusal of his disciple.

We entered the SAC building.

"I am disappointed that talented people are not participating."

"At least it was not true for the senior batch." Gautam was correct.

"Yes, to an extent, all three of them had contributed to their field and were respected."

"Equation between Rocky and Vatsal though remains unclear. Am sure Kaushik will let us know when the time is right." Gautam had not forgotten it yet.

"We will soon get to know next year. Sid will get it from Kaushik! Anyway, there is one thing which was very satisfactory for me." I was thinking about the future.

"What?"

"The way the teams from the first year have shaped. They have loads of enthusiasm. If we can get the right talent in the next year, I believe the combination will have the potential to help Kara achieve wonders."

"The first year is surely a lovely group of people. Am sure the poltu for club reps would have led to new development within the batch," Gautam was talking from experience.

"Yeah, I already witnessed some interesting developments." I could recollect my conversation with Dixcy.

"What do you think for the future?" Gautam was again thinking forward.

We had crossed the squash court and reached the open area behind the SAC building.

"Don't know. As of now let's concentrate on getting the BRCA and BHM trophies. Let's execute our plan of building accountability at all levels. Let's prioritize areas to target next year basis the talent available in the house. Let's give our best to achieve the vision we have. I hope people in our batch will not take it to their heart and become a bottleneck to our plan. But the overall equation will surely change depending upon the dynamics next year. The current coalition may or may not stand as every group will have a chance to be active next year." I summarized.

"Completely agree. If *poltu* in second year required so much of energy and time, how much of energy will the third year politics will demand!"

"I don't want to think about that now!" I was tired.

"But you can't ignore it as well."

"Understand you completely. It will include taking care of an innocent batch who are our immediate juniors and then a batch which is yet to join. It's funny to imagine we are referring to the important role a set of people, who are yet to join, are going to play. Interestingly, we are talking about ones for whom final decisions to join the campus are yet to happen! As TK had rightly once said, they, whoever and wherever they are, don't have any clue what is in store for them if they will end up here after a couple of months."

We sat down on the boundary wall from where the stairs went down to the Open Air theatre. "Indeed, it's funny. In fact, I got reminded of your *Mahabharata* reference. New characters will join soon with new events. And each of them will have a definite role to play. But you still didn't tell me what you think about the future?" Gautam wanted a definite answer.

"As of now, it's very far off Gautam. And I am not even sure what role I am going to play at the end of the next year." I was holding myself to think in the direction.

"I may be forcing you for this, but sitting today, what are the possible options that you can think of?" Gautam was not going to leave me so quickly.

I started applying my mind. After a pause, I replied, "Gautam, if I look back, it all started for me with one aspiration – to win anything and everything for the house. For me, it's the BRCA trophy." I drew a big circle with 'BRCA' written inside it on top of the boundary wall in the space between us while we were sitting there on the fence. "Now over a period, I realized that to win the same, personal enthusiasm is not enough. I need the power to be able to influence and instil accountability in others."

"Today you can proudly say you have got both - the enthusiasm for the house as well power in the house." Gautam summarized it.

I drew two more circles with 'Enthusiasm' and 'Power' written inside them respectively. I then drew arrows connecting these two circles with the 'BRCA' circle drawn above.

"Absolutely, and so the main motive is to leverage them to win BRCA and possibly BHM trophies for the house. The results, the energy and the batch dynamics are sure to play a big role. The journey after that will depend upon three parameters – BRCA results next year, my energy and batch dynamics." I drew three more circles with 'Results,' 'Energy' and 'Batch dynamics' written inside them respectively. I then drew arrows to connect these three circles with the previous two circles of 'Enthusiasm' and 'Power.'"

"I like your way of thinking." Gautam was listening.

"Now if we can win the BRCA trophy next year, I don't know how it will impact my enthusiasm after that. It will be an important factor to decide my journey for power."

"Got it."

"My energy is at its peak today. After a year of continual 'fight', next year, I don't know where it will end. Will it remain the same as it is today or will it be like what happened to TK who ran out of steam? It will also depend on our juniors who have been a great source of energy for me even today. And so I will remain in contention for even stronger power, or I may support someone else personally to stay relevant in the house like Guru who supported Shashi."

"I remember at the end of first year, you spoke about 'survival of the fittest' playing out over the years with the funnel of posts to remain relevant getting only smaller. So many characters that were relevant at the end of first year like Utkarsh, Rahul, Barnwal and for that matter may be Edison may not be relevant going forward as far as gunning for any political post is concerned. With the next year the funnel even getting smaller, sustaining energy may not be easy. Understood. What about this third circle of batch dynamics?" Gautam pointed to the third circle.

"Standing today all four groups are active. Groups or individuals who have lost may try to come back even stronger – may be few of them or all of them. There will be many who will prepare for the future. During the year, we may have better clarity about everyone's game. They will surely impact our game and thinking and so the plan for the future."

"But you should not forget the motivation to leverage the power for the larger good," Gautam reminded me.

"Agree, but still, standing today I think all four options are possible – I go for power for the larger good, I go for power to continue to enjoy the control that I will have next year, I support someone else to remain relevant, or I give it up completely. And the final answer will depend upon 'Result,' 'Energy' and 'Batch dynamics' impacting my 'Enthusiasm' and so the quest for 'Power.'" I summarized while pointing towards the connected circles that I had drawn on the top of the wall.

"Will tell you only one thing Abhimanyu – if we want to go big next year, we will have to do a set of things through the year. We can't just take a call at the very end. Because unlike this time, it will be beyond our batch."

I nodded to him and said, "Too much for me to think tonight!"

"Ok Ok. Let's go. You have two months of free time to think about this. Edison and Sid would be cursing us by now. By the way, are you thinking about joining consulting after the campus?"

"Why?"

"The way you have started structuring your arguments and whatever I have heard from the final year seniors preparing for the placements, I am getting a feeling you are heading in that direction."

"Come on Gautam! I don't know anything about consulting yet. But now that you have said it, I will try to understand it when am back into the campus after the break."

We had a long dinner followed by a long bakaiti session that night. Bansal also joined us for the same. Sid made sure that we didn't talk about poltu anymore.

When we took leave from each other that night, looking forward to a two month long deserving break, I was thinking 'Today surprisingly Gautam and I spent more time talking about power, ambition, and poltu in the House than discussing our plan to bring BRCA trophy to Kara."